Fox and Lucien,

Beyond

The Gates of Hercules

Perry Vayo

Fox and Lucien,
Beyond the Gates of Hercules

Perry Vayo © 2015, All rights reserved
ISBN: 978-0-9882680-6-7
Published: July, 2016
Publisher: Infonouveau™
Createspace Edition

Library of Congress Control Number: 2016911630

Find out more about Infonouveau™ and upcoming books online at http://www.infonouveau.com

Infonouveau
353 Oxford St.
Rochester, NY. 14607

info@infonouveau.com

Printed in the U.S.A.

Table of Contents

Table of Contents (con't.)

infonouveau™

Browse our other titles at:
www.infonouveau.com

Chapter 1

A Letter Home

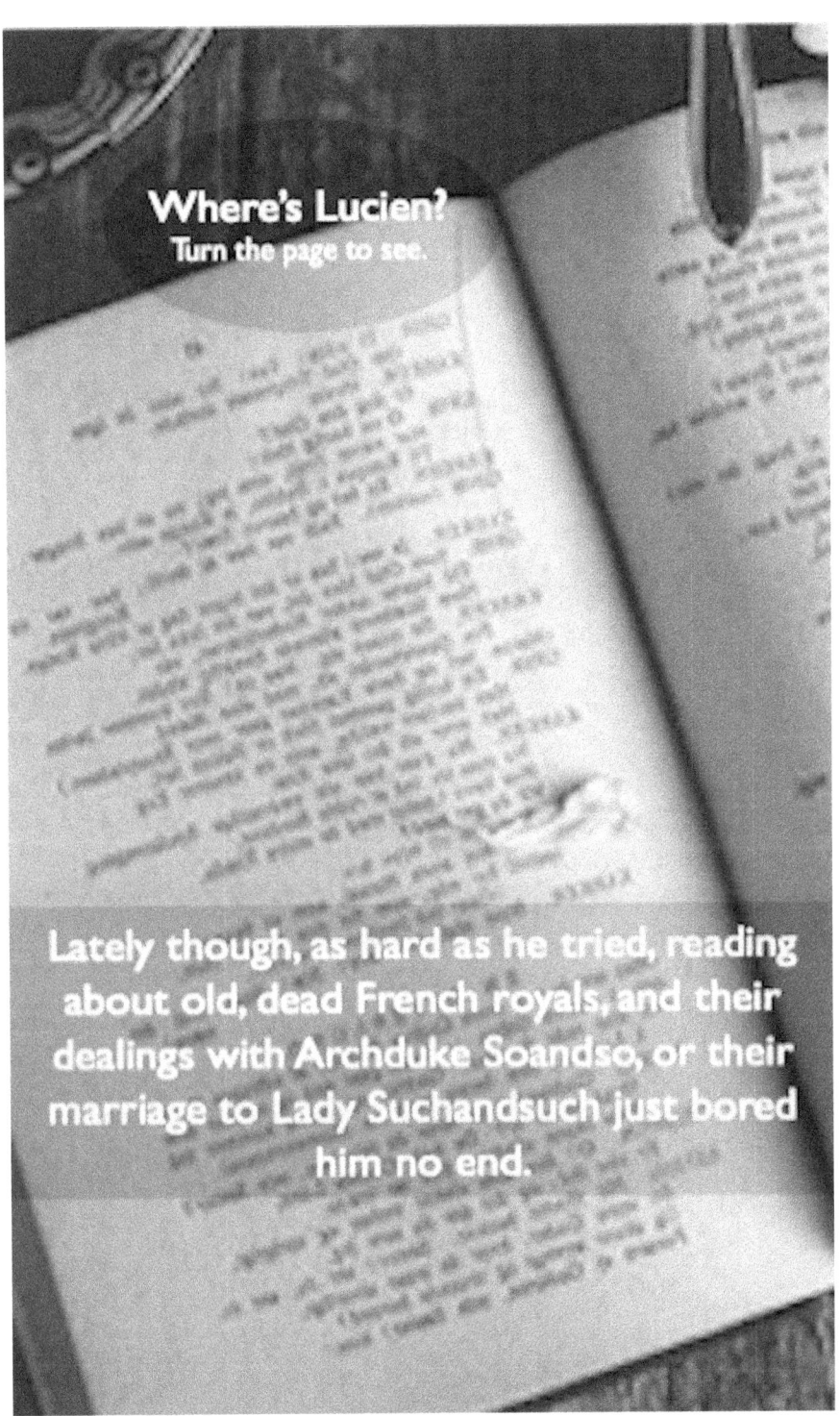

Where's Lucien?
Turn the page to see.

Lately though, as hard as he tried, reading about old, dead French royals, and their dealings with Archduke Soandso, or their marriage to Lady Suchandsuch just bored him no end.

I'm right here!

The thick history book claps shut with a heavy thud, launching a fleet of little dust particles into the air like tiny ships adrift on unseen oceanic currents. Lucien had always loved to learn, and did well on all his examinations. Madame Marboeuf was so proud of his successes, that he wanted to do his best for her as well. Lately though, as hard as he tried, reading about old, dead French royals, and their dealings with Archduke Soandso, or their marriage to Lady Suchandsuch just bored him no end. More and more, he caught himself thinking about the exciting days he had spent with Fox in Paris – escaping the guards at the Tuileries, or performing together on the street to help their friend, the old blind man. Playing the old man's violin had totally changed their fortunes, and reminiscing about it now made him want nothing more than to be home with his best friend, exploring the gentle hills and busy streets of Bordeaux, rather than being cooped up here in this dingy school library, surrounded by nothing more exciting than stacks of old, dusty, leather-bound books.

As important as his education had been to his uncle, when he was alive, Madame Marboeuf, who had adopted him as her own, was even more keen on giving Lucien a "proper" education, and he didn't want to disappoint her. After all, it was Madame Marboeuf who had given up her life in Paris to bring them back to the only real home he had ever known. She had rehired all his uncle's former staff and began the long restoration of the old house, just so that he could grow up in the good old surroundings his uncle had first provided for him.

It was a fine home again. The old gardens were as green and lively as his brightest memory of them. Mr. Raimond, who was now Lucien's step-father, took great joy in maintaining them. On many mornings, Lucien would watch him, from his bedroom window, outside with the gardener, his shirt-sleeves rolled back, tending proudly to his plants. Father Raimond, would still travel to Paris on business quite often, staying in the new house he had built there on Lucien and Fox's old "island", but he was always anxious to get back to Bordeaux, to his new family and his gardens. He seemed to really love the home he now shared with his new wife, just as much as Lucien did. It made sense to Lucien that his new father, after losing his own son and then his first wife, would want nothing more than this comforting and secure new life for himself and every member of his family.

It was for them, as much as for himself, that Lucien worked so diligently in his new school, but lately it had become so hard to pay attention; he missed Fox, he missed home, he even missed his old tutor – his new professors were so strict and dismal. "How would any boy be able to pay attention to all this boring old stuff," Lucien thought. But, he checked himself, after all his new parents had done for him, their pride in him made all the hard work worth the effort. Today however, it was just too much. "Enough studying for now," he said as he pushed the book aside and carefully extracted a letter from the inner pocket of his jacket, which was hanging from the back of his chair. He gently removed the folded paper from its envelope and began to read it, again:

"Dearest Cousin,

I hope this letter finds you, and our little friend Fox, in good health and spirits. I do apologize that it takes me so long responding to you these days, especially because our aunt informs me that you are doing so well at your studies, and has told me how proud she is of your accomplishments at college. I must admit, I don't think I was quite up to your standards during my time there. Hopefully, I am making a better account of myself now. God and I both know that I have a great deal to account for."

Lucien stops reading and thinks to himself, "Poor Gustave, when will you accept that all is forgiven? When I write him again, I will remind him of how fortunate I am to have a cousin that I can consider a brother." He turns back to the letter:

"Our officers are keeping us busy these days, which has left me little time for correspondence. We are currently in pursuit of the Moorish criminal, al-Qadir. He has fashioned himself into a sort of warrior-priest, and his people follow him with a blind faith that puts one in mind of Attila, if you can believe it. To his credit, he has proven an elusive target. Rather than choosing to stand and fight, which he knows would mean defeat, he has engaged in a campaign of harassment, attacking and quickly retreating back into the desert where he feels safe. We have adopted the same tactics – to "fight fire with fire" as the saying goes, which brings me to my own good news, of sorts. Thanks to my riding skills – for which I can thank my father, your uncle – I have been promoted to the cavalry. The training is rigorous, but, I have to say, it is far preferable to being a foot soldier, like our old friend father La Tuile. (My admiration for the old soldier grows with each passing day I am here in conflict.)

I wish I could tell you where I will be tomorrow, but, in truth I don't know. Our agents report back to the commanding officers who then quickly plan their attacks. We ride light and fast, and engage al-Qadir wherever possible. The fighting is furious at times, and I have already been in a few bloody scrapes (please don't repeat that to your mother) but have, so far, fared well.

The nights, camped in the desert are my favorite times. The air becomes very crisp and clear, revealing wonders in the heavens that I never knew existed. It allows the mind to expand and develop a better understanding of God's creation. I must say, that reflection has also humbled me, and made me all the more ashamed of my past. I have grown enough now to stand as a man and take responsibility for the wrongs I have committed, especially against you Cousin, and I will redeem the debit I have incurred. On this, you have my solemn word.

Tomorrow, early, I must be ready to go out on patrol for several days, so I will say goodbye for now. I will read a few more pages of your good old book tonight and hope for pleasant dreams.

Until we meet again, your devoted cousin,

Gustave

Lucien puts the letter down slowly and looks off into the Algerian deserts, imagining the sounds of the galloping horses, the brilliant stars and the strange dark people who Gustave has spoken of so often. He imagines his cousin on horseback vanquishing the evil outlaw al-Qadir, under the pale light of a cold desert moon. After a moment, he folds the letter and slips it back into his jacket, and with a sigh, dutifully pulls the old text book to him. Opening it, he leans back into his studies.

Chapter 2

Holiday!

Where's Lucien?
Turn the page to see.

Moments later Lucien and several classmates emerge into the bright sunlight of the Bordeaux spring through the heavy ancient doors of the school.

The sharp crack of the ruler on Lucien's desk startles him out of his reverie, sending one of his textbooks tumbling loudly to the floor. There is a chorus of snickers from the rest of the class as Lucien scrambles to retrieve the book, and quickly reopen it to the correct page. He looks sheepishly up at the rather rotund, red-faced professor glaring down at him. "I beg your pardon, sir," Lucien says apologetically. "Perhaps young Monsieur Lehun," the teacher pronounces loudly, "would be kind enough to share today's daydream with the rest of us? I'm sure we would all benefit by knowing what it is that is so potent it trumps my lesson?" The corpulent instructor steps back, inviting Lucien to speak. Lucien looks around the room, and addresses the class without hesitation, "I was thinking about my cousin..." "Ahhh...," interrupts the teacher, "I should have known. She must be a lovely young girl to have cast such a spell." "No sir." Lucien replies quickly, his face flushing at the suggestion. "My cousin is a horseman in the legion, fighting in the campaign in Algeria at this very moment. I have just received a letter from him, and I am very concerned for his safety; he is the only cousin that I have." The professor looks disappointed that Lucien slipped his snare so easily. "Well, Mr. Lehun, as concerned as we all are for your cousin's well-being, please remember why you are here, and leave your cousin's business at home," he snaps. "Yes sir. I will try sir," Lucien replies. The school-master retrieves a pocket watch from his vest and glances at it quickly. He sighs tiredly before speaking,

"I can see that you are all rather anxious to get home for your holiday, and I fear, that as with Monsieur Lehun, I have lost you all for today. So, I will dismiss class early." He pauses for effect, then continues, "I am sure you will all be happy to know that Monsieur Lehun will be giving us a lecture on the Algerian campaign when we return to class after the break. Mr. Lehun," he says, turning to Lucien, "do you have any objections?"

Lucien looks up at the professor, the surprise showing on his face, then replies dutifully, "No sir, of course not sir."

Moments later Lucien and several classmates emerge into the bright sunlight of the Bordeaux spring through the heavy ancient doors of the school. As they walk down the well-worn stone steps one of the group remarks, "Oye, lucky Lucien's not so lucky today!" Another adds, "Not much of a holiday for you...a lecture, on top of our other lessons! That old puff-ball! Good luck." Ever the optimist Lucien responds, "It's not so bad as you think. Gustave has told me so much about the desert and its people in his letters that I feel almost as if I've been there myself." "Has he told you about the harem girls?" one of the friends interjects playfully. "Harem girls? No. Not at all," Lucien replies. "He tells me only about his adventures riding out after the outlaws in the desert." He pauses thoughtfully for a moment, then continues, "If something were to happen to Gustave, my mother, his aunt, would be devastated. She has worked so hard to make a family of us again, and treats Gustave as her own, just as much as me. She worries about him terribly." The classmates walk along the boulevard leading away from the college in silence, not knowing what to say to their friend, until one asks, "So, tell us more about these harem girls." "What's a harem?"

another asks. A third boy speaks up authoritatively, "Well, I happen to know that these desert men all have harems, which are really no more than herds of girls. They can have as many as they please." "A herd of girls?," comes the reply, "It sounds awful." Another boy chimes in, "Why would you want to be surrounded by so many girls at all? What do they do all day?" They continue along in silence as they ponder the mystery before them.

Chapter 3

The Sentinel

Where's Fox?
Turn the page to see.

Fox stares, transfixed, at the front door, watching keenly for the slightest hint of movement...

I'm right here!

Fox stares, transfixed, at the front door, watching keenly for the slightest hint of movement in the ornate brass doorknob. He has sensed for the last two days, as Madame Marboeuf has become increasingly agitated, that something is going on. Now, he can smell it, literally taste it, in the air. Ever since moving into this big old house in the country, and his friend Lucien had gone away to school, Fox had always been able to sense when the boy would be home. He hated letting Lucien go off on his own, but, having visited the school several times, Fox had quickly determined that it was a place best left to Lucien and all the other humans. Their separations still made him desperately sad, but he had quickly learned that they were temporary, and that his closest friend would always come back for him. So today, it is not just the woman's growing impatience to get everything in the house spotlessly clean, and free of all the good old smells that linger there, that gets his attention. The dog already knows that the boy is coming, he feels it, and he knows to sit and wait, until he can smell it, too. The heavy door may have no window, but he "sees" right through it, sensing far beyond it. Any slight puff of air that creeps in beneath it is a breath of new information. As the boy gets closer, the currents in the air paint a picture in Fox's head, showing him exactly where Lucien is; out on the road passing the dairy cows, taking their secret path across the field of rye, turning onto the drive that leads right up to that door. So, he waits patiently for Lucien's pre-ordained arrival, using his nose and ears to mark the boy's progress. He can be patient, because for the little spaniel there is nothing in his entire world more important to do than this. "Honestly Fox," Madame Marbocuf comments as she suddenly materializes behind him, swishing out of one room and into the next, in constant motion, "you've been sitting there for hours. I have no idea when Lucien will arrive, he's walking again. It's so odd how he prefers to walk these days rather than be driven." Fox looks at her for a moment, then, turns back to the door, as if to say, "Do you really not know that he is almost here?" Madame Marboeuf notices the look on the little dog's face and continues, "Yes, I know how you miss your friend. You wait there as long as you care to." With that she sweeps off into the house, calling out to one of the kitchen staff as she goes, "Martine, has the silver been polished yet?" A woman's voice can be heard from another room, responding impatiently, "Oui, madame, of course, it's all been tended to." Fox ignores the exchange, focused entirely on the door knob now. He begins to pant. His tail starts to sweep the floor behind him. He waits and watches and smells. He gets to his feet. The door makes a slight movement and then the knob shifts with the weight of a hand on it. He crouches down. The knob turns and the big old door begins to swing open, pulling a fresh infusion of scent with it. The smells explode into the dog's nose and head. Fox lunges, leaping exuberantly toward a spot in space that he knows will be filled in a moment by his best friend.

Lucien steps through the door and before he can announce his arrival he is accosted by a dark furry shape arcing through the air toward him. "Oh!" he exclaims in surprise, dropping his bag to the floor, just in time for his arms to be filled to capacity by the squirming body of his faithful companion. "Fox!" he laughs, "you've surprised me again! How's my little friend? Have you missed me?" It's a rather silly question really, given the shower of licks the boy is enduring at the moment. Hearing the commotion, Madame Marboeuf sweeps excitedly out of the dining room, where she has been inspecting the shine on the silver, and stops in the doorway looking on as Fox welcomes Lucien home. Having never fully understood the bond that has developed between the two, at this moment she knows that understanding isn't important, so she waits patiently for her turn to greet her adopted son.

That evening, long after the commotion of Lucien's arrival has subsided, Lucien, Madame Marboeuf, and Mr. Raimond are having dinner. Fox is at Lucien's feet looking content, not only because of the return of his pack leader, but also from the tasty treats Lucien spirits from his dinner plate to the dog. The table itself is a glowing treasure of silver and crystal − the silver candlesticks shimmering radiantly, thanks to Madame Marboeuf's overzealous attentions. As they dine and talk they are attended to by several servants of the house staff, who also seem quite happy to have Lucien home again. Not only does his presence lighten their employers mood, it keeps her distracted and gives them a bit of a respite themselves. Lucien, has known them all since he was very young, and although he is careful not to become too cordial with them, as his uncle had insisted, they all, nevertheless, feel much more relaxed when he is at home.

Madame Marboeuf and Mr. Raimond look on, impressed, as Lucien eats his meal. His appetite, even without his long walk home, is impressive, but now he eats as if he hasn't seen a crust of bread in weeks. Martine, a middle-aged woman, who has been in the house for as long as Lucien can remember, and now over-sees the entire staff, is happily refilling Lucien's plate from a sideboard behind him that is overloaded with the tasty dishes for the evening meal, as he (and Fox) inhale everything placed in front of them. Finally, Madame Marboeuf has had enough of his single-minded focus on his dinner, interjecting, "Lucien, do please remember to breathe in between mouthfuls." Lucien catches himself, just as he slips a tidbit of goose meat to Fox. He looks up sheepishly, "I'm so sorry for being rude Mother. This dinner you've made is so good, I feel I could eat it all. The meals at school are nowhere near so delicious." "It makes me happy to hear it," Madame Marboeuf replies, "and to see you with such an appetite, but remember, it's no longer just you and Fox living together in your little hovel." Mr. Raimond chimes in immediately, "My dear, that is no hovel, that is a castle fit for royalty. I dare say, old Father La Tuile and his dog are very happy there. Lucien and Fox transformed that old lot into a quite proper estate." Lucien looks thoughtfully at Mr. Raimond, adding, "I do so miss Father La Tuile and my other good friends in Paris. Is he well, Father?" Mr. Raimond replies, "Lucien, when last I saw him he was as stalwart as ever. He and his Austerlitz were keeping a firm guard on your old island." Madame Marboeuf interjects, "Lucien, would you care for more food? "Yes, please Mother," Lucien replies quickly, before turning back to Mr. Raimond, "Father, when might I go back to Paris with you? I would so like to see my old friends again." As he speaks, Madame Marboeuf signals to Martine, who quickly removes Lucien's plate without him taking any notice. "It would be a pleasure to have you return to Paris with me" replies his step-father. "Perhaps we will all go together, but, I don't think we can talk about that until your session is done for the year. It's a long way to Paris, and I don't want you missing any of your lessons." Martine places a new plate of food deftly in front of Lucien, but, the boy takes no notice of her, as he goes on with Mr. Raimond. "But sir," he says, while cutting a bite of food, "that seems so far away, and I learned more in Paris than in...," he stops short with his fork, seeming to suddenly notice the fresh plate in front of him. He turns deliberately to Martine, saying, "Thank you so much, Martine," then continues with Mr. Raimond, "any of my classes." Mr. Raimond considers this for a moment, then turns to Martine, trying to get off the subject of Paris, "Yes, Martine, everything is splendid. I don't recall ever seeing the silver shine so brightly."

Martine replies diplomatically, "Thank you, sir. Madame wanted to be sure that everything was perfect for your son's return." Madame Marboeuf is pleased at the flattery. Mr. Raimond gives her a quick wink, at which she begins to get up from the table, saying, "Lucien, my dear, let me get you something more to drink." But, before she can get out of her chair, Martine is there, whisking Lucien's glass away to be refilled, saying, "Oh no madame, please. You don't pay me to stand idly by and chat." She expertly pours a bit of wine into Lucien's glass and then fills the rest with water. Mr. Raimond jumps back in, "Martine, no one can ever accuse you of being idle." The servant replies, "Madame knows how to keep her staff busy, sir," raising a knowing laugh from Monsieur Raimond, who adds archly, "Of that there can be no doubt Martine. Of that there can be no doubt." Madame Marboeuf joins in with mock offense, "That will be quite enough out of you, you insolent woman." Lucien jumps to Martine's defense, "Don't listen to her Martine, she loves you as much as any of us."

While Martine is touched by his words, and her inclusion in their conversation, she is an old hand at her duties, and knows when a line is being approached that should not be crossed. She addresses Madame Marboeuf, "Madame, if you have no need of me, I will go see to the dessert now." Madame Marboeuf excuses her, and Martine heads into the kitchen, giving Lucien a little pat on the shoulder as she does. After Martine has left, Mr. Raimond remarks, "She is quite a prize my dear, you'd better be good to her, or the neighbors will steal her away." "That will be quite enough out of you as well," snaps Madame Marboeuf.

With that, Mr. Raimond turns to Lucien and remarks lightly, "My boy, a gentleman knows when to argue and knows when to change the subject...What shall we discuss now? You've not yet given us a report on your classes..."

Lucien hesitates a moment before answering, "They are going well enough I think. We will be getting our reports soon, and then we will all know. I do love to learn, and you have told me how important it is to be educated, but, he hesitates. "But, what Lucien?" asks his mother. Lucien looks at her, then back to Mr. Raimond, "It isn't so easy to pay attention all the time. The professors can be so boring." Mr. Raimond smiles, saying,

> "Lucien, we have all had poor teachers and had to sit through uncomfortable lessons. It seems endlessly tedious at times, but, like any good business venture, you profit by your exertions. The more you put into it, the more you will get out of it."

Lucien replies, "Yes sir. Mother," he continues hesitantly "please don't be angry with me, but, I was caught by my professor just yesterday not paying attention in class. He has given me a special work assignment to do while I am here as punishment." Madame Marboeuf looks at her son kindly, "Lucien, there are consequences for everything that you do. If you are not paying attention to your lessons and get found out, you will bear the consequences. I'm sure you will do an excellent job." Mr. Raimond, aware of Lucien's normally sharp focus asks him, "Why were you not paying attention, Lucien? That's not like you." Lucien replies forthrightly,

> "I was thinking about Gustave, sir. He has sent me another letter, and it was full of all the adventures he is having in Africa. But, it made me fear for his safety. He made it sound like nothing at all, but, the men he is fighting against sound so uncivilized and dangerous. I could not stop thinking about what we would do if Gustave were to be hurt, or worse. He is trying so hard

to atone for himself, that we will be proud of him, and, that I will forgive him. He won't believe that I have already done so. He is my beloved cousin and brother now. If he were to fall on misfortune in Africa, I don't know what I would do. This is why my thoughts wandered. I am sorry, sir."

Madame Marboeuf, is quite touched by her son's explanation, and she bristles at the idea of Lucien being punished for his concern over his cousin. "Lucien," she says, "you have nothing to be sorry for. It is only your caring nature that has tripped you up. I will not stand for such unfair treatment for you. Tomorrow I will go speak to this professor of yours and let him know how things are!" Lucien is shocked, "Oh no, mother, you mustn't! " he implores. Mr. Raimond jumps in on his behalf, "My dear, Lucien is right. No matter the reason for his daydreaming, he was in the wrong for not paying attention, and his professor must run his class as he sees fit. Lucien understands this. Lucien, what is your assignment?"

Lucien replies, "Algeria sir. I must report on Algeria and our campaign there." Mr. Raimond replies, "Well then, you will show your professor what type of student you are by standing up and delivering the best report you can. That will serve you the best, in the end." Madame Marboeuf interjects, "Well, nevertheless, I don't like the idea of my son being punished for an innocent daydream." Mr. Raimond replies, "My dear, just a moment ago you told Lucien he must bear the consequences of his actions. Lucien knows that he must account for himself. Do you agree Lucien?" Lucien responds, "Yes I do sir, completely. You have taught me that." Mr. Raimond continues, "In this case then, the best way for you to do that is by demonstrating your excellence to your teacher." Before Lucien can reply, Fox, who has been sitting patiently at Lucien's feet has had enough. He puts his front legs up on Lucien's thigh so he can see above the table and barks, as if to say, "Of course we will. Now, how long must I wait for my next bit of goose!" Lucien obliges him immediately, "Of course, you want the rest of your dinner, too. All this talk is nothing to you, is it Fox?" The dog grabs the tidbit from Lucien and ducks back down under the table with it. Madame Marboeuf looks on disapprovingly, but says nothing. Lucien continues, "I think I will take Fox to visit Uncle's grave tomorrow. I haven't been there in so long." Madame Marboeuf chimes in, "That sounds like a splendid idea Lucien. I will ride along with you." Her unexpected gesture puts Lucien in an awkward spot. Lately, he has been missing his uncle dearly, and had planned to visit his "father" on his own, with Fox, just the two of them. With Madame Marboeuf along, everything would feel so much more stiff and formal, not at all what he hoped for. "Mother," Lucien begins tentatively, "would you be terribly disappointed if Fox and I went on our own?" His aunt looks at him puzzled and a bit hurt. She looks at her husband, who nods his head slightly in answer to her silent question. "No, Lucien," she says in a measured tone, "that would be fine. I understand that you would like some private time with your uncle. I will have the carriage ready for you in the morning." "Oh, thank you mother! I knew you would understand, but, if you don't mind, we would rather not be driven. We will walk on our own. It will be a fine adventure for us." "Honestly Lucien," his mother replies, with more than just a hint of frustration in her voice, "why you would want to walk all that way and back is beyond me. But, if that is what you want to do...do not be late," she scolds, not having anything better to say.

Chapter 4

Visiting "Uncle"

At the gate of the ancient cemetery, Lucien looks around for the old knotty tree that marks the area of his uncles grave.

The next morning, Fox is up with the first warm rays of the sun streaming into the bedroom, peering down at Lucien, who still sleeps soundly beside him. Sensing that something is planned for the day, the dog is anxious to get the ball rolling, so he nudges Lucien lightly with his nose to rouse him, but gets no response. Fox waits and then tries again, this time pawing at Lucien's shoulder, which achieves nothing more than his friend rolling over and continuing to sleep. Clearly, not the result Fox is looking for, he tries a gentle bark, but it comes out sounding like a hoarse whisper, and when that does no more than his previous attempts to wake his friend, he's had enough. Stepping back, he takes a breath and barks out a loud, piercing wake-up call, that rouses Lucien with a start, as he cries out, "What? What is it?" Rubbing the sleep from his eyes, he looks over at the dog who is staring at him intently, tail wagging. "Fox! I should have known you would understand that we are going on an adventure today. You just can't wait, can you? Alright," the boy says, stretching, "be patient. I have to get up and get my clothes on for the day." In reply, Fox bounces around playfully on the bed, trying his best to get his sluggish friend moving.

A few minutes later, Lucien and Fox bound down the big, old carved staircase that delivers them into the large greeting hall of the house. Several rooms open off this one, and in one Martine is busy straightening things up. When she sees Lucien and Fox, she stops what she is doing and speaks to the boy, "Lucien, your aunt warned me to not let you leave without having your breakfast, and she had me pack up something for you to take along as well. So, come on into the table and eat." Lucien, with Fox at his side, steps into the doorway and replies, "Thank you Martine, but perhaps you can add some breakfast to what you've already packed. It is such a beautiful day, that I am anxious to go. We'll eat it along the way, I promise you. I'm sure Fox won't let me forget our breakfast." Martine puts her hands on her hips, knowing that it is no use to try to dissuade him. "Well," she says, "you must promise to eat it. I'll just be a minute. Let your dog have some water while I pack it up for you." Lucien follows her toward the kitchen door as he replies, "Thank you, Martine, you are too kind to us." He stops at the door, and lets Fox go in to get some water, while he sits at the dining table, and talks through the door to Martine, "Where has my mother gone so early this morning?" From through the door Martine responds, "She and Mr. Raimond don't confide their business to me. When you didn't appear for breakfast, they didn't want to wake you and went into town to take care of some errands." Lucien replies, "It was so nice to be in my old bed, with Fox sleeping at my feet, that I just couldn't get up. Fox finally got impatient and woke me, he's so eager to go." Martine emerges from the kitchen with the cloth bag well stuffed with food, which she hands to him, saying, "I don't want you to bring any of it back, do you hear?" Lucien smiles at her, "Yes Martine, we will eat every bit, I'm sure of that," he says, taking the bag.

A few minutes later, the big old doors creak open, and Lucien and Fox emerge into a glorious Bordeaux morning, setting off down the drive to the road. The bright sun and the moist ocean air conspire together to create a fine haze that softens the lines of everything, making the countryside look like the work of a master landscape artist. Martine watches after them as they walk off, slowly becoming part of the grand painting, then closes the door and returns to her chores.

Later, slowly winding their way up into the rolling hills above the city, Lucien and Fox are enjoying the breakfast that Martine has packed for them. Lucien rips off pieces of fresh baguette and cold meat which he eats himself or tosses to Fox. The dog for his part, is having a hard time deciding between the food, or the opportunity to explore the fragrant surroundings. Behind them, the entire expanse of Bordeaux is clearly visible in the distance. Turning around to have a look back. Lucien remarks, "My, look at how the city grows Fox. Why soon it will be just like Paris!" Fox's alarmed barking interrupts the reflective moment and he quickly turns to his friend confronting a large black cow, who stands unperturbed, meekly looking at the little invader from the other side of a low stone wall. "Ha! Fox, you have corralled her," Lucien shouts merrily, "But, now let the poor thing have her own breakfast! Come along, we've still a ways to go you know." Fox gives the cow one last bark for good measure, then tears off after Lucien who has continued up the road.

It is late morning when they finally arrive at their destination. Lucien has been to the cemetery only once since his uncle died, just after they had all moved back to the big house. Things were still in disarray, and the visit was quick and too crowded with other people for him to do more than feel ill at ease. He had decided right then that he would come back again as soon as he could, just the two of them. However, once his classes began, and he was stuck at school most of the time, he had neglected his promise until today. He knew his uncle would understand, but, it made him feel guilty somehow. After all his uncle had done for him, how could he not have come to check on him before now? "Shame on me for it," he thought to himself.

At the gate of the ancient cemetery, Lucien looks around for the old knotty tree that marks the area of his uncle's grave. Spying it a short distance away, the two set off through the maze of monuments and markers toward the old oak. "Uncle's grave is over here," Lucien says to Fox, as he steps around the craggy trunk, where he finds the stone marker that stands guard over his uncle's grave. Although obviously newer than many of the surrounding markers, it is still beginning to show some age and lack of care. Lucien immediately sets to work pulling the weeds that have sprouted around it and clearing away the wind-blown debris.

"Oh Uncle," he apologizes, "I am so sorry that I haven't been more diligent. I promise I will come back more often to take care of your little home. Auntie will come too. She wanted to accompany us today, but, I asked to make the trip alone. Uncle, she has been so good to me since we were reunited in Paris, you would be proud of her. She and Mr. Raimond have married and moved here just so that we can all be back in your fine old house."

He sinks down to the ground and leans against the stone, as he chats on to this uncle.

> "Mr. Raimond still has his new house in Paris that he built on the old "island" where Fox and I lived, but, he is here as much as he can be. I wish you could have met him Uncle, he saved us from a terrible fate, and has taught me so much. I wish you were here to know him...I wish you were here..."

Trailing off, Lucien says nothing for a long while. Fox finally breaks the silence by dropping a stick down beside Lucien, and then stepping back to wait, in his demanding dog way, for Lucien to pick it up. "Yes, Fox," Lucien says softly, "I wish Uncle could have met you. He would have been so happy to know that I was in your care." With that, he lofts the stick for the dog, who tears out eagerly after it. As he watches Fox pounce on his prize and trot happily back to him, Lucien wonders if his uncle might have had a hand in Fox's sudden appearance that awful day so long ago at the Tuileries. He tosses the stick again and watches Fox bound after it on his tireless legs.

> "Uncle," Lucien continues, "Gustave is in Africa with the Legion. After all the misfortunes that occurred in Paris, he vowed to turn over a new leaf, and at the urging of Father La Tuile he enlisted to show that he was earnest in his intention to change his fortunes. I know that he also wants to think that you would be proud of him. In his last letter he has told me that he is now a dragoon, thanks in large part to the outstanding riding skills that you gave him. I hope that is enough to bring him safely back to Bordeaux. I am so afraid for him. He is my brother now, more than my cousin, and I wish there was some way I could help him."

As he speaks to his uncle, Fox waits anxiously for Lucien to throw his stick again.

"His adventures sound so grand and important. Sometimes, it makes me miss the life that Fox and I had in Paris, on our own. By remembering all the lessons you taught me, we managed so well. Now Gustave is on his own, and in danger, in a dark, treacherous land. We should be together, taking care of one another as brothers do."

Fox, having now given up his stick and their game, is more than happy to be the recipient of Lucien's gentle neck rub, as he sinks to the ground beside the boy. But, just as the dog's eyes are about to close in relaxation, something suddenly has him on full alert. Eyes wide, ears pricked up, he stares at a grave stone between them and the old tree, and in a sudden flash of motion he is away, bounding toward the stone. The squirrel concealed behind it wastes no time darting for the safe haven of the tree trunk with Fox in hot pursuit and closing fast. At the last second, the squirrel leaps for the tree, landing on the trunk several feet up, as Fox crashes to a halt at its base. The squirrel makes a mad leap for the first branch and perches there, tail twitching, scolding Fox, from high over the head of the franticly barking dog. Lucien laughs loudly at the spectacle, all traces of his previous despair seemingly wiped away in an instant. "Fox," he calls, "come back, you've been beaten. One day you'll get one, but come here now. Let's have our lunch, and then we must start for home. It's a long walk, so you must save your energy. Come here." Fox looks over at Lucien and sees that he is opening the bag they brought with them. Knowing what that means, he gives the squirrel a look of contempt, then turns and walks back to where Lucien is pulling their lunch from the bag.

Chapter Five

The Violin Player

Picking up the beat from the metronome, tapping his foot to get in time, he draws the bow gently across the strings once more.

Later that night, after having dinner with his mother and Monsieur Raimond, Lucien is in his room, poised with his violin in front of a music stand that holds several pages of sheet music. A beautiful rosewood metronome, sitting on a small desk he has piled high with his school books, clicks out the time as he works his way through the piece. After completing just a few bars of the rather complicated song, he hits a sour note and stops. Clapping the violin under his arm to hold it steady, he shakes out his hand to loosen his fingers. Then, leaning into the music stand, he studies the sheet music for a few moments, takes the violin from beneath his arm and mounts it to his shoulder again. Picking up the beat from the metronome, tapping his foot to get in time, he draws the bow gently across the strings once more. The music pours sweetly out of the instrument as Lucien makes another attempt at the song. His tentativeness fades the farther into the piece he plays, until he finally relaxes and begins to think that he's got it. He misses another note. Undeterred, he pauses just long enough to take a deep breath, then, tapping his foot to get back in time with the metronome, he returns to the beginning to start again.

Downstairs, in the sitting room, Madame Marboeuf and Mr. Raimond are enjoying some Cognac, nestled into two elegantly upholstered chairs that face the ornate fireplace, where Fox relaxes happily in front of the fire. Lucien's playing filters down through the house from his "practice studio" upstairs. Mr. Raimond remarks, "He has gotten quite good, don't you think? I almost regret telling him that he doesn't have the skill to be a musician."

Madame Marboeuf replies, "Yes, he has improved so much. He seems to have set a goal for himself to learn as many songs as he can by heart." From upstairs, the sound of the violin stops, and a loud, joyful shout of triumph fills the air. Mr. Raimond remarks, "You don't suppose it's because of what I said to him that he is working at it so hard, do you?"

Back up in his room, Lucien takes up the bow again, and speaks to himself, "Alright, you did it once. Now do it again, this time, without the music. You can't carry sheet music with you everywhere you go." He turns to face away from the music stand, takes a moment to get in time with the metronome and then, draws the bow across the strings one more time.

Chapter Six

Reunited

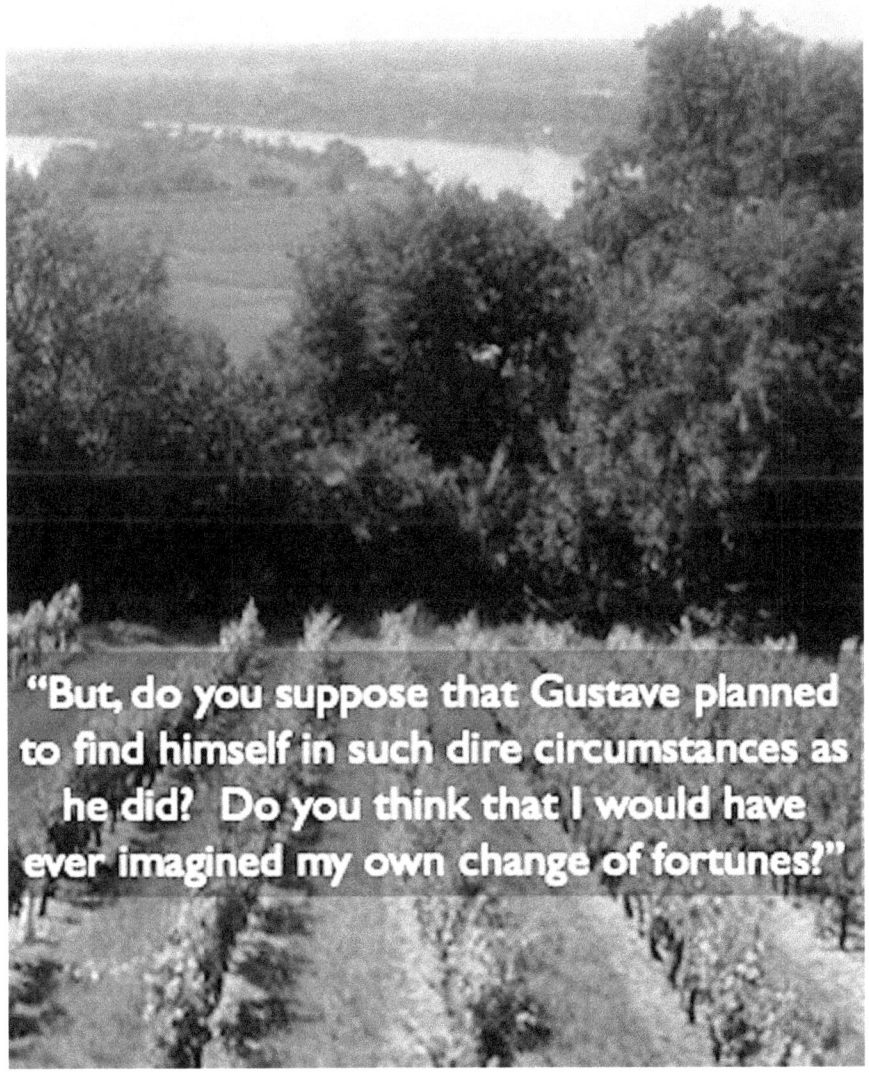

"But, do you suppose that Gustave planned to find himself in such dire circumstances as he did? Do you think that I would have ever imagined my own change of fortunes?"

The sinuous rows of dewy grape vines that blanket the hills beyond the house's kitchen garden glisten in the morning sun, creating elegant silvery green strands across the countryside. Madame Marboeuf and Monsieur Raimond are having their breakfast on the terrace overlooking the gardens and the vineyards, enjoying the enticing sun and cool Atlantic breeze. "Such a beautiful day," Madame Marboeuf remarks, "Look at the vineyards glow in the sunshine." "Splendid," Monsieur Raimond agrees, taking a deep breath, "the smell of the ocean is in the air, as well." They both look up and smile as Lucien comes outside to join them. "Good morning Mother, good morning Father Raimond," he says as the takes his place at the table. "I am sorry to be so late." "Not to worry Lucien, you have no classes today," his mother says. "Have something to eat dear," she continues, as Martine brings over a platter of pastries, fruit and cheese for him to choose from. "Thank you, Martine," Lucien says appreciatively. "We were listening to you practicing your violin last night Lucien," Monsieur Raimond comments, "I must say, you've improved tremendously from when I first heard you play outside the cafe." "Thank you, sir," responds the boy. Mr. Raimond continues, "Maybe I was not quite correct in my assessment of your musicianship. You seem to be quite driven to succeed at it." "Oh no! You were quite correct," Lucien replies, "I don't think I would ever be able to walk on stage in Paris, or even Bordeaux, and perform. But, I do remember the night I was able to help my poor old friend raise the money he needed for his family, and I could only play four songs then! I just imagine what I might have earned if I could play a great many lively tunes!" "So, you are considering life as a street musician then?" Mr. Raimond adds wryly. "Oh no, sir, not at all," the boy shoots back. "As I said, I think you are right that it would not be a good vocation for me. But, I have thought that, if I should ever find myself in need, perhaps I could earn money that way, as I did for my friend Marie's father," adding thoughtfully, "Fox and I had such fun that night."

Madame Marboeuf looks shocked at the suggestion that Lucien would ever need to become a street musician. "Lucien," she declares, "you will never be in such need that you will be fiddling for your supper. I will see to that." "Yes, Auntie," Lucien replies, "I know that you love me too much to allow something like that," Lucien assures her. "But, do you suppose that Gustave planned to find himself in such dire circumstances as he did? Do you think that I had ever imagined my own change of fortunes?" Monsieur Raimond adds, "My dear, it seems our Lucien is being quite practical. I am impressed with his forethought. Even if he should never have to perform for a meal, there is no harm in being able to." His mother just heaves an exasperated sigh of resignation, "Just be sure that your practicing doesn't interfere with your other studies."

Once she has finished, her old butler Phillip, who has been waiting patiently just inside the open doorway, approaches the table, "Yes, Phillip, what is it." The butler replies "The postman has just delivered a package for Master Lucien. Would he like me to bring it in now?" he says to her. She replies sharply, "We are in the middle of our breakfast, I am sure..." Phillip interrupts her, "Pardon

Madame, but it is from Master Gustave." Hearing this, Lucien exclaims, "Oh yes, do. Bring it at once! Auntie please, let's see what it is." "Yes, of course dear," she replies, knowing this is a skirmish she will never win, "I am just as curious as you are." Turning to Phillip, she continues, "You may bring the parcel in." "Of course Madame," he replies, turning to Martine who hands him the parcel which she has been holding the whole time. "Master Lucien," he says, giving him the package. Madame Marboeuf gives Phillip a dour look, "Well, you seem to have me all figured out don't you?" she grouses good-naturedly. "Not at all Madame," is his wry response. Mr. Raimond takes a pen-knife from his pocket and hands it to Lucien saying, "Lucien, let's leave them to their bickering, and have a look inside your package." Lucien gladly weighs in with the knife, first cutting away the binding twine, then quickly unwrapping the parcel and joyfully pulling out his old copy of "Robinson Crusoe", which he raises excitedly into the air, exclaiming, "My book!" As he does so, a letter falls out of it onto the table. Seeing the letter, he hurriedly thumbs through the book to be sure there is nothing else hidden inside its pages. "Lucien, dear, leave the book, and let us hear what is in the letter," implores his mother. "Yes, you're right," he says putting the book down and picking up the envelope. He quickly extracts and unfolds a single sheet of paper, which he begins to read silently. His aunt interjects, "Lucien, you are being rude, share the news from Gustave?" Lucien reads the note aloud.

"Dearest Cousin,

I trust that this note will find you well, as I'm sure our aunt is keeping you well scrubbed and better fed. To be honest, I would welcome a bit of that here!

Your old book has been a great companion to me, and puts me in mind of better times whenever I pick it up. But, it is now time for it to go back to its rightful place with you. We will be marching tomorrow, and I don't know when I will next have a another chance to post this home. Thank you so much for the lending of your book. I hope you will forgive me the "slight" damage. Be assured that neither my faithful horse nor I are any the worse for it. Thankfully, the book and my saddlebag took the brunt of it, and preserved us for another day. It was a ricochet and took us by surprise...

Lucien drops the letter and picks up the book. He turns it over and sees something he missed initially, which makes his eyes go wide: a hole penetrates the back cover of the book and continues about halfway through the pages before stopping. The reality of Gustave's situation had never completely registered with him – with any of them – until this moment. He looks at his aunt, "Oh my Auntie, do you think my book has saved him from a musket ball?" He just stares at the hole in the back of the book, transfixed. "Lucien!" Monsieur Raimond says forcefully, bringing the boy's focus back to the table, "Gustave was fortunate to have your book with him, but, he is living a soldier's life now and this is the reality of it. Now, please read us the rest of the note." Lucien picks up the letter again and continues, somewhat tentatively now:

...but, it did no more than startle my brave mount, who quickly regained his composure and bore me safely from the fight. I do hope you like your souvenir of the Algerian campaign!

56

I have a great deal to do before we march tomorrow, so I am unable to write more now. Please give my love to our aunt, and to Monsieur Raimond, who I am sure is watching over you both. I long for the day that we can all be back together in Bordeaux, and I can reestablish myself as the honorable heir of my father.

Your devoted cousin,

Gustave

He sets the letter gently on the table. The stifling silence now hangs heavy in the air. Overhead, a few clouds have moved in, intermittently blocking the bright sunshine, giving the morning a darker cast. They continue their meal, each lost in their own imaginings. Finally, Lucien speaks, "Gustave is a fine horseman." Madame Marboeuf casts a concerned look at her husband, and adds, "Yes, of course he is Lucien. He will be fine."

Chapter Seven

A Secret Stash

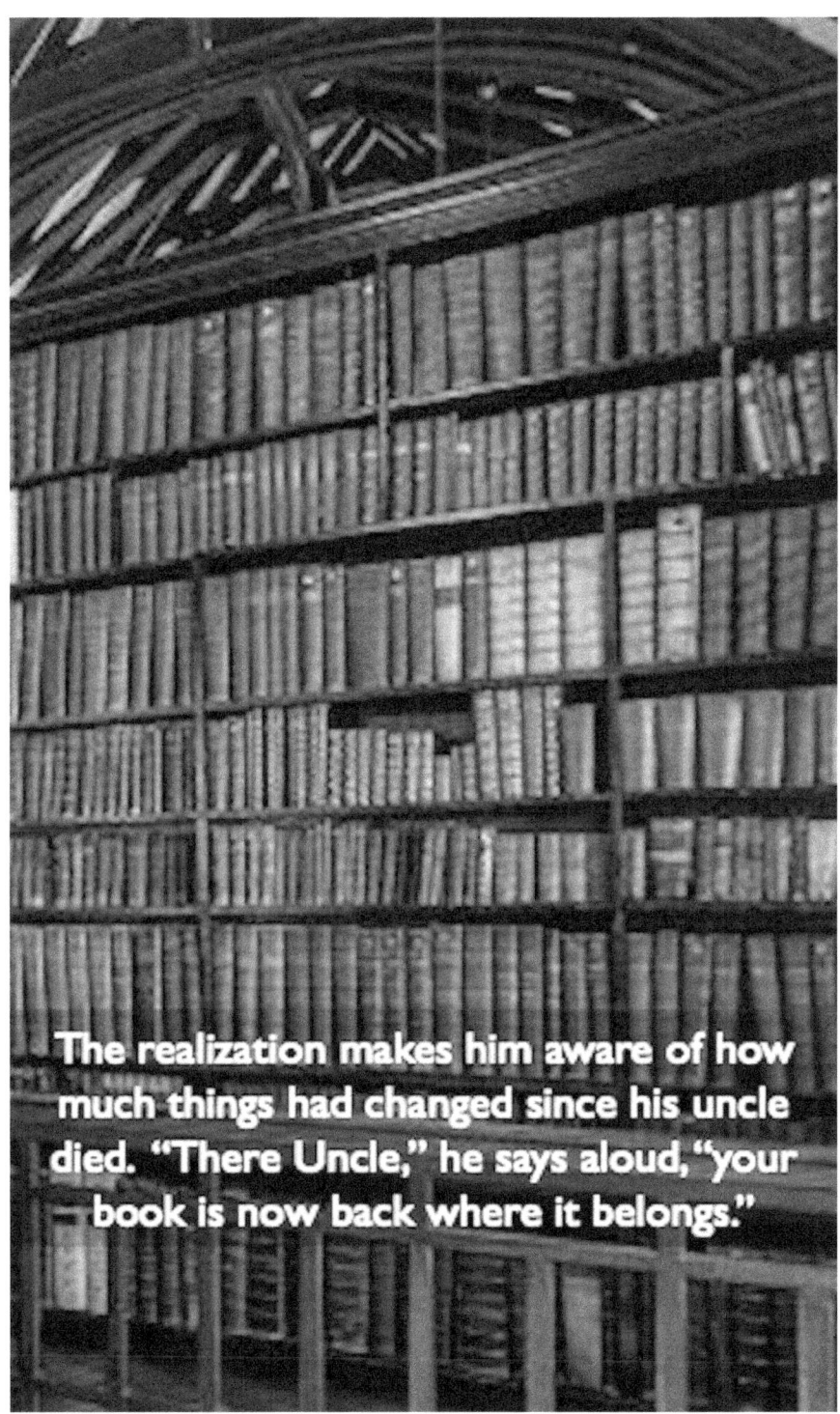

The realization makes him aware of how much things had changed since his uncle died. "There Uncle," he says aloud, "your book is now back where it belongs."

That night, with the moon casting a pale silver light into his room, giving it an eerie glow, Lucien lies in bed, with Fox curled up contentedly at his feet. He has the blankets pulled up high, and his newly returned copy of "Robinson Crusoe" is open in front of him. As he flips through a few pages he speaks to Fox, who does no more than rotate an ear in Lucien's direction. "You know Fox," he says, "it's been such a long time since I've read this, it doesn't seem like the same story anymore." He turns the book over and runs his finger carefully around the new hole in the back cover, then begins paging toward the front, counting the number that have been punctured by the piece of hot lead. He stops when he finally reaches the spot where the damage is no more than an indentation, and continues, "Fox, can you believe it? That ricochet went through 50 pages of my old book! It must have gone through a heavy leather saddle bag before that and who knows what else!" He thinks about this for a moment, before going on, "Oh poor Gustave, please be so careful. You are an excellent rider, but I don't think you can outrun musket-balls!" He gently closes the book, and turns it over to examine the hole again, then sets the volume carefully on the reading table beside the bed and turns down the oil lamp and snuggles into the blankets to sleep. His hand finds Fox's head, which he rubs gently for comfort. "Good night Fox," he says, as he gazes thoughtfully out the bedroom window at the moon.

Hours later, the early morning darkness finds Lucien awake. He reaches for the bedside table and picks up his book, examining it again, then, with one hand he throws the blankets aside and sits up on the edge of the bed. Fox, startled by the coverings landing on him, gives a little yip, to say, "Get these off of me, if you please." Lucien obliges, "I'm sorry Fox, I didn't mean to wake you. Go back to sleep. I'll be right back." With that, he slips out of bed and crosses to the bedroom door, clutching the old book in one hand, and turning the knob with the other.

The hallway outside his door is shadowed and silent. The servants are off in their own quarters, and his aunt and Mr. Raimond are sound asleep in their own suite. The moonlight streaming in the windows at the end of the hallway offer the only light as Lucien walks carefully and quietly along the passage, stopping finally in front of his uncle's old study. He instantly remembers that cold day, so long ago now, when he stood at that door begging his cousin to let him in, just so he could have some company. "How much Gustave has changed since that day," he thinks to himself. Opening the door, he steps into the familiar old space. It still looks much the same as it did then and he can imagine seeing his old uncle by the fireplace, reading one of his cherished books, and looking up warmly to greet him. Lucien had always marveled at all the fascinating volumes in his uncle's collection. It was a fine library, worthy of any scholar. His uncle had always encouraged him to read any of the books that were there, saying, "Lucien my boy, if you can read it, you may read it. If you can't read it, all the more reason to try." It was from this collection of dark leather and gold embossing that his uncle had extracted the book that Lucien now held. It was the last thing his uncle had given him, and he always treasured it, keeping it with him through thick and thin. It had been his anchor and his best remembrance of those better days. But, now, it felt different. Now that he finally had the book back, and it had that big hole in it, Lucien realized that that the book should be put it back into the collection that it came from. It was time to find something new.

Still remembering the exact spot the book was pulled from, he walks carefully, but purposefully, across the shadowy room, and stops in front of one of the towering walls of books that encircles it. Reaching for the step ladder he begins to climb, then, thinking better of it, stops and steps down. Raising the old copy of "Robinson Crusoe" up over his head, and lifting himself up on his toes, he is able to use the edge of the book to make room for it in its former spot, pushing it back into place, stopping just when the spine was even with the the spines of the books on either side of it. Stepping back to have a look at his handy work, he realizes that not long ago he would have needed the ladder to reach that spot, but now, the shelf was within his grasp with almost no stretching at all. It makes him aware of how much things had changed since his uncle died. "There Uncle," he says aloud, "your book is back where it belongs." Then adds, "Time for a new story now." Walking to the desk in the center of the room, he stands a moment to look all the way around at the magnificently loaded shelves on all sides of him. Then, moving as close as he can to the exact middle of the room, he spins around several times, with one arm outstretched, as a pointer. He stops twirling, opens his eyes, and walks in the direction of his outstretched arm, stopping in front of one of the walls of books. Considering them for a moment, he thinks to himself, "'Always reach beyond your grasp,' Uncle, you told me that," and shifts his gaze up to the higher shelves, the ones just beyond his reach. He retrieves the library ladder and rolling it quietly to the spot where he had been standing, immediately climbs to the top shelf, where he begins looking through the books.

The warming light of day is replacing the hard silver rays of the moon, and the library is now beginning to glow in the waxing sunlight as Lucien continues searching through the titles on the top shelf, but isn't too pleased with what he has found so far. "Oh Uncle," he laments, "these books up here sound so boring, is that why you put them up here out of easy reach?" Smiling at the thought, he adds, "Are you saying I should keep to the lower shelves, Uncle?" Losing his focus, he also loses his balance and has to quickly grab the ladder to steady himself, but in so doing, he drops the book he is holding onto the floor where it lands with a loud thud. "Quiet Lucien!" he thinks, "You will wake the whole house!" Slipping lightly down the ladder to retrieve the errant tome, as he stoops for it, he notices that one of the cabinets beneath the shelves has been knocked slightly ajar. Peering inside, he discovers a stack of books too large or oddly shaped to fit on the regular shelves, laying on their sides in the cabinet. "I don't recall these old books," Lucien is thinking as he begins to examine this new stash. Spying one book off to the side, leaning against the end of the cabinet, he carefully pulls it out, "What's this?" he wonders as he turns it over to look at the front cover. In old, flaking gold letters, it reads, *"The King of Pirates: Being an Account of the Famous Enterprises of Captain Avery, The Mock King of Madagascar."* He sets his new find aside and quickly returns the fallen book to its place on the upper shelf. Satisfied that everything is back in order, he picks up his newly discovered old book and steals quietly back to his bedroom, where, much to Fox's annoyance, he is forced to vacate Lucien's pillow, where he had taken up residence. Lucien turns up the reading lamp beside the bed, and opens the book.

Later that morning, Fox comes bounding down the stairs, with Lucien in hot pursuit, and his new discovery clasped tightly in one hand. When they reach the bottom of the stairs, he laughs, "Fox, I think you win this time, perhaps I should have gotten more sleep." Martine who is just on her way to the kitchen when the two of them come racing down, scolds them dutifully, "It won't be so fun when one of you falls down and breaks your neck." Lucien looks up at her, "Oh Martine," he says, to her slyly, "I know you do care for us. We will try to be more careful." "Yes, I am sure you will," she replies, not convinced. "What's that book you have there?" she enquires, crossing to them. Lucien holds the book up for her to see. "I found it last night in the library, Martine. I decided that it was time to return my old book to its place, and it was then that I chanced upon this one," he explains. Martine examines the book, warning, "You take care of this book Lucien, it's old and fragile. Your uncle brought this home long before you first arrived here. He developed a sudden interest in pirates. Who knows why? He was interested in so many things. I remember he came home with this book and sat down and read it right through, saying it was research." She hands the book back to him, adding, "Dusty old thing. Now go on and get your breakfast, your parents are outside." "Yes, of course Martine," he replies, "Come Fox," and with that they bolt from the room, toward the terrace and breakfast.

Chapter Eight

Captain Avery

He leans his head back against the pear tree, and lets his mind wander out to sea and grave pirate adventures. Behind him, away off in the distance, the white dots of sails litter the surface of the ocean beyond the "Port of the Moon."

Out behind the house, Lucien and Fox sit beneath one of the splendid fruit trees that border the kitchen garden, separating it from the vineyards spreading out down the gentle hillsides toward Bordeaux, and its bustling trading port, "The Port of the Moon." The area takes its name from the crescent shaped bend in the Argonne river where it is located, upstream of the union of the river with the Atlantic Ocean. Beyond the city and the river that runs through it, the vast sprawl of the Atlantic looms large and omnipresent, separated from the river by a thin strip of land that points to the junction of the two.

Beneath their fruit tree Lucien and Fox lay sprawled, taking advantage of the shade the old pear provides. Lucien reads aloud to Fox from his new book, and the dog seems perfectly content to lay in a sunbeam and listen passively to Lucien's commentary.

> "Why Fox, this Avery was quite an ambitious fellow. Do you know that he made himself King of his very own island! He took the whole of Madagascar for his own. Can you believe such a thing?" he says, adding thoughtfully, "Of course, he was an Englishman."

He goes back to his reading, not noticing that Fox looks to be sound asleep nestled in a little hollow between the roots of the tree. Lucien continues,

> "Captain Avery was abducted by sailors as a boy, at almost the same age as I, when I was cast-away in Paris. His parents had intended for him to be an educated gentleman as well, but he was kidnapped out to sea and never returned. Can you imagine it, Fox?" Lucien continues, "He was befriended by the captain of that ship, who took him under his protection and taught him the sailing life. It's as if Captain Avery had his own

Monsieur Raimond, don't you think Fox?" Lucien remarks, with a hint of excitement rising in his voice.

Fox lays still, content to listen and twitch his ears at the fly that is pestering him. "This Avery is very much like us Fox. We had our island, and he had his. We were taken from our homes, as he was. We made our own way in Paris, and he made his own way at sea. Fox, are you listening at all?" Lucien turns back to the book and begins to read;

> "The Captain, by this time being awaked by the noise of the conspirators working the ship, rung the bell, inquiring what was the matter, to whom Avery and some of the crew replied, "Nothing. Are you mutinous in your cups? Can't you lie down, sleep, and be quiet?"
>
> "No," saith the Captain. "I am sure something's the matter with the ship. Does she drive? What weather is it? Is it a storm?"
>
> Saith Avery: "Cannot you lie quiet while you are quiet? I tell you all's well; we are at sea in a fair wind and good weather."
>
> "At sea," saith the Captain; "that can't be."
>
> "Be not frightened," saith Avery, "and I'll tell you. You must note, I am now the Captain of the ship; nay, you must turn out, for this is my cabin, and I am bound for Madagascar, to make my own fortune as well as my companions'."

Lucien looks up from the book, "What a bold fellow this Avery was," he exclaims. "I guess I am not much like him after all. Avery commanded men and fortunes. All I know how to do is play my violin. Not much of a pirate am I, Fox," the boy laments wistfully, as he turns his gaze toward the deep blue, beckoning ocean off in the distance. "Fox" he begins, "I think tomorrow..."

Leaning his head back against the pear tree, Lucien lets his mind wander out to sea and grave pirate adventures. Behind him, away off in the distance, the white dots of sails litter the surface of the ocean beyond the port.

Chapter 9

The Shuttered Door

Where are
Fox and Lucien?
Turn the page to see.

As he ventures in he catches a glimpse of
the dog, digging at the ground beneath what
appears to be a shuttered up doorway. He
calls to the dog again, just as Fox disappears
through his excavation and is gone.

Fox waits patiently outside a fragrant little Patisserie on a bustling side street in the heart of Bordeaux. After a moment, Lucien emerges from the little bakery with a package containing various crusty, sugary treats. Fox, immediately smelling its tempting contents waits obediently at Lucien's feet, ignoring the passers-by. The look on his face, so open and earnest, says, "Come on, we both know you are going to give me something good, why make me beg." Lucien, as if in reply to the dog's gaze says, "Yes, of course Fox, do you really think I would forget about you while buying good things to eat?" He gently retrieves a nice warm croissant, and breaking it in half tosses one to Fox, who snaps it deftly out of the air. Lucien takes a bite of the other half and says, "Come along Fox, we're almost there. We'll find a place to sit and have another bite in just a few minutes I think." With that, they start off down the street, Fox beside Lucien, his leash hanging slack between them. Fox often wondered why Lucien bothered with the thing, "It's all so silly," he would think. "Where else would I want to be?" As they continue along, Lucien notices more and more sailors amongst the crowd, either talking boisterously with their shipmates, happy to be ashore for a time, or lugging provisions and pushing barrows laden with supplies. "We must be very close now Fox," Lucien exclaims, "See all the crewmen rushing about. I can't believe that we haven't been here before now." At that moment, a rather course looking sailor bumps into Lucien as he passes, knocking him aside, unconcerned. "Pardon me, sir," Lucien says, with the well-practiced manners that have been drilled into him, first by his uncle and now his aunt, "I did not see you." The rough sailor replies with a gruff growl, too absorbed in his own business to stop for Lucien, continuing down the street, and disappearing into one of the many storefronts that line the way. "I think sailors must be rather rough men Fox," Lucien continues. "Do you suppose that one might have been a pirate?" Fox replies with a curious look, to which Lucien adds, "Yes, I think so too." They continue exploring the bustling street a ways, until stopped by an intersection. Lucien turns to look down the cross-street and freezes in his tracks, awestruck at the sight before him.

Lucien and Fox are now literally face to face with a forest of wood, rope and canvas formed by the masts and rigging of the long line of fine, tall sailing ships tied up to the piers of the port. The bow sprits of some of the ships extend out right over the street that runs along the shoreline creating a canopy of rope and wood. The painted hulls of the ships, with their tall masts and long cross trees, from which the sails are hung, makes Lucien think of a forest in winter, all the leaves long since blown away, leaving just the branches, in all their glory. The rigging running between this tangle of "branches" is so thick that it actually blocks the sun in spots. Lucien, with Fox at his side, wanders toward this armada of ships, trying to stay out of the way of the rushing longshoremen, with their carts and barrows, wheels clattering over the cobbles of the street. Reflexively, Lucien scoops up his friend for fear of him getting trampled beneath this throng. Fox looks just as happy to be up where he can get a better view, as they walk along among the confusion of ships and horses and sailors, and slowly melt into the crowd.

Making their way along the waterfront, they emerge from the crowd at the mouth of a narrow, dark alleyway between two dirty stone warehouses. Lucien, absorbed by the sights and sounds around him, doesn't notice when Fox suddenly pricks up his ears and quickly turns his head toward the alleyway. A moment later, with an unexpected burst, the dog leaps out of Lucien's grasp and bolts into the passage, in hot pursuit of a dark, ghostly little shape that quickly vanishes into the shadows. Lucien, unprepared as he is, cannot stop the dog, and calls desperately after him, "Fox, where are you going? Fox come! Fox! Come here!" But Fox, focused on his prey, at the mercy of his instincts, seems to have completely forgotten Lucien. "Fox, come!" the boy tries again, but gets no response from the dog. "Fox," he cries, as he starts down the passage after the dog, "where have you gone?" Once his eyes adjust to the dark, he sees that one side of the narrow gap is an unbroken stone wall, but on the other, what looks to be the older of the two building, the wall is punctuated by boarded up, locked windows. As he ventures in he catches a glimpse of the dog, digging at the ground beneath what appears to be a shuttered up doorway. He calls to the dog again, just as Fox disappears through his excavation and is gone. "Fox! Stop! Come here!" he cries desperately, but the dog is gone. Lucien runs to the opening and kneels down to get a better look. He can squeeze no more than his head through the hole, and inside can see nothing in the darkness. He can however hear Fox, still in pursuit of whatever it was that got his attention. As the dog moves around inside, from time to time Lucien hears a gentle metallic clinking sound, which concerns the boy. "Fox, come back right now," he implores. As his eyes adjust to the dim light inside he begins to make out strange shapes in the large mostly empty space. The dusty, spotty light that filters through the gaps in the shutters, supply just enough illumination for him to make out several ghostly structures. He's not sure, but he thinks he can see chains hanging from a heavily built scaffold that runs down the middle of the cavernous space. Some of the chains reach almost to the ground, and these knock together as Fox runs beneath them, creating the strange metallic sound. Lucien turns his head as best he can to see more of the room, but the light is too dim to make out much else, but he senses that something also hangs from the wall beside the doorway where his head is. Before he can make it out, the clanging chains get his attention and Fox appears in front of him. Lucien is relieved and admonishes the dog, "Fox, there you are. How could you just run off like that? Come outside this instant!" With that Lucien extracts himself from the hole and waits for Fox to crawl back through. Once the dog is out, he proudly lays his prize at Lucien's feet. Lucien recoils when he sees that his friend has brought him a freshly killed rat! "Oh my goodness Fox! Is this what you were so intent on! You must leave these filthy creatures alone. They are dirty awful things. Now come along, we must get home, and I think, give you a good bath too!" He picks up Fox and heads quickly out of the alley, saying, "I think we've had our adventure for today Fox.

Time to go home before Auntie sends the whole staff out to search for us!"

At dinner that evening, Lucien excitedly recounts the day's adventures to his parents. His aunt is none to pleased with the report of their exploits that day. "I do not want you poking around at the port Lucien, there are dangerous people around the docks, and, how could you let Fox go chasing off after a filthy rat like that? He could have been bitten, and you too! Honestly, I thought you had better sense than that." Lucien makes a desperate attempt to defend himself, "But, Mother," he begins, "nothing did happen. Fox caught his rat, and we were home in time for supper. I am sorry that I have worried you." He pauses to gauge the success of his plea. "Well, nevertheless," Madame Marboeuf replies, "something might have happened, and I would not have heard of it for days!" she exclaims. "Yes, Mother, I am sorry, I will be sure to tell you where I am in the future," he says, "but, what about the old warehouse that we found? Isn't it odd, the strange sound I heard when Fox was inside? I do wish I could have seen better what was there." Monsieur Raimond interjects, "Perhaps it was a holding area for convicts waiting to be sent to the colonies. Many types of cargo ship out of the Port of the Moon." Madame Marboeuf adds, "Criminals being sent to their punishment, nothing so mysterious about that. I want you to stay away from that place." she says, punctuating her statement with a stern look. "I agree, Lucien," adds Mr. Raimond, "that is no place for a young gentleman to be poking about. You could have been robbed or abducted and never seen again." Martine who has been standing by in silence now unexpectedly speaks up, "I beg your pardon, sir," she says stepping to the table, "but, that building was not for prisoners, at least not as you describe. I have spent my whole life here in Bordeaux, and I am well aware of what has taken place over the years at the port. With your permission, I can tell Lucien all about it." Mr. Raimond gestures her to continue, "Of course Martine, we would all like to know a bit more of the history of our new home. Please continue." Martine turns to Lucien and speaks,

"When I was a girl, about the same age as you are now, I once accompanied my father to that area in the early morning. He was on an errand for his employer, and we were there before most people were out. At the piers, he went off to do his business, and I was left on my own. While I waited for my father, I watched from behind a barrel as a group of Africans were taken off a ship, and marched right into that very warehouse. They were not criminals, but they were prisoners." Lucien looks confused, "If they were not criminals, then why were they being kept as prisoners," he asked. Martine continues, "They were African slaves being sent to the King's colonies to work on the sugar plantations. Many slave ships sailed from Bordeaux in those days. It was not normal for them to come back to this port with such cargo aboard, but it would happen occasionally because of weather or to change ships. They would use that building to keep them secure and out of sight," Martine says, concluding, "No one likes to talk about it much, but many high families in Bordeaux made their fortunes in the slave trade."

Madame Marboeuf looks stricken, "Slaves! We do not participate in the slave trade in France. How dare you say it." Mr. Raimond responds, "My dear, Martine is telling the truth. Until only a few years ago, France sent a great many ships into that business, and many French fortunes were made there. Even today, it is rumored that the colonies are furnished with workers that way. It is reprehensible, but, not untrue. I dare say, Lucien, your uncle at one time or another had contact with slavers." At the suggestion that her former employer had anything to do with the slave trade, Martine jumps to his defense, "I beg your pardon, sir. It is not my place, but, I knew Monsieur Armand for many years. He was a very good man, and never did I suspect he had any dealing in that business," she says passionately. "No, of course not Martine," Mr. Raimond replies, "I was simply suggesting that the slave trade was a large and well-established concern for many years in Europe, and as an astute trader, Armand would surely have come into contact with it at some point." Madame Marboeuf has heard quite enough, "No more of this sordid conversation. Martine, make yourself useful; we shall have our dessert now." "Yes, Madame," comes Martine's well practiced reply, and with that she is gone. "Lucien," Madame Marboeuf continues, "your uncle was a good man, and would never do business with those who profit from the imprisonment of others. Thankfully, our great country has turned the slavers out, and is no longer involved in that godless trade." The conversation is over, and Lucien knows it.

A few minutes later, as he sits and quietly eats the fine dessert that Martine has brought out from the kitchen, he thinks back over the events of the day, and the now even more enticing warehouse, and is already planning his next visit to the old slave chamber.

Chapter Ten

The Conspirators

Where's Lucien?

Turn the page to see.

To that end, at his first chance, he gathered his three closest friends and told them the story of the dark, mysterious warehouse at the docks.

Their holiday break now behind them, and back at their desks, Lucien's classmates were anxious to hear his report on Algeria. Being boys of a certain age, their primary interest was in bearing witness to any mistakes or stumbles Lucien might commit that they could taunt him with later. They were the best of friends, but, there is an unwritten code among classmates that had to be respected, so, to their disappointment, "Lucky Lucien" pulled off his presentation admirably, supplying his friends with little ammunition for later use. He had written his report, based in part on the tales that Gustave had related to him in his letters, as well as news accounts of the campaign, and his own vivid imagination. In the end, even his stern professor had to give him grudging credit for a job "well enough" done. Lucien was pleased with the praise, although, he knew it was not his best effort. He had pulled together just enough to get by, which was not like him, but, he had been so distracted while he was back home. After Martine had enlightened the family about the former use of the warehouse, Lucien had questioned her about it more fully, listening carefully to her recollections, if not her warnings to avoid the place. Of course, all he could think about then was going back again to see the awful sight once more. He could not understand the thinking of his countrymen, who had just endured a terrifying revolution in the name of freedom, dragging innocent people from their homes in chains, and shipping them off to the ends of the earth as slaves. This did not jibe with the picture that he had been raised to aspire to, and he wanted to know more.

To that end, at his first chance, he gathered his three closest friends and told them the story of the dark, mysterious warehouse at the docks. Who would go with him to visit the place, he demanded. Adding, in good pirate fashion, "Who has the stomach for it?" None wanting to be outdone by the others, all three agreed. So, the plan was laid to sneak out and slip away to the docks that same afternoon.

The sun is lowering itself toward the horizon when they arrived at the port, with Lucien quickly leading his band along the river to the deserted old building, mindful of the dark characters that are just now emerging into the waning daylight.

The alleyway between the old buildings is looking even more mysterious now, with the light of day being replaced by the creeping shadows of night. "Come on," Lucien whispers, "the broken shutter is just down this alley." He walks boldly into the dark trench formed by the walls, with his comrades close behind. "Here," Lucien exclaims, "look. This is the spot where Fox went in." As the others huddle around to see, Lucien kneeling down, notices that the hole has been repaired. "Oh," Lucien exclaims quietly, "someone has nailed the hole up again!" One of Lucien's classmates complains, "We've come all this way, and now you say we can't even look in." Another chimes in, "Quiet you. Lucien would not have brought us here if he knew we could not go inside. All we need to do is check the other windows and see if we can't find another way." "Yes!," Lucien agrees, "Come on, let's start looking." With that the four of them spread out along the alley, tugging and kicking at the shutters in hopes one of them might be loose. But, whomever repaired the first one, did a thorough job, and made sure the others were all good and stout. Having no luck finding another way in, and gathering back around Lucien, they are wondering what to do next, when suddenly, out of a shadow steps a menacing looking man, who has been watching their explorations. "Well, hello there lads!" he scowls, "Having a hard time breaking in?" The boys are caught off guard and panic. "Run!" someone yells, and they rush as one past the watchman and escape, all but Lucien. He doesn't run. He stands his ground, defiant. "We've done nothing wrong, sir, so if you don't mind stand aside and let me pass." "Why, I don't think so, pup," says the other, "What if I hadn't covered that hole over, I suppose you'd still be singing the same song?" He grabs Lucien by the collar and begins to haul him down the alley toward the street. "I think I'll turn you in as a thief." "Unhand me!" Lucien commands, "I've done nothing. How dare you imply I'm a thief." "Well boy, I think you're just what a thief looks like, so off we go." Lucien struggles to break free and finally twists loose, jumping back from the man's frantic grab for him. "Leave me to my business you oaf, or I shall call for an officer and have you arrested for kidnapping," he cries defiantly. "Good luck!" the watchman laughs, "they won't be back until after sun up, if then." "No matter," says Lucien, "for you won't lay a hand on me again!" With that, the boy lunges frantically past the watchman, who is now standing between him and the street. At the last second he feints one way and dodges the guard, leaving him grasping at thin air. The guard spins around just in time to see Lucien disappearing around the corner and out onto the street. He doesn't bother to chase him, thinking he had put a sufficient scare into the boys to keep them away. He had done what he had been paid to do and that was enough for him.

The next morning, back at school, Lucien catches up with his cohorts in the large, noisy dining hall. The conversation comes to a standstill when Lucien sits down, the boys casting guilty looks at one another as they eat their breakfast. Lucien takes a few bites, before breaking the heavy silence. "That was a fantastic adventure we had last night, don't you think?" One of the other three weighs in, "Lucien, we could have been killed. That guard looked like quite a rough man." Another boy joins in, "We would be expelled from school if we had been caught!" There is another long pause, as Lucien looks around the table, taking stock of each of his comrades, before continuing, "When I was there with Fox, the shutter was broken and there was no one paying any mind. I never dreamed anyone would be watching now." One of the other boys counters, "Is it so hard to believe that the owner of the building wants to have his property protected from vandals?" "What if that scoundrel had gotten a hold of one of us?" interjects another of the boys, "My parents would have been very angry, to say the least." "It's true," Lucien replies, "but, we don't have to worry about that, because it didn't happen. We will just need to be more careful next visit. Now, we will know to be on guard." "Next visit?" another interjects incredulously. "We won't go back with you Lucien." "I should say not," another agrees, "it's not an adventure for a proper young man, who will need to become a professional in just a few years."

Lucien is disappointed. "Where is their sense of adventure?" he thinks to himself. "They already sound like old men!" He is beginning to realize that he is no longer like all the other boys who had been so well looked after every single day of their lives. As good as his life had been with his uncle, and now with his aunt, his time in Paris had changed him. He wasn't afraid of the unknown anymore. As brave as his uncle had taught him to be, it was always bravery within the confines of his comfortable existence. He wore the right clothes and therefore he could expect deferential treatment. But, in Paris, that had all been taken away. He had gotten by on the strength of his heart and mind; on his kindness and generosity to others; on his abilities alone. He had made it on his own, and he now realized that he would be going back to the warehouse on his own as well. Who needed them running away at the first noise in the dark. He would go back, but, he would go with his only real friend, the one who had already shown him that he would never run, never leave him. Fox would go with him, and together they would discover the secrets of the old, dank, warehouse.

Chapter Eleven

The Slave Chamber

Where are
Fox and Lucien?
Turn the page to see.

Inspecting it with his fingers he makes out a metal cuff, attached to an old chain, which is then bolted firmly into the stones.

Fox sits in the front hall, attentive, ears perked up, staring at the heavy wooden door, listening. From time to time he lifts his nose, sniffing at the faint breeze that creeps in beneath the closed door. The dog knew that once the upstairs maid had changed the sheets on Lucien's bed and closed the door, that the boy was gone again. Lucien had said goodbye to him, promising to come home soon, but once the bedroom door had been shut, the dog knew it was back to the normal routine and to his own fluffy bed beside the big fireplace. It was a good life for a dog; food, comfort, companions, all the important things, and he was content but for his best friend not being there. There had been no change in the routine of the house since Lucien's departure, no extra cleaning of rooms, or fussing over the silver, but today, when he woke up, Fox had a sense – even though the house seemed the same – that things were going to change. The feeling had gotten stronger throughout the morning, so after eating some food around noon, and rather than curling up in his bed for an afternoon nap, he wandered to a spot in the front hall, where he stood for a moment looking at the door, and then calmly sat down on the floor to wait.

There's no rush. He knows what he knows. He'll wait. "Fox? What are you doing there?" calls Madame Marboeuf, puzzled. "Go lie on your bed, that's no place for you." The dog turns his head to her as if to say, "Isn't it obvious what I'm doing? I'm waiting," and he turns back to the door. She walks over to his spot and leads him, reluctantly to his bed by the fireplace, where he obediently sits down. "Now you stay right there, so you're not underfoot. We can't have Martine or one of the others falling over you." He does as he's told, just long enough to watch her leave the room, but once she disappears into the house, and he's sure she isn't coming back, he picks himself up and heads back to the front hall, to his spot, and plops himself down on the floor again to watch the door, to sniff at the air, and to wait.

It is about an hour later that Madame Marboeuf finds him in the front hallway again, in the same spot, watching the door. "Fox!" she calls from across the room, "what are doing there again..." But, he can't hear her. He is up on his feet now, nose in the air, pulling in the scent. He knows his tail was wagging now too, he can feel it, even if he can't control it. But, why would he want to? He's happy, and wants to show it. His tail actually pulls him back and forth now, as the scent grows, and he begins to feel the vibrations in the floor coming through from beneath the heavy door. "...Didn't I put you on your bed!" Madame Marboeuf continues, as he readies himself. Then, just as the door begins to open, the dog is right there, springing toward the widening gap with a happy bark. She calls out again in some alarm, "Oh my!" But it's too late, Fox is airborne, leaping for the door, just as Lucien steps through. As always, Fox hits him before he can even make it inside, and as always, Lucien is ready for the attack. He catches the dog in one clean, practiced motion, and brings him into his body in a warm bear hug. "Hello Fox! How's my good boy?" Lucien exclaims, petting the dog and setting him back on the ground. Fox leaps for him again and again, barking happily. It is Madame

Marboeuf's voice that punctuates their warm greeting. "Lucien? Oh my, what on Earth are you doing home now? Are you sick?" She rushes to him and lays her hand on his forehead to check for fever. Lucien replies, "No mother, I'm not sick. I'm fine." She hugs her son, then pushes him to arms length, "Then, what are doing here?" she asks, concerned, "You've only been gone a week." He looks at her archly, "Shall I go back then?" he asks. She gives him a disapproving look. "Mother," he continues, "I was given permission to come retrieve my violin. I had intended to take it before. So, I've come to get it, but, I will stay here for the weekend if you will have me." "Oh my, don't be silly," she snaps, "If I will let you indeed!" Lucien had considered many different excuses for his return home after such a short absence, but it was after rejecting several other defective reasons, that he decided on his violin. He knew that she would love the idea of him playing his violin at school, which might even allow him to join the school's orchestra, and he was confident he could get permission to go home for it too. "Violin it is," he thought. "No other reasons are needed."

It was bright and early the next morning that his real reason for coming home began to play itself out. Lucien and Fox, creep quietly down the big staircase that lands so grandly in the main hall of the house. Once they are sure that no one is about, the two conspirators move quickly to the front door. Lucien swings the door open for Fox, who slips out quickly, with Lucien right behind him, gently latching the heavy door behind them, the heavy iron knocker tapping gently against the strike plate. Inside, at the morning table, Monsieur Raimond responds to the thud from the front door, looking up from his reading for a moment, then hearing nothing more, turns back to it again. Outside, Lucien and Fox make good their escape, running together down the great long drive from the house, toward the old road that winds its way down into the city, and to the mysterious old warehouse.

They arrive at "Le Port de La Lune" with the sun high, amid the normal crush of activity. Vendors and longshoremen lug and push handcarts full of various cargos to and from the many ships moored there. The carriages of merchants and ship owners jockey for position adding to the energetic chaos. Lucien carries Fox protectively as they make their way through the throng, both seeming to be enjoying all the sights and sounds that swirl around them. When they finally arrive at the alleyway that runs beside the old warehouse building, Lucien pauses at the corner, and peeks around it cautiously, scanning for any sign of the watchman who interrupted their previous attempt. Seeing no one, he sets Fox on the ground and they disappear into the dark alleyway together.

Walking slowly and cautiously Lucien remains alert for any sign of the watchman, while Fox busily sniffs along the old stone foundation of the building. Stopping at one of the shuttered windows Lucien tries to get a peek inside by pulling himself up to the sill to get a look. Unable to suspend himself there long enough to find a suitable peephole, he drops back to the ground and notices that Fox is back sniffing and pawing around at the boards covering the hole where he first got into the building. Joining the dog, Lucien observes, "It's no use Fox, the hole has been repaired." But, as he reaches the doorway he sees that the new boards have already been chewed up by the rats who, obviously not happy to have their front door sealed up have taken the matter into their own hands and restored their passage. Thanks to their handiwork, Lucien can just get his hands between two of the boards where they meet the ground. He yanks on one of them, but it doesn't budge. He tries again. It flexes a bit but still doesn't come free. Looking around, Lucien runs to the back of the alley and picks up a leftover scrap of lumber. Returning to the doorway, he jams this new tool into the space between the boards, then pushes on the opposite end, and sees that the board over the opening flexes further. Excited, he tries again, this time using his feet. The board again flexes, but still doesn't pop free. With a quick look down the alley toward the street, to be sure they haven't attracted any attention, Lucien gives the lever a sharp "all or nothing" kick. There is a sharp snap of breaking wood as the lever splinters and falls to the ground. He picks up the broken pieces to examine and quickly drops them again when he realizes they are useless. Frustrated, he turns back to the opening, where he sees, to his delight that his lever was not the only thing that broke. The board he had been prying on has split down the middle and been pulled partially free. He grabs the board and yanks on it and with quite a bit of pulling and twisting manages to wrench it free, opening a gap, just large enough for him to squeeze through. Noticing how black his hands have become from his exertions he looks about for something to wipe them clean.

Seeing nothing, he reluctantly uses his jacket. "Don't tell Auntie," he says to Fox, who replies with an uncomprehending tilt of his head. With that, Lucien says, "Okay, let's go," and Fox darts through the opening with Lucien right behind him.

As his eyes adjust to the murky light inside the warehouse, Lucien begins to make out the fixtures in the room that he had seen so dimly before. The smell of the place is all mildew and stale air, and the dim light filtering through the gaps in the shutters that seal up the place illuminates the thick clouds of dust they have stirred up. Lucien walks carefully, creeping forward, calling out quietly, "Fox? Where are you?" Hearing Fox's excited snarling mixed with a loud clatter of chains just ahead of him, he tries to move toward the commotion calling quietly, "Fox? Come here." Feeling his way along the wall, his hand runs into something metallic. Inspecting it with his fingers he makes out a metal cuff, attached to an old chain, which is then bolted firmly into the stones. As he lets it drop, the old rusted shackle makes the same eerie rattle that he heard before. It is at that moment that Fox appears at his feet, depositing his prize on the ground for Lucien to see. The boy looks down, better able to make out the dog now. "Fox! There you are! Don't tell me you've caught another rat!" He nudges at the dark shape at his feet, "Oh my! Fox! You must leave those filthy things alone! Stay with me."

His eyes now adjusted to the faulty light, he is perplexed by what he sees; they are in a large, mostly empty room. It has windows along one side, that are shuttered tight. Along the other walls and in between the windows he makes out more of the hanging iron chains, all bolted in place to the stones. Down the center of the room, is a heavy wooden framework about eight feet tall, that is fastened to the floor of the warehouse. The same old heavy chains and cuffs hang from this sturdy wooden gantry as well. Lucien makes his way to a spot where a thin sliver of light breaks through one of the shutters and onto the chains to have a closer look. Walking curiously through the cavernous room now, trying taking it all in, reaching up to touch and examine the hanging manacles, he wonders about the people who had been so mercilessly confined here. Fox meanwhile is exploring around the edges of the large room, where he begins pawing the ground again. Lucien, seeing this, makes his way over to the dog. "Fox, what do you have there?" he asks, curiously. Fox continues digging at the dirt floor, where it meets the old stone walls.

As the two continue their exploration inside the old prison, they are unaware that they have attracted an unwelcome visitor out in the alleyway. The watchman, who had almost caught Lucien and his school friends, has returned. Noticing the broken board laying on the ground, he stoops down to investigate, and quickly sees the splintered and dislodged shutter board. "Well, back for another look, eh?" he says to himself. "What are we going to do about that, I wonder?" He takes a position beside the hole where he can't be seen from the inside and settles into wait. "You're gonna have a surprise when you come out, I'd say."

Oblivious to the "surprise" waiting outside, Lucien is entranced by what Fox has unearthed. Picking it up and brushing the dirt away, he sees it is a small carved figurine, like nothing he has seen before. He holds the little figure up to the light to try to discern its shape, and realizes that it is a figure of an animal, crouched and ready to pounce. As primitive and stylized as it is, the thick mane around the animal's neck and its powerful features are unmistakable. "Fox," says Lucien, "it's a lion! I think you have found something that belonged to one of the people who were kept here. They must have dropped this little figure as they were being..." He stops and reflects on the artifact for a moment, then adds solemnly, "Fox, we should go home now." Seeing Lucien heading for their opening, Fox, darts ahead and leads the way back to the hole in the old door. With a quick glance back at Lucien, he plunges excitedly through the hole, and disappears from view. Lucien hears him yelp in alarm, and calls out, "Fox!, What's the matter? Are you hurt?" "Not yet he isn't, boy. Not yet," comes the chilling reply. "Hello, who's there?" Lucien cries in alarm. "Leave my dog alone." As he runs across the room and lunges into the opening, he hears the watchman say, "Let's see how it sits with you to be stolen from." Lucien's head pops out the other side in time to see the man disappearing around the corner and onto the street. As he tries to scramble through the opening, his jacket gets caught on one of the bent over nails that had, just a short time ago held the shutter boards in place. He yells, "Stop! We've stolen nothing! Fox!" Lucien yanks at the jacket, and with the sound of tearing material he is freed. He jumps to his feet and rushes after Fox and his kidnapper. At the street corner, he looks frantically around but seeing no sign of them takes off running in the direction that he saw the man go. At the next corner he calls out at the top of his lungs, "Fox! Fox!" He strains to hear, when suddenly his heart jumps at a response, a sharp bark from further up the street, closer to the ships.

Up ahead of Lucien, the sailor rushes through the crowd. He hears Lucien calling from behind him, "Fox! Fox!" The dog struggles to get free, but he is clamped tight in the man's sturdy arms. Fox manages to pull his head free and give out a sharp bark. "Quiet you!" comes the harsh response from the sailor, "Your young master will think twice before he goes about trespassing and thieving again!" As he passes an unattended cart, he quickly grabs up an empty sack that is draped over the front of the barrow and proceeds to stuff Fox inside. Fox, for his part, manages to give the man a good nip as he is pushed into the bag.

Lucien, meanwhile, rushes along through the crowds in hot pursuit, but has not actually caught sight of his prey, simply running toward the barks he has heard in the distance. He stops to call again, "Fox!, Fox! Where are you?" This time there is no answer. With increasing panic, Lucien lunges forward pushing through the people, stopping right beside the wheelbarrow where the watchman had grabbed the sack, only now, the owner of the cart is back, hard at work piling it high with cargo from one of the nearby ships. Lucien calls out to him, "Sir, excuse me sir, have you seen a man carrying a dog rush past here?" The longshoreman shakes his head, "No. I've just returned to my cart this moment. Perhaps you've seen who has stolen the sack that I left here?" he says indignantly. "No sir, I'm sorry, I've not," replies Lucien, rushing off even as the longshoreman speaks, "It's a sad state of affairs," he says as he grabs the handles of the wheelbarrow and shoves off with his load of goods. Meanwhile, continuing toward the piers, Lucien suddenly catches a glimpse of the watchman in the distance. The man is rushing up the gangway of one of the ships, but, now instead of a dog in his arms, he has a sack slung over his back. Even at this distance, Lucien is certain that he can see the sack moving and jerking about on the man's back. "Fox," the boy says to himself as he rushes after the kidnapper.

Reaching the bottom of the gangway, Lucien charges up the incline. He makes it about two steps before he is stopped dead in his tracks by the burly second mate, who is overseeing the cargo and personnel that are being brought aboard. "Slow down there young gent. What business have you on this ship?" he asks assertively. Lucien answers breathlessly, "Sir, you have allowed my stolen property onto this ship, and I demand that it be returned to me, or I shall go and fetch the police and you can return it to them." The sailor is both amused and somewhat impressed by the boys confidence and demeanor. "Now, slow down young master. I've not allowed anything aboard that isn't listed on my manifest. I will swear to it, so be on your way, you are holding up our provisioning." Lucien won't be deterred, "If you refuse to help me, then I demand to speak with your captain." The sailor replies sharply, "Captain LeFevre is busy preparing his ship for departure. He has no time for this." Without warning, a voice comes booming down from the quarter deck of the ship, "Mr. Artaud, why are you not seeing to the provisioning of my ship? I will not be put off schedule before we are even underway." Lucien jumps in, "Captain, Captain, a minute of your time!" The captain looks down over the rail at the boy standing at the bottom of the gangway and addresses the sailor, "Mr. Artaud, what is this boy's business?" Artaud turns to Lucien, "Well now you've done it," he hisses. He signals to a sailor at the top of gangway to come down, "See that this boy stays here." The burly sailor takes a position to block the gangway, and Artaud walks up to confer with the captain. From where he is standing, Lucien watches their conversation, but does not hear a word of it. After a moment, Artaud returns, and speaks to Lucien, "I have told the captain of your charges, and assured him that nothing has come aboard that is not accounted for in the manifest. The captain says you should go away." Lucien looks up at the captain and calls out to him, "It is my dog, sir! My dog has been taken from me, and brought illegally aboard your ship." The captain, obviously unsympathetic to Lucien's plight replies to his second mate, "Mr. Artaud, please tell this lad that there are no dogs on my ship, but, if I do find one by and by, I will be happy to float it home to him." The captain turns and disappears, leaving Lucien, facing Artaud. With tears beginning to well up in his eyes, Lucien implores, "But, he's my dog sir." The sailor is not without sympathy, but, he is adamant, "Boy, I've told you, no dogs have come on board this ship. Perhaps you've mistaken this one for one of the others. There are quite a few tied up in the Port of the Moon now. You should try one of them." With that, he eases Lucien down off the gangway, and goes back to his work of loading the ship. Lucien stands for a moment in shock, not knowing what to do. Slowly, he turns away and walks along the wharf, toward the bow of the ship, then quickly ducks behind several barrels that are stacked for loading. He watches with interest as sailors and longshoremen roll their casks and barrels up the gangway and then down into the hold of the ship, one after another, a seemingly endless procession.

Chapter Twelve

Rescued!

Where are
Fox and Lucien?

Turn the page to see.

The blackness is so thick that Lucien feels it clinging to him, like the tar that clings to the barrel that now holds him....The choking smell of the stuff adds to his misery, but, he dare not move, not yet.

We're right here!

The darkness is complete. The blackness is so thick that Lucien feels it clinging to him, like the tar clinging to the barrel that now holds him, filling every crack and seam. The choking smell of the stuff adds to his misery, but, he dare not move, not yet. After almost losing his grip on the lid, and nearly spilling out of the barrel as it was rolled roughly up the gangway and onto the deck of the ship, he can't let himself move, and he desperately wants to move. The most he has allowed himself, out of fear of being discovered, is a tiny opening at the edge of the barrel lid to allow some fresh air in. For Fox's sake, he needs to hold on a bit longer, and so he does. Trying to make the best of things, Lucien imagines how much harder it would be if he had come to rest upside down, or worse, at the bottom of a whole stack of barrels! "Be thankful for small miracles," he reminds himself while passing the endless minutes in his dark, self-imposed prison cell.

Finally, after what seems like days, but has actually only been hours, Lucien can wait no longer. Not only does the barrel seem to be shrinking in closer by the minute, but his mind is now racing at the thought of Fox's plight at the hands of the sailor, or watchman, or whatever he actually is. He must get out of the barrel to save his little friend, thinking to himself, "There's no point in avoiding the inevitable." So, very slowly and gingerly, he repositions himself in the barrel as best he can, then gently pushes up on the lid. It doesn't budge. "Oh my, what shall I do if I can't get out of this barrel?" Lucien thinks. "I will have to let my presence be known, and then who knows what might happen to me!" He tries the lid again, this time with a bit too much conviction, as the wooden disc springs up out of its place and pops into the air. Lucien grabs after it wildly, managing to get control of it before it can thud down on the top him. Lowering the heavy wooden disk carefully and quietly back down, he listens intently for any sound before gently tilting it just enough to peek out over the rim. The sun is gone now, but, his eyes being already accustomed to the dark inside the barrel, he can see well enough. In front of him he makes out only the dark, sea-water cured wood of the side of the ship. Realizing that he is facing the wrong way, he carefully lowers the lid back down and works himself around toward the opposite direction before once again lifting the barrel end. This time, what he sees is the dark, mostly empty deck of the ship. His barrel was not lowered down into the hold, but instead is standing by the rail, mid-ship, just forward of where the captain had stood earlier in the day.

Seeing no one anywhere on deck at the moment, he carefully stands up. After so many hours bent and cramped inside the barrel his legs scream in pain as he forces them to straighten out. Taking a moment to rub the blood flow back into them, he then ever so quietly and carefully, pushes himself up, with his hands on the rim of the barrel, and lifts first one leg and then the other over the side. Dropping gingerly to the deck, wincing at the pain still throbbing in his joints, he notices that his barrel is one of three, sitting at the rail, and he ducks behind them for cover. From his new hiding place, he takes a quick look around, and realizes he can't linger there, he must get out of sight and find Fox. Making sure the coast is clear, he darts across the deck to a dark companionway. Pausing to listen, and hearing no sounds coming from below, he slips quickly down the steps and disappears into the ship. On the lower deck, crouching behind the stairs, it strikes Lucien as odd that the ship was so quiet, after the flurry of activity that had swarmed around it earlier in the day. "Perhaps they are all off to dinner somewhere," he thinks, remembering how his old friends the masons had loved to carouse in Paris at night. "Fox, if only I can find you while the ship is empty, we will be away from this dock in no time, and having our supper at home!" He is sure that Madame Marboeuf would soon be missing them, and will be up waiting for them when they finally walk through the door, but, as cross as she is certain to be with him for returning to the warehouse, he knows it will be anger born out of concern for them, and Lucien thinks he will suffer it gladly. He knows how lucky he is to have Madame Marboeuf as his new mother, and any scolding by her, they will happily bear, just to be safely back home again.

As he creeps off down the passage toward the front of the ship, he moves carefully between the many shadowed corners and alcoves created by the dim light of the oil lamps that burn sporadically along the lower deck. After slipping down the passage further, he stops and listens for any sounds of motion or conversation, and when he is sure he hears nothing, he softly calls Fox's name, hoping for a reply. Hearing nothing, he creeps carefully past several unmanned workshops, that from the looks of them belong to the ship's carpenter and the chandler. He whispers as loudly as he dares, "Fox?...Fox? Do you hear me? Fox?"

but still hears no reply. Rounding another set of stairs he reaches the crews quarters; hammocks hang from the great deck beams like a tangle of jungle vines, awaiting the sailors to return for the night. Calling out one more time, Lucien freezes, when he thinks he hears a sound. He hears nothing. "Fox?" he whispers again, and then, there it is again, a scratching noise coming from the darkness in front of him. He instantly recalls the scuttling, scratching noises made by the rats at the warehouse, and it makes him hesitate. "Fox? Please let that be you, and not more of those filthy creatures...Fox?" Hearing it again, he walks toward the sound, and now thinks he hears a well-muffled whimper coming from a heavy gear locker affixed near the hull of the ship. The door of the locker is latched, but not locked, so he slowly opens it and peers cautiously inside. With the lid open the whimper instantly becomes clear. "Fox!" Lucien whispers excitedly, "That is you! I've found you!" A quiet little yip is the reply. As Lucien pushes several large hanks of rope out of the way, saying, "Good boy Fox, stay quiet, and I will have you." A moment later he is pulling at the canvas sack that holds Fox, even as the dog struggles to find a way out. Lucien quickly unties the rope holding it shut, and Fox's head immediately pops out, attacking the boys face with licks and kisses, so happy is he to see his friend again. Pulling Fox from the sack, Lucien exclaims, "My poor Fox, who would do such a thing to you? Come now, we have to get out of here." He picks the dog up, and closing the locker behind them, they steal quickly back down the dingy passage.

At the bottom of the companionway Lucien first descended, the sound of loud laughter and conversation freezes them in their tracks. Heavy footfalls can now be heard moving about on the deck as some of the crew return from their time ashore and begin to spread out across the ship. Hearing this, Lucien rushes for the stairs, hoping to make a mad dash off the ship before they can be stopped. But, as they reach the steps, he looks up and sees a sailor standing in the opening, about to start down. The two of them quickly back into the darkness to stay out of sight, and as they do so, Lucien recognizes the man standing in the companion way is none other than the brute who snatched Fox at the warehouse. As the awful fellow and his friends begin down the stairs, Lucien makes a head-long dash down a nearby set of steps, with Fox held tight, and they vanish into the cavernous, dark belly of the ship to hide until they can slip away and run home.

The sailor, who stole Fox, reaches the crews quarters before the others file in behind him, and immediately goes to the rope locker to check on his hostage. Opening the lid to look inside, he is immediately shocked to see the canvas sack empty, laying atop the pile. He begins looking around furtively, not wanting to attract the attention of his shipmates who are now filling the space and climbing into their hammocks. The sailor quickly closes the the locker and glances about furtively, hoping to catch a glimpse of Fox cowering in a corner, or beneath a table somewhere, but it's no use, the dog is nowhere to be seen. His mind races with the possible repercussions, until finally he convinces himself that the dog must have gotten free and followed his nose off the ship and to shore. "Smart little dog," the sailor thinks to himself, "I'll bet that boy is worried sick." He slides up into his hammock, "Well, serves him right, breaking in where he ought not be. I hope the little cur gets home. Oye!, and now I won't be worrying about getting some fool dog ashore without Captain LeFevre or Mr. Le Beau getting wind of it. Good riddance, and the same to that stink'n old warehouse too. I'll stick to making my wages at sea from now on." Satisfied that all is again right with the world, he closes his eyes to sleep.

Not far below him Lucien and Fox listen silently as more and more of the crew return to the ship after their various adventures ashore. "Fox," Lucien whispers, "these men sound very rough, even more so than the masons, who were also rather hardy types." Fox listens as Lucien continues, "If they should get their hands on us, who knows what they might do? They could throw us over the side as thieves!" Lucien continues, "We will stay here and wait for them to go to sleep, then creep off this miserable ship and be gone before anyone has a chance to see us. Don't you agree?" Fox shakes his head as if to say, "You're the boss. I'll do what you tell me." "Yes, we will wait awhile, or maybe wait for daylight then find the captain, and I will prove to him that you were captive on his ship. He will have that sailor arrested!" With that, Lucien moves to get a bit more comfortable, pulling Fox closer to him and Fox doesn't complain one little bit.

Chapter Thirteen

The Stevedore's Report

After waiting patiently for several minutes, the door swings open again and Martine quickly ushers the man in, latching the door behind them.

Martine stands on the threshold of the kitchen door, framed by the herbs and flowers that grow so abundantly to either side of it, thanks to Monsieur Raimond's careful attention, speaking quietly to a stranger. The man is dressed in plain, heavy work clothes, and has the hulking build that attests to many years spent in heavy lifting. He holds his hat nervously in his hands as he talks to her about whatever business they are discussing. Martine becomes increasingly distraught as she listens to the fellow, finally motioning for him to remain where he is as she closes the door and disappears. After waiting patiently for several minutes, the door swings open again and she quickly ushers the man in, latching the door behind them.

Once inside, Martine directs the man into Madame Marboeuf's sitting room, and introduces him, continuing, "he is a stevedore at the port, and has..." She is cut off by Madame Marboeuf, who is obviously anxious to hear whatever it is the man has to say. "Well, let the man speak, will you Martine!" she snaps. Catching herself, she continues, "I am sorry Martine, that was uncalled for." Martine says nothing, being well aware of how worried everyone in the household is about Lucien and Fox. When it was discovered that they had not returned last night, Madame Marboeuf had gone into a fit, having every inch of the property searched, and servants dispatched to all the neighbors to spread the alarm. Martine is every bit as affected by their absence as Madame Marboeuf, and she steps back silently to let the man speak.

The stevedore takes a step toward Madame Marboeuf, "Madame, my name is Pierre, and I work at the port. I have worked there for many years, and have even been employed by your late brother from time to time in the past. He was a fair and decent man. "Yes, yes, of course," Madame Marboeuf snaps, "What of my Lucien, and little Fox?" "Yes Madame," the stevedore continues, "though having never met your son, I was familiar with him, having seen him in the past with his uncle, and after his amazing return from Paris, he is known to many people. So, I took notice when I saw him yesterday at the port." He sees her about to interject something and anticipates her question. "I know it was him, for he actually spoke to me Madame. I had just finished loading my barrow with goods when he stopped to ask me if I had seen a man carrying a small dog. He was very excited and out of breath. I told him that I had seen nothing. It was then that he spied something down the quay, and quickly thanked me and ran off. He tried to board a ship that was being loaded for departure, but was stopped by one of the mates. The captain was called, and I heard him send your boy away. But, I don't know that he went on his way. I watched him walk along the pier and then duck and hide amongst some cargo that was waiting to be loaded. That is all I know, because I went back to work. When I returned, I saw no more sign of him. Knowing who the boy is, and who his family is, it was my wife, Madame, who convinced me to come and report to you what I have seen."

Madame Marboeuf is on her feet, aghast at the news. "Good heavens, are you saying my boy is on that ship?" she exclaims anxiously. "He had Fox with him...oh my goodness." She turns to Martine sharply, now firmly back in control of the moment, "Martine, have the coachman bring up my carriage immediately...with four. I must get to the docks!" Before Martine has a chance to move, Madame Marboeuf continues frantically, "What are you waiting for! On your way!" Martine rushes out of the room and Madame Marboeuf grabs her purse from a side table near the door, and addresses the stevedore again, "And you...you must run to the police right now and tell them what has happened. Tell them, I will meet them at the port." She opens her purse and pulls out a couple gold coins. Handing one to the stevedore, she says, "This is for your invaluable information," then handing him the second, continues, "and this is for your speed in your new task. Come sir, I will see you out." The stevedore looks at her a moment, understanding the deep fear she is working so hard to cover up. As he walks with her toward the front door he says, "Of course Madame, you have my word that the police will be summoned." At the door, the man stops deliberately, and continues, "Madame, the name of the ship is the *Argo of Bordeaux.*" Madame Marboeuf takes a breath and steadies herself. She suddenly realizes that in her excitement to get to the dock to find Lucien and Fox, she had almost plunged recklessly forward, without even knowing what ship she was looking for. "Thank you, sir," she replies gratefully, "You are truly my savior today." "I understand your distress Madame, and hope your son is soon home with you."

Chapter Fourteen

Sailed!

She turns frantically back to the dock, to a gaping hole in the line of ships where the Argo of Bordeaux had been. "Where is it?" she shouts, "Where is the Argo of Bordeaux!"

A gleaming black carriage, pulled by a team of four grey horses charges down a cobbled street, toward the Port of the Moon, careening through the crowds with a violent clatter of hooves on ancient well-worn pavers. People jump out of the way as the coachman weaves the swaying rig skillfully, but aggressively toward the river, finally charging across the wide plaza that runs beside the water. Weaving through the confusion of cargo and people the coachman brings his coach and the breathless horses to an abrupt stop beside the docks. He quickly jumps from his perch atop the carriage, and rushes to open the door and put down a step for his passenger, but, he's too late.

Madame Marboeuf is in a panic, and is already halfway through the door by the time the carriage lurches to a halt. She jumps down from the high carriage, without waiting for the step, and is caught by the driver when the heel of her shoe twists on one of the pavers. "Madame, please," implores the driver, as she rushes past him toward the water and the row of merchant ships tied there, stopping just a few paces further on. She turns to the driver, "Are we at the correct place?" she asks emphatically, "IS THIS THE CORRECT PLACE?" The driver replies with defeat in his voice, "Yes Madame, this is the spot. I am certain Madame." She turns frantically back to the dock, to a gaping hole in the line of ships where the *Argo of Bordeaux* had been. "Where is it?" she shouts, "Where is the *Argo of Bordeaux*?" She charges toward a longshoreman, who is engaged in coiling mooring lines, nearby, "You there," Madame Marboeuf storms, "Where is the *Argo of Bordeaux*?" He looks up at the domineering woman with the fine carriage, and isn't impressed. He's seen too many women and men just like her arriving late to their ships, storming about as if the world will end because of it, to care much. He answers her in a low voice, "She sailed at the turning of the tide, while you were safe in your bed, Madame." The indifference and condescension in his tone immediately combine with her unfocused frustration to infuriate her further. She steps toward the man with every intention of venting her full fury on him, when a gentle hand on her arm distracts her. She spins sharply to come face to face with her coachman, who speaks calmly, "Madame, we must go to the harbor-master...Madame?" She glares at him, as the sense in his words slowly take hold. Her face softens as she realizes that he is right. Glancing back over her shoulder at the empty spot where the *Argo* had been, she turns back toward the carriage. "Come, we must get to the harbor-master, immediately," she repeats, as she sweeps past the driver toward her carriage. He rushes to open the door for her, at which she storms, "Stop fussing over me Louis, and get to your horses. I'm not an invalid!" As she pulls herself up into the carriage, she pauses to turn back to the coachman, "Remind me to give you a raise, Louis." The coachman replies knowingly, "Yes, of course Madame, now may we go?" She steps into the carriage and he closes the door behind her, then climbs deftly to his perch and takes up the reins. With a sharp whistle from him and a light flick on their leathers the horses surge ahead, the iron-rimmed wheels of the carriage and the pounding hooves raising their cacophony again as they tear off.

Chapter Fifteen

Beyond the Headlands

Where are
Fox and Lucien?
Turn the page to see.

As the mouth of the Garonne and the French coastline shrink into the distance, the crew of the *Argo of Bordeaux* are busy at the rigging, piling on sail to take advantage of a favorable wind.

As the mouth of the Garonne and the French coastline recede into the distance, the crew of the *Argo of Bordeaux* are busy at the rigging, piling on sail to take advantage of a favorable wind. Captain LeFevre watches over his well-practiced crew from his place beside the helm. He checks their heading at the binnacle, and makes a slight adjustment to the wheel, giving the helmsman a good natured clap on the shoulder as he does so. Like all captains beginning a new voyage, over-seeing the first setting of the sails in a fair wind on a clear day has him in high spirits. This is heaven for captains and crews alike. The captain settles into his place, content for the moment to listen to his first-mate barking orders to the deck, and adjusting his stance as his ship leans leeward and picks up speed. It is only the distant booming from astern, and a cry of "Sail ho!", that breaks his trance. "Sail ho, astern" comes the cry again. The captain turns to look off behind the ship, and sees the sun-bleached sails of another vessel coming on behind them. His first mate, Le Beau, joins him, handing him his telescope. Through the glass a small, heavily-canvassed cutter comes into focus. There is a flash of light from the small deck gun mounted to the forward deck of the boat, and a moment later, another boom echoes out over the waves. The captain notes that the boat flies the colors of the Port of the Moon. "The Harbor Master? What the devil does that man want?" scowls LeFevre to his first mate. "We will not waste this fair wind, Mr. Le Beau," he asserts, and after a moment of consideration gives the command to the first mate, "Lighten the sails...don't make it to too easy for them."

The first mate replies, "Oui. Not too easy," and turns from the captain, walking forward, shouting new orders, which are repeated along the length of the ship, as the crew jump once more to the rigging.

It is some time later when the stout little cutter comes alongside the "*Argo*," then pulls slowly ahead of the lumbering freighter, to launch her boat. The boat carries the harbor-master, a roundish, older man, with a great face-framing white beard, and two young sailors to man the oars. They earn their pay getting their cargo delivered to the other vessel, needing to navigate the large chop that had blown up, as well as the intersecting wakes being given off by the two sailing ships. But, through hard exertions and solid skills, they come alongside and are thrown a line, which the harbor-master, demonstrating the uncanny balance earned of a lifetime in heaving boats, gets cleated with surprising dexterity. After the harbor-master and one of the sailors are brought aboard, the line is then payed out, letting the launch and the other sailor drop in behind the ship, to wait with the boat and enjoy the ride.

Wasting no time, the captain immediately addresses the harbor-master, "Monsieur Veilleux, I had hoped to be out of your company for the better part of a year, to what do I owe this visit?" "Captain," replies the harbor-master, with a blustery air of authority, "I have been informed by a good citizen of Bordeaux that you may have a stowaway aboard your ship, and, I have been empowered to search your vessel in order to ascertain if this person is indeed on board, and if so, to return him to shore. Therefore, please heave-to, so that I may conduct my examination."

The captain replies, "A stowaway, you say?" He thinks for a moment, then adds, "If this stowaway is a boy of about 12 years that you are looking for, I have some bad news for you." The harbor-master listens intently, as the captain continues, "As we were completing our provisioning, a boy of that age came to the gangway and tried to board, saying that he was looking for his dog. He was stopped, and I myself sent him away. Any number of my crew watched him walk off down the pier to the next ship to try the prank again. So, I'm afraid you have come a very long way for nothing." The harbor-master looks annoyed at this, "A damn rascal no doubt," he says, "but Captain, I am bound to have a look just the same, so please heave-to, so we can have our search." "No sir," replies the captain firmly, "I will not. You and your man are free to search in order to give a good report when you finally get home, but, I have a fair breeze and intend to drive on. I have already lightened my sails for your sake, and will take in no more. I will not lose my schedule before I have even left sight of my home port. So, search if you must, but I suggest you make it quick, because my ship, like the day, rolls on. You will have a long tack back to Bordeaux." Veilleux replies, somewhat deflated, "Very well." The captain adds, "I will not ask you to crawl about in the bilge, I will have one of my men go below, where they are already accustomed, and give us a report." "That is kind of you, sir." comes the polite response.

With that, they begin their canvas of the ship, starting at the bow and working aft, the harbor-master and his sailor open every hatch and barrel and locker they see.

The captain meanwhile picks out one of his crew and directs him to go below to search. "You there," barks the captain to one of the crew assembled nearby, listening to the goings-on, "get below and give it a good scrub, and report back when you have. Get to it." "Aye, Captain!" the sailor barks obediently and disappears down a dark companionway. Unknown to the captain, the man he has chosen to search for the stowaways is the very man who stole Fox away at the warehouse!

Once below deck, and on his own, the sailor finds a secluded spot and sits down on a box to examine his situation. "Well," he thinks, "this is some luck for me. If they find that dog and the boy I'm done, but," he considers further, "if they are aboard, they are surely down below, and here I am looking for them. If I find them, I'll just clap them both up where they are and deal with them once we're good and away. If I don't find them, then, my problem's solved. Even if they do pop up later, once we're away, I've nothing to worry about, my mates will take my side in all of it." He grins slyly, then mutters, "Yes, sure, I'll look for 'em, just not too hard," and whispers, "Ahoy boy. Ahoy dog. You here?" The sailor laughs at his own cleverness, as he begins to walk casually about, looking under buckets and inside small boxes, "No, nothing in here, nor here either," he says, still snickering to himself.

Further below, unaware of any of the goings on up on deck, Fox and Lucien lay side by side against the hull. The gentle motion of the ship and the muted hiss of the water as it slips past the planks have lulled Lucien into a sound sleep after so long in the dark. But, Fox is wide awake, his eyes open wide, his ears perked up listening, and his nose taking in a familiar scent. A low growl begins in his throat, and it stirs Lucien, who starts suddenly, not realizing that he had been sleeping. Fox's growl continues, "Oh, what is it Fox? What's there? Not some vile rat I hope." From where they are hidden Lucien can see between the barrels and crates, toward the hatch they escaped through. He quiets Fox with his hand, giving him a gentle "Sssshhhhh..." just as the drawn, sinewy head and neck of the sailor pops through the hatch over head and lowers a lantern down inside to beat back the darkness. Fox struggles in Lucien's arms, but, the boy holds him still. The head in the hatchway pivots around from side to side following the lantern light. Then he quietly calls out:

> "Here doggy. Come on out, boy. I won't hurt 'ya. I'm here to send you home." The sailor snickers again. "No? Not here? Well, all the better for me...and for you too. Why, you and your young master are probably home snug in his little feather bed, with a couple good licks to his backside to boot."

He laughs a bit more heartily at his own wit, but is cut short by a voice booming from above, "Ahoy below! On deck now and report!" At the sound of the first-mate's voice, the sailor takes one more quick sweep of the hold, then jerks his head hastily up through the opening, colliding with one of the framing members of the hatch as he does. Lucien listens, too afraid to move, as the sailor curses in pain, and stomps off to report to the captain and the harbor-master.

Back up on deck, Mr. Veilleux has completed his inspection and stands with the captain, awaiting the sailor's report. Emerging from a companionway the man is walked over to them by Le Beau. As they approach, the first mate speaks up, "Captain sir..." The captain and his guest turn around to face the two new arrivals. The captain speaks, "What have you found? Where are my stowaways?" The sailor speaks up authoritatively, "I found none, sir. No dog and certainly no boy sir. They must have scampered on home after you sent them off." The captain dismisses him, "Very good, return to your duties." and then addresses the harbor-master, "Well, there you have it. The boy is not here. I am afraid you have come a long way for nothing, and from the look of the sun and the direction of the wind, you will have a long and dark journey back. I am truly sorry that I can't send the boy home with you. I feel for his poor mother, but now, if you will allow me, I must put my ship and crew back to our business." The harbor-master understands that the captain is inviting him off his ship, and to be honest, he is relieved the boy is not here. It would have meant extra work for him, and he will be more than happy to get back to port, and home to a hot meal by morning.

A short time later, Veilleux climbs aboard his stout cutter, and the launch is tied to the stern. As the "*Argo of Bordeaux*" tightens her sails and picks up speed away from them, the smaller boat comes about, and sets its course for the first of many brisk tacks that it will take to get back to the mouth of the Argonne river again.

Chapter Sixteen

In the Bilge

In a flash the little dog darts after the dark shape, and a moment later he has the rat in his mouth, giving it a violent shake.

After their close call with Fox's kidnapper, Lucien decides that it would be a good idea to slip further into the ship, away from any hatches or stairways, until they can be sure they are no longer being hunted. To that end, they creep to a spot up against the hull, shielded on the other three sides by well-secured barrels and crates of cargo. Nestled in this new redoubt, leaning against the heavy hull planking, Lucien holds Fox and gently rubs the dog's head, wondering aloud what they should do. "I'm getting so very hungry Fox," he says to the dog, "you must be famished, and thirsty too. We must figure out how to sneak off this ship before we perish down here. If we could only find a barrel of meat and a cask of water, well then, we could have a grand feast!" he muses. A low growl rising in the dogs throat silences Lucien, and he suddenly jumps up with a start, dropping Fox, as a small, furry, dark shape scurries across his leg and disappears into the dark maze of cargo. In the dimness Lucien can't see the little rodent, but Fox, with his keen senses can. In a flash the little dog darts after the dark shape, and a moment later he has the rat in his mouth, giving it a violent shake. Fox then flips the rat into the air, and catches it again. Unable to see what's happening, all Lucien hears of the rat's dispatch is the muted crunch of bone as Fox's teeth close, finishing the job. "Fox!" Lucien cries as loudly as he dares, "Come back! Where are you?" Standing with one hand on the hull to steady himself, he strains to hear, as another skirmish breaks out closer by, and Fox lunges after another rat unfortunate enough to be within his unerring aim. This one ends in the same fashion and just as quickly.

"Fox," Lucien whispers harshly, "Come back," just as his little companion emerges from the surrounding stacks. Lucien grabs him, "Are you alright? You didn't get bitten by one of those vile rodents did you? Let me look." Fox gives Lucien's face a reassuring lick to say, "What's the fuss? It's my job." As he leans against the side of the ship, inspecting Fox for injuries, he suddenly becomes aware of a sensation he hadn't noticed before coming up through his back, up through the ship, a vibration, a slight shudder in the *Argo*'s planking. Suddenly, all too clearly, it makes sense to him. "The ship is moving Fox!" Lucien cries in alarm. Far down in the belly of the vessel where they are hidden, in complete darkness, sleepy, hungry, and preoccupied, he hadn't noticed the clues, until now. "Fox," he cries with growing distress, "We are moving! We are sailing! We must get off this ship right now, no matter the danger!" Trying hard to keep his thoughts straight, and not panic, he continues, "We must find the captain, and tell him what has happened and hope for the best." With that he picks up Fox and begins to feel his way purposefully back toward the hatch and the ladder. Fox, gives another low growl at the darkness as they go. "Leave those awful creatures to themselves Fox, we must get home now!"

Chapter Seventeen

Captain LeFevre

Where are
Fox and Lucien?
Turn the page to see.

The captain regards Lucien dourly, "Kidnapped? How's that? I sent you off this ship myself, our search found no sign of you, and yet," he adds incredulously, "here you are."

Up on deck, the excitement over the harbor-master's search has long since faded and the crew has settled back into its well-practiced routines. All sail has been run out again and the helmsman holds a steady course. The crew go about the endless business of keeping the canvas trimmed, to the ever-shifting wind, as the captain holds vigil over the entire scene from his place on the quarter-deck, content to simply watch the unconscious workings of a well-regulated crew as his ship plows on into the open ocean. It is into this smooth running nautical machinery that a boy and a dog emerge suddenly from the dark, depths of the hold.

As they step out of the companionway, Lucien takes a deep breath and makes an attempt at straightening up his disheveled clothes. He runs his hand over his hair, and then he and Fox proceed to march purposefully toward the stern of the ship, where the captain resides. The two walk right past several sailors, who don't know what to make of this unexpected sight. Lucien says nothing, keeping his eyes fixed on his goal. It is not until they've climbed the few short steps up to the quarter-deck that a burly hand clamps down on Lucien's shoulder and stops him. "That's far enough, boy." booms Le Beau, the first-mate. Lucien responds boldly, "My name is Lucien Lehun, and my dog and I have been kidnapped. I demand to speak with the captain. I insist you take us to him." Le Beau looks stunned; had the ship not just been searched, and no stowaways found? Now this boy was claiming to be kidnapped! The mate responds a bit anxiously, "Oy, I think I will boy. The captain will sort you out. Come with me." he commands, herding the two up the steps and over to the captain, who has watched the entire interchange between the boy and his mate. "Captain," Le Beau reports, "this boy has come up from below and claims to have been kidnapped." The captain regards Lucien dourly, "Kidnapped? How's that? I sent you off this ship myself, and our search found no sign of you, and yet," he adds incredulously, "here you are." "Kidnapped, sir," interjects Lucien. The captain holds up his hand, "We will discuss this matter in my cabin, away from the crew." With that he marches away and disappears through the hatchway leading to his personal offices below the quarter-deck. Le Beau brings Lucien and Fox along and they all disappear into the captain's quarters.

The crew having all seen the boy and his little dog talking to the captain, watch curiously as they disappear behind closed doors for interrogation. The well-regulated nautical machine, grinds slowly to a halt, as the men begin to move aft and congregate near the quarter-deck to hear what can be heard. The second mate, who has remained on deck, sees this and is quick to jump to action, booming out, "Scalawags, back to work! You will hear what you need to hear, when you do! Now jump to it! Back to work, I say!" The crew disperses to their stations, but all ears, and any sideward glances they can manage, are trained on the captain's cabin.

No one emerges from inside for a long while, and it causes increasing conjecture among the crew. There is one sole sailor who doesn't seem at all interested, as he busies himself with adjusting the rigging, recoiling lines, and doing whatever he can to look like he has no interest in the goings on in the captain's quarters. This is the sailor who brought Fox aboard, and then was charged with searching the ship for them. Now, he is hoping against hope that, somehow, the boy hadn't seen him clearly enough to identify him, and surely, he notes to himself, "That little dog won't say anything." He smirked a bit at the notion, "A talking dog, I'd pay a franc or two to see that," he thinks.

Chapter Eighteen

The Moonlighter

With all eyes upon him, the accused protests, "Oy, why it's just a dog. What court in France takes a dog as a witness."

After what seems, to the anxious crew, to be an eternity, the captain, the first mate, Lucien and Fox re-emerge from the captain's quarters. Le Beau immediately signals to the second mate to assemble the crew. Artaud promptly turns and bellows out, "All hands aft! All hands aft! Snap to it! Roust yourselves!" At the sound of his voice, crewmen rain down from the rigging and pour up from the lower deck, assembling in front of the captain and the others. Once all are present the captain steps forward to speak,

> "One of our company stands accused of theft and kidnapping. This boy has told me the tale of how they came to be on my ship. Shall I believe him? It is a song quite similar to the one sung by the harbor-master. But, neither of them are a part of this crew, so, I ask you, my men, how is it the boy and his dog came to be here? How is it they remained undetected in spite of the search of the *Argo*? There is a man among us who knows the answers, and I will now give that man a chance to step forward."

The captain stands, hands clasped behind his back, looking out at his crew sternly, waiting for the guilty party to step forward. There is no movement in the crew, just a sea of stoic, sun-dried faces looking back at him. The captain continues,

> "Then, shall I have the boy point you out like a common criminal, to be clapped in irons? Or, in manly fashion, will you step forward and claim your own actions? It will only serve your cause to do so."

He pauses to allow the guilty man one more chance to step forward and confess.

There is an excruciating pause, causing the men to shift about uneasily in the hot sun. Finally, when no one makes a move to step up, the captain turns to Lucien, "Step up here to me Lucien. I will have you point out the man who is responsible for your being here?" Lucien steps forward, holding Fox with him, and looks carefully at the hard, weathered faces. The captain, sensing the boys reluctance adds, "Have no fear of these men, my boy, most are honest and god-fearing." Finally, Lucien addresses the captain, "I am sorry sir, I cannot. I was not able to get a clear look at the face of the man who took Fox, and your crew are all men of the sea, many of whose faces and beards look similar to me. In good conscience I can not say one or another is the culprit." Fox begins to squirm impatiently and Lucien, out of habit, sets him down. The dog barks defiantly at the crew, then looks up at Lucien, trying to let his friend know that he can pick out the man. Seeing the confused look on the boy's face, and before Lucien can stop him, Fox leaps down to the lower deck and runs through the crowd to one of the sailors, where he stops and begins to bark and growl. The rest of the crew step back, leaving Fox and the sailor alone in the middle of a circle of sailors. With all eyes upon him, the accused protests, "Oy, why it's just a dog. What court in France takes a dog as a witness." The captain descends imperiously to the lower deck and steps over to the sailor giving him a hard look before responding, "Perhaps, but, we are not in France. We are on MY ship. Tell me, were you not also charged with searching the lower decks for Lucien and Fox when the harbor-master waylaid us? How peculiar that you could find no sign of either of them, and yet, just a short time later, here they are," he says, waving a hand in Lucien's direction. The sailor looks about tremulously and blurts out, "I didn't kidnap anyone! I didn't bring that boy aboard, just his dog. Just to give him a good scare for snooping about in the old holding house where I was moonlighting to help my family. I ran the boy and his friends off a few days ago, but, this one decides to come back and trespass. So, I snatched the dog to give him a good scare, that's all. I didn't mean for him to get stowed aboard, Captain," he beseeches. The captain considers his plea for a moment before replying sternly, "Your intent is of no importance. What is germane is the fact that, had you not taken the boy's dog and brought it aboard my ship, while in another's employ, neither the dog, nor the boy, would be here now. I am now obligated to see to their safety for the duration of our voyage, or until I can return them home." The captain pauses for a moment then continues, "I would be within my rights to have you flogged." He turns and motions the first mate to him. "Mr. Le Beau, please mark down in the ledger that this man's share will be reduced by one quarter, in order to compensate the company for the additional expense of passage for our two guests." He now addresses the assembled crew again, "Further, the boy and the dog are now under my care, until we make the colonies and I can arrange for their passage home. So," he says, addressing the guilty sailor, "should any harm befall either of them, by anyone's hand on this ship, you," addressing the sailor specifically, "poor soul, will be held accountable, as well as the offender." He raises his voice to be sure everyone assembled hears him, "IS THAT UNDERSTOOD?" A chorus of unenthusiastic, grunted, agreements rise in reply.

Lucien, who has been listening silently, has crept forward to retrieve Fox, and looks around at all the hard faces glaring at him. He speaks up to the captain, "Captain, sir, I must ask you for leniency. This man needs his wages, and it is true what he said, I, and my friends, had indeed gone into the warehouse. I knew full well that I should not, but I did it for an adventure and to see the strange things it contained. I was always taught that a gentleman never allows another to suffer for his own actions, so I ask you to please reconsider." The captain is impressed by Lucien's noble gesture. "My boy, you were well-raised. I am sure your parents would be proud of your courage." Lucien replies, "My uncle, sir, who is now dead, always said, 'Personal responsibility is the heart of true liberty.'" "Your uncle," the captain continues, "was a wise man. I appreciate you stepping forward, in front of all these men to admit your part. However, the punishment stands. This man could have called an officer to take you home for just punishment. But, instead, his thinking went to mischief, and that I will not countenance." Turning to the sailor, "The punishment stands, unless you would prefer something...more immediate?" The sailor shakes his head sullenly. "In that case," the captain says, "I am done with you. Do not try me. Now, back to work all of you!" He turns back to Lucien and Fox. "My boy, Mr. Le Beau will show you to a cabin, and you will dine with me and my officers for the duration of your passage with us." "Thank you Captain," the boy replies, "I hope that I will not be imposing on you for more than a day or two." The captain looks at Lucien kindly, understanding that the boy has no idea what he is in for. "It will be a bit longer than a day or two Lucien. I am sorry for that."

Lucien looking surprised and perplexed asks, "But, sir, will you not turn the ship around and return to Bordeaux? Was it not just yesterday that we were in port?" Answering gently, the captain explains, "We are two days at sea, with a fair wind driving us the whole time. I can not turn back now. I must use the wind while I can. As much as I am the master of this ship, I am obligated to the owners, as well as my crew, to produce a profitable voyage. If I do not, I will lose my ship and my livelihood. Do you understand, my boy?" he asks. Lucien, suddenly struck by the immensity of it asks with a quaking voice. "But sir, when may we...go home?" "When indeed," comes the captains reply. "I have already been thinking on that, and I am hopeful that with luck, we will be able to divert to Lisbon, and set you on your journey home, without losing too much time, if God and the wind are with us. Until then," the captain continues, "make the most of your new adventure. You have the freedom of the ship, but I would advise that you stay aft, and not go below. That would not be wise."

Chapter Nineteen

A Letter From Home

Madame Marboeuf, looking drawn and tired from the ordeal of recent days, sits quietly at her writing table, lost in the midst of composing a letter to Gustave.

Madame Marboeuf, looking drawn and tired from the ordeal of recent days, sits quietly at her writing table, lost in the midst of composing a letter to Gustave. Outside the window of her office, the sky darkens ominously as a thunderstorm drifts in from the ocean and threatens a deluge. Martine comes in with a coffee service, which she sets down carefully and pours a cup of the hot liquid, which Madame Marboeuf accepts gratefully. "Thank you, Martine," she says, "you and the others have been a blessing to me and my husband." Seeing that Martine looks a bit surprised by her praise, Madame Marboeuf continues, "My Lucien has taught me that I must let people know they are appreciated, and to try to be less stern." "Madame," Martine responds kindly, "some of us have cared for Lucien since he was a young boy. We are all very worried about him and pray for his safe return to us," adding thoughtfully, "He is just the sort of boy I would want for my own son." "Thank you Martine, you are kind," Madame Marboeuf replies. There is an uncomfortable silence, as each woman's thoughts turn to Lucien and Fox, broken finally by Martine, who excuses herself diplomatically from the room, "Well, I've got to get back to my work, and I see you are in the midst of a letter. Do you need anything Madame?" "No, thank you, Martine," Madame Marboeuf replies, "you have cared for me excellently." She waits for the servant to leave the room and then turns back to the letter, dreading the news it will deliver. She writes;

My dear, brave Gustave,

I do so hope that this letter finds you in good spirits and in good health. I can not begin to imagine the hardships you must endure in that unforgiving place. Please remember that we are all very proud of you, and the way you have dedicated yourself to turning your situation around. It is clear that you are becoming a man that your father would be very proud of. Do whatever you need to do to come home to us safely. (I am told that you have been in regular contact with old Father La Tuile, and that he has been advising you on martial matters. I do hope that you are able to avail yourself of the old soldier's long experience at arms.)

I must confess, I am writing to you with very distressing and sorry news. I am quite beside myself over these recent events, and hope that the matter will resolve itself shortly and happily, but I have a terrible feeling that it won't. To the point, your cousin, Lucien, and his constant companion Fox, have gone missing this last week. I am aware that the two of you have (I am gratified to know) become quite close and share letters frequently, and so I know this news will be as distressing to you as it is to me. It was several days ago now, that Lucien came home from school unannounced, and the very next morning he set off with Fox on some adventure or other that I was unaware of. (He has taken to wandering the countryside with Fox on a regular basis, and it always concerns me.) It was not until the next morning, after I spent a sleepless night, that I got news from a stevedore that he had seen Lucien and Fox at the port. (I suspect that he had gone back there, after my admonishments to stay away, in order to poke about an old warehouse, that had once been used by the slavers that sailed from Bordeaux.) This man thought Lucien and Fox may have been taken aboard a ship there. I alerted the authorities and rushed to the port, but to my horror, the "Argo of Bordeaux" had sailed, and Lucien was nowhere to be seen. It was then that I reported the matter to the harbor-master who promised to chase the vessel down and search her. I have just gotten word, that the search was completed days ago, but no sign of Lucien or Fox was found aboard the ship. All the other ships in the port were also held there, and searched, but to no avail. I am now left here in misery to wonder where my son has disappeared to. I cannot bear the thought of him alone and cold somewhere, where I can't help him. I take some comfort from the fact that my Fox is with him. As you already know well, Lucien has no more loyal friend in the world than Fox, and neither will ever leave the other to harm.

Gustave, I want you to know, that although you are not legally my son, I consider you to be, just as much as Lucien. Now, I am here alone with my husband still away in Paris and my two boys lost to me. I wish that you would come home now. This house is your home, and it is in need of you both.

Please be careful and safe, and listen to the counsel of your officers. Most importantly, come home safely to us.

Your loving Aunt

Chapter Twenty

The Sailing Life

Where are
Fox and Lucien?
Turn the page to see.

Then, with another quick, calculating touch
of his nose, he springs again and in an
instant is out on the open deck once more.

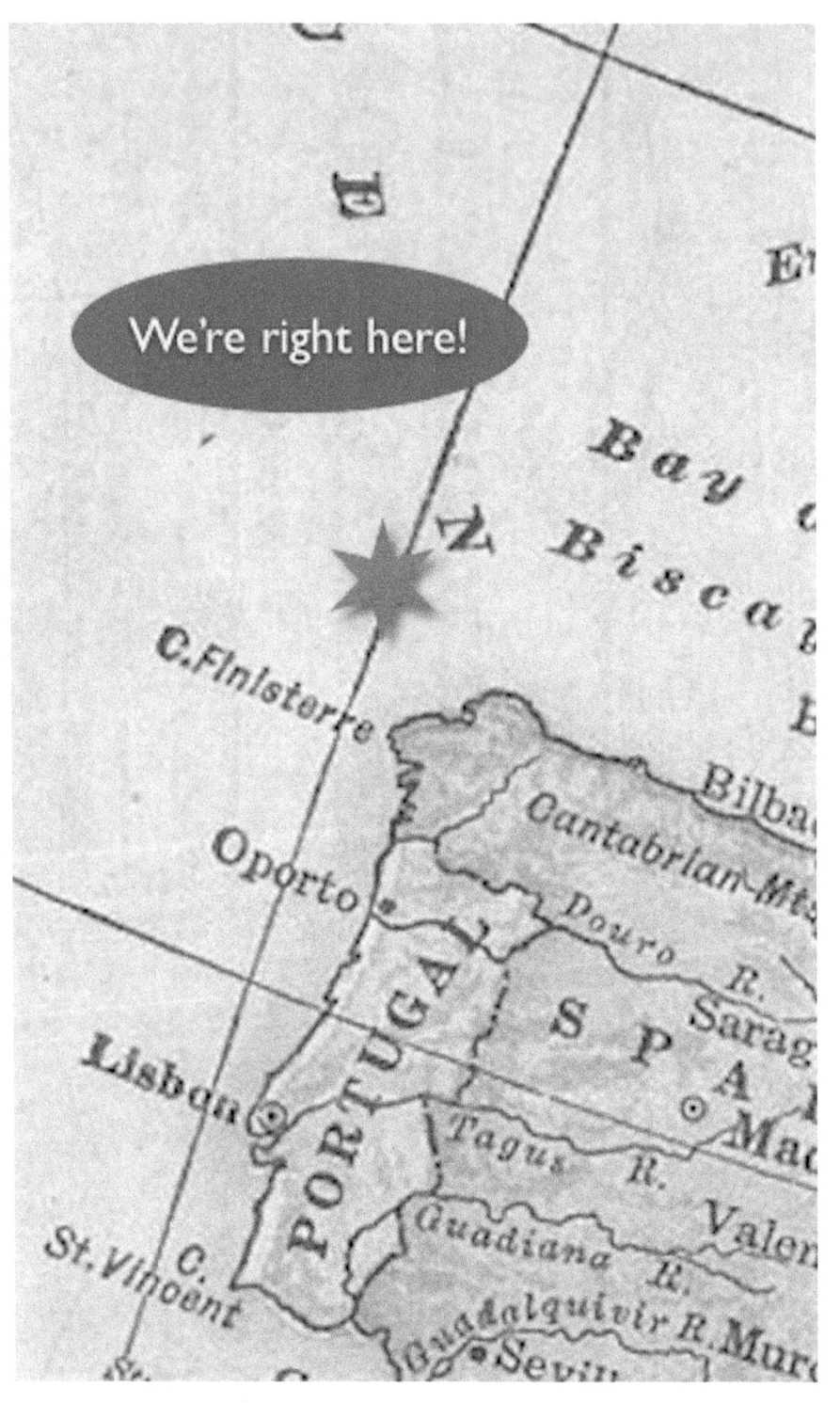

Fox stares up at the small, dimly lit hatch leading out of the ship's hold, and considers the treacherous path he must take up the steep, open steps, to get to the deck above. He's made this trip several times since being aboard the *Argo*, but it still scares him – a few memorable missteps being mostly responsible. He touches the bottom step with his nose to get a better sense of it, then, with no more hesitation, he picks up his prize and bounds upward, springing from one step to the next with such speed that he literally pops up through the hatch, landing a good foot away. A sailor, working nearby in the ship's chandlery laughs at the dogs acrobatics, "Back at it again are you? That's a good doggie." Fox, glances in the man's direction, as he trots quickly off toward the next obstacle - another steep set of steps - he must navigate to get back to the main deck. Reaching them, he pauses again at the bottom to consider his path. Although every trip up and down the steep treads becomes easier, even as the ship pitches and rolls in the waves, Fox thinks, it would be much better if he didn't have to go so far to do his job, and decides that he will try to avoid that deep, dark place in the future. Then, with another quick, calculating touch of his nose, he springs again and in an instant is out on the open deck once more.

The now familiar sounds of shipboard life come rushing full force into his ears, along with the ever-present smell of the ocean that fills his nose. That smell soaks everything – a good strong scent that is equal parts life and decay at once. Back at home, he would often raise his nose to this scent as it came floating ashore on the afternoon breezes. He didn't know then that it was the smell of the ocean, only that it was always there, lurking mysteriously in the background, and now, that same smell is inescapable, overwhelming everything. As Fox lifts his nose to the air, the breeze on deck shifts slightly, carrying another familiar smell to his brain, the smell of the boy, intermixed with that of the captain and a swirling mess of odors that are the sailors going about their work. He knows them all now, and with a sweep of his nose, knows the direction each is coming from. So, even though he doesn't yet see his friend, he knows just where to find him. Of course, he already knows where Lucien will be, they had taken to spending their time with the captain at his place by the rail, on the raised quarter-deck. The captain, for his part, had taken a liking to them both, and was happy to pass the time instructing his eager student in some of the many skills needed to be a sailor. So, Fox had a pretty good idea of where they would be, and his nose confirmed it. He trots proudly toward the stern of the ship, avoiding the men as they go about their business, trying his best to stay out from underfoot. He's become so adept at it that most of the sailors don't even know that he's creeping about or dodging out of the way.

Making quick work of the final set of low steps that lead up to the quarter-deck, he practically leaps from the bottom to the top in one light-footed bound, springing into view not far from the wheel. The helmsmen gives Fox a warm greeting, "Hello little hunter," the sailor says good-naturedly, "Got something for the captain do you?" Fox looks past the man and spots Lucien and the captain at their expected spot. With their backs to him, they have no idea he is approaching. "How do they get by in life, not being able to smell, or see, or hear well enough to know what's about them," Fox thinks to himself. As he approaches, he sees that Lucien's attention is absorbed by a shiny contraption that the captain is demonstrating, pointing off to the horizon and then up at the sun, as Lucien peers through the shiny thing, and moves it up and down in an odd fashion. Fox stops a few feet away and sits down to wait, but, when Lucien fails to sense his presence the dog is finally forced to give a little bark. Lucien and the captain turn around at once to see Fox sitting there at their feet.

  "Why Fox," Lucien exclaims, "there you are." Then eyeing Fox's trophy, laid at their feet he adds, "Oh, Fox, you have been down in the belly of the ship again! Will I have to put you on a string to keep you out of there?" The captain on the other hand looks perfectly thrilled, "Nonsense! Fox, you are a great addition to my ship. Why if I had you in my crew, this ship would float several inches higher!" As the captain bends down to pick up his trophy, Fox jumps about excitedly, as if to say, "Yes! I've got you another one, and it wasn't even hard!" Captain LeFevre picks up the prize by the tail, and says, "Thank you Fox. You are certainly paying your way on our voyage. I fear that I will owe you a share of the profits!" He slips his free hand into his pocket and pulls out one of the treats he has taken to having ready for the dog, and tosses it to him as he flings the dead rodent over the side. "Fox, you stay here with us now," admonishes Lucien, as he picks the dog up,

"We can't have you getting underfoot and causing trouble for the captain or the crew." The captain replies, "Fox is no trouble at all. He is an outstanding ratter my boy, and that makes him welcome on any ship at sea. My crew suffers him gladly, I can assure you." With that the captain reaches into the pocket of his coat and pulls out another morsel and tosses it the dog, who snatches it quickly out of air and inhales it appreciatively.

"Sir," Lucien goes on, "I am very happy to know that Fox is no trouble to you. You have been very kind to us, and I would hate to think that we are putting you out any more than can be helped. In fact, I feel rather badly that Fox is able to contribute so well, while I do nothing more than distract you from your duties by teaching me all about sextants and stars and the like. Perhaps there is something I can do." "Lucien," the captain reassures, "you are my guests, but, I appreciate your offer. What can you do?" Lucien chimes in, "I can play the violin sir, if there is one aboard. I have practiced quite a lot and know a good number of songs." The captain considers this, "Is that so? That would be a fine gift for the crew. I will have Mr. Le Beau inquire about a violin." "Thank you, captain," the boy replies excitedly, "it would be my pleasure to entertain the crew before we reach Lisbon," then pausing he asks, "How long will that be, sir?" The captain furrows his brow, as he makes a few calculations in his head, replying, "The wind has been good to us so far. If it holds, we may be able to make Lisbon in another two days. You and Fox will soon be on your way home to your aunt." "That is wonderful news sir," Lucien exclaims,

"Don't you agree Fox?" The dog, sensing the lightening of Lucien's mood, gives him a happy lick on his face.

Chapter Twenty-one

The Musician

Where are
Fox and Lucien?
Turn the page to see.

Some, not content to just listen, jump to
their feet and dance, transported to joy by
the music and the softly rolling ship.

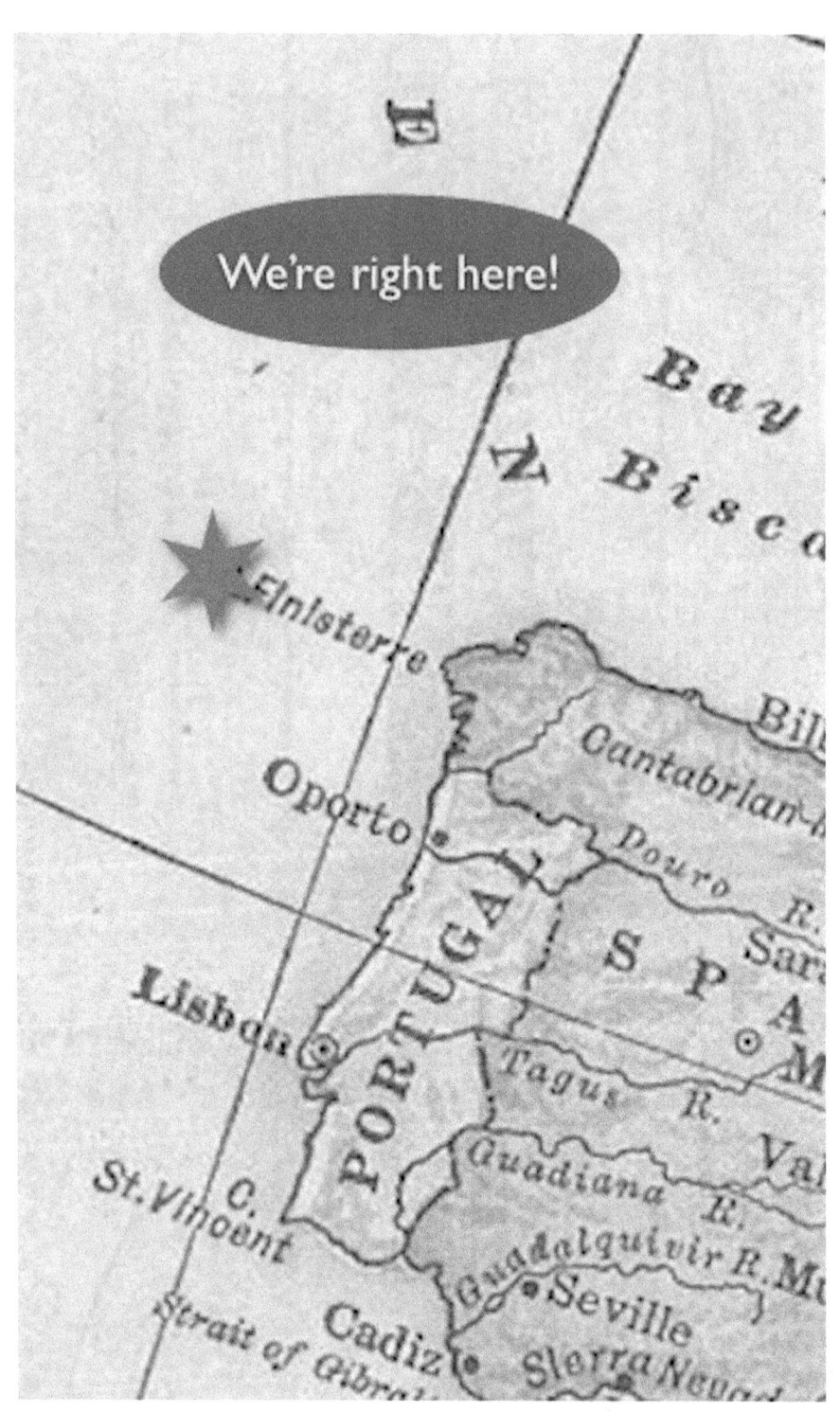

The deep darkness of the night sky is punctuated by countless stars, and a brilliant crescent moon rising from the horizon, revealing the ocean with an endless dance of shimmering silver sparkles. The *Argo of Bordeaux* plows along through the darkness with only the hiss of the foaming water rushing along her planks, and the slap of the waves on the bow to mark her passage. As she emerges from the obscuring dark, another sound begins to rise, faint at first, muffled by the noise of the wind and the water, then slowly rendering itself into music. The closer the vessel gets the clearer the tune becomes, eventually revealing itself as the lively notes of a violin and the rhythmic stomping of feet on the ships heavy planks. Lucien and what looks to be the *Argo's* entire crew are up on deck together. Lanterns have been strung from the rigging, giving the ship a bright festive glow. Accompanied by several of the sailors, Lucien plays a rollicking tune on a violin, as the rest of the crew listens, stomping and clapping to keep time. Some, not content to just listen, jump to their feet and dance, transported to joy by the music and the softly rolling ship. Fox, too, capers happily amongst the men, barking and jumping and flipping in the air, to the rousing applause of everyone.

As the ship passes on, the captain can be seen, standing with the helmsman, at his place by the wheel. In a moment of generosity Captain LeFevre relieves the helmsman, sending him down to join the fun, taking the wheel himself, holding their course, while still taking in the joyful sights and sounds coming from Lucien, Fox and the crew. It is a happy crew and a well-tended ship that surges onward, driving relentlessly out into the darkness, taking its music with it.

Chapter Twenty-two

Pirates!

Where are
Fox and Lucien?
Turn the page to see.

The fight, such as it is, is brief, as the raiders set upon the Argo without warning and overwhelm her crew before any real resistance can be mounted.

Lucien and Fox are sound asleep in their little compartment, sharing the bed that seems to fill most of the tiny room. The square port-hole a few feet above the bed glows in the early morning light, supplying the only daylight to the space (At night Lucien has taken to gazing through it at the countless stars that fill the sky so far out at sea, trying to memorize the constellations that he's learned from the captain). On this particular morning however, scant sunlight filters through the portal, not for the sake of a sunless sky, but rather because the view to the sun has been blocked from the outside. Having been up well into the wee hours of the morning playing his violin and dancing with the rest of the crew, both Lucien and Fox collapsed into bed, happy and exhausted, and now lie fast asleep, oblivious to the dark craft that has slipped up beside them under cover of night, and now blocks the morning sun from Lucien's window as it rests uneasily beside the *Argo of Bordeaux*.

With a sudden jolt, the door to the compartment bursts open. Like a wave, the sound and fury sweeping the deck floods in to the little compartment, causing Lucien to bolt up in bed, startled awake by the noise. Fox is already barking and growling in alarm at the dark, sinewy man, sun-burnt and sea-water washed, now standing in the doorway. He holds a menacing, curved sword in one hand, and a flintlock pistol tucked into his belt. Before Lucien can move the man is on him, grabbing the boy and pulling him from the bed. Fox lunges at the burnished, powerful stranger, but he sweeps the dog aside with a quick movement of his arm, and drags Lucien out of the cabin.

On deck the chaos subsides quickly, finished almost as soon as it began. The fight, such as it is, is brief. Their captain had managed to navigate his ship up beside the *Argo*, un-noticed by her tired and sleeping crew, and launched a daring night time attack. The merchant ship was taken before most of the crew even knew it. The raiders set upon the *Argo* without warning and overwhelmed her crew before any real resistance could be mounted. As the last of the crew are hauled up on deck and placed under guard, the shouting and the general mayhem dies down quickly. Now, where only a few hours ago, music and laughter filled the air, a tense silence hangs over the ship. Lucien is led through this scene in stunned disbelief, and placed in a row with the other members of the ships crew, along with Captain LeFevre, guarded by a gang of burly, fiery-eyed sailors in various degrees of disrepair. As they watch helplessly other raiders from the pirate ship scour the *Argo*, hauling whatever they think is of value out onto the deck and piling it in front of their prisoners. This goes on until they are satisfied that they have found whatever is worth finding. As the pillaging goes on Captain LeFevre speaks to Lucien in a hushed voice, "The rascals followed us through the night Lucien," he whispers. "The music and the lanterns led them right to us. They stood off until the crew was asleep, then were on us before we knew." Lucien replies quietly, "Has my playing for the crew caused this?" The captain is quick to reply, "Of course not Lucien. We had a rousing bit of fun last night. It is my fault that we were unprepared. I am responsible for you, not the other way round." "Quiet!"

shouts one of the pirates when he becomes aware of the two of them talking. "You talk to the captain, when he comes aboard, until then, quiet!" He holds the tip of his sword up to the captain's chest to emphasize his point. The captain glares back at the man, fixing him with a steely gaze, until the pirate lowers his blade and moves on.

A moment later, Lucien spies Fox, creeping out of the cabin, tail between his legs. He tries to make his way unseen along the edge of the deck toward the side of the ship, closer to where Lucien is, but doesn't get far before another of the pirates sees him and lunges for him with a frightening charge and drawn sword. Fox yelps in fear and runs for his life. Lucien, without thinking, seeing only the fear in his little friends eyes, instantly jumps to his aid, rushing recklessly across the deck toward the dog. "Fox! Come here," he yells. The terrified dog, rushes to him, and leaps up into Lucien's arms. Just as Lucien grabs him and pulls him in, he is knocked forward by a blow to his back, and sent sprawling across the deck, never letting go of Fox. He regains his footing, just as he is roughly grabbed and spun around by one of the over-zealous guards, "So, you want trouble, boy? Well, I'm happy to oblige." The pirate raises his hand to hit Lucien, but before he can, he is stopped short by a booming command, "Avast there sailor! Avast! Leave the boy be, or by Poseidon you'll answer for it!" The pirate stops and instinctively turns toward the command, expecting his captain to be standing in front of him, instead, he is confronted with Captain LeFevre, who fixes him with a cold, steely gaze, one honed to razor sharpness from years spent at sea confronting and containing unruly men. The pirate knows the look, and the meaning: *"You are on my ship, I am your master and commander. You will obey, or suffer for it."* He loosens his grasp on Lucien and Fox, before it dawns on him that he needn't heed that look, not now, not on this ship. This man is HIS prisoner. He defiantly tightens his grip on Lucien again, and gives him a good shake for emphasis. Captain LeFevre takes up the challenge, striding toward the pirate, but is quickly yanked back into line by another of the guards. The pirate casts a victorious sneer at LeFevre just to drive his point home, and waves the blade of his dagger menacingly in front of his captives, enjoying his moment of dominance. His victory is short-lived, for at that instant, he is struck on top of the head by a big meaty fist. He staggers and spins around spitting rage, to confront this new assault, still holding tightly to Lucien and Fox. A huge, rather well-dressed man, with a flamboyant black beard confronts the pirate coldly, speaking quietly, "Are you deaf fool? Did you not hear the captain's command?" He leans in closer, speaking slowly, "Must I repeat it for you?" The sailor is confronted once again by that steely, unwavering gaze, only now, it blazes from two obsidian orbs, glaring out from beneath equally dark eye-brows, that are themselves framed by a wide-brimmed black hat, worn low to block the sun. The dark eyes glaring out from beneath that hat leave no room for questioning, only for strict obedience, and not much room for that. The sailor capitulates without hesitation; this is the man he knows he must obey or suffer for it. Letting go, he shoves Lucien back toward the other prisoners, adding gruffly, "Back with the others you." Lucien quickly obeys and steps back in line beside Captain LeFevre, who put's a reassuring hand on his shoulder. Meanwhile, the standoff between the sailor and the pirate captain is not over. The pirate captain, who seems ready to burst with the power he emanates, holds that sailor's gaze, and will not release it, until the sailor not only has released Lucien, but has also lowered his own head in capitulation and steps back deferentially. Once the pirate captain is satisfied that he has completely over-powered the sailor with his force of will, he turns to his prisoners. "Captain," he says, with dark cordiality, "please accept my apologies. My crew is high-spirited and can run amok at times. It is a constant struggle for me, but, I would not want it any other way." "No, of course not," LeFevre replies. "Your civility is appreciated, but that unfortunately brings us to the business at hand. My ship and my crew are your prisoners, and I ask that you release them, and take me for ransom. They are a good crew, and I will not see them abused." "Rest assured, captain," replies the other, "that once I have taken stock of your vessel and her contents, I will decide your fate, fairly. I am only interested in prizes and treasure. So, whether I seize your vessel, and sell your crew to the Turks; or feed you to the sharks, and burn your boat to cinder, be assured the decision will be made with MY best interests in mind." Captain LeFevre considers their predicament before responding in the only way he can, "Then sir, our fate, for now, is in your hands."

Chapter Twenty-three

The Pirate Life

Where are
Fox and Lucien?
Turn the page to see.

Birdy is taken somewhat aback by this demand, and snaps, "Well, young Lucien, unfortunately for you, I am no gentleman from Bordeaux!", he says, laughing at his own wit.

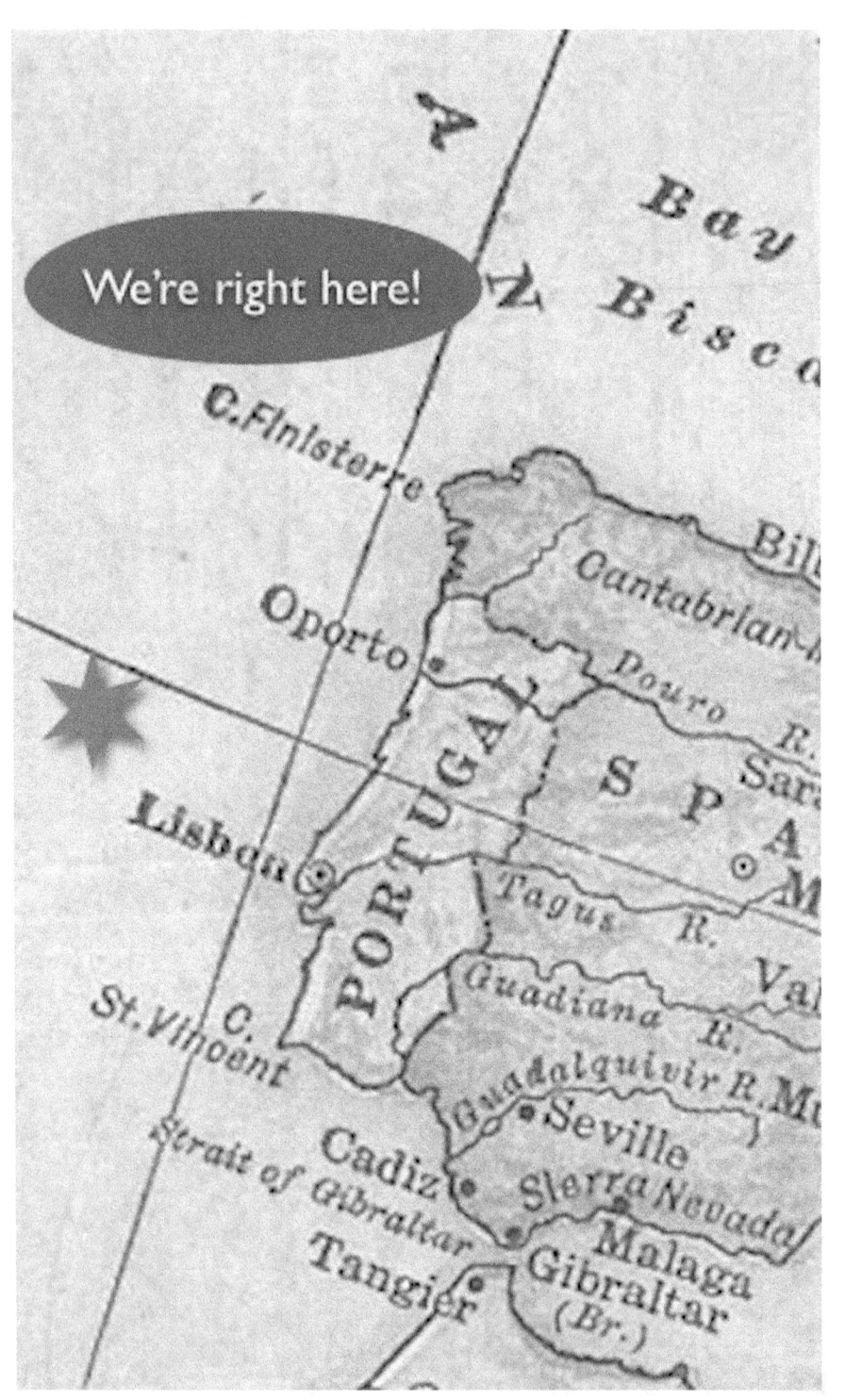

We're right here!

Lucien, Fox, and Captain LeFevre stand silently at the rail of the pirate ship, watching helplessly as the *Argo of Bordeaux* recedes into the distance without them aboard. All around them activity on their new vessel is picking up as the crew hoists sail, and makes ready for their escape from the area. As the sails are set and trimmed, the ship begins to creak and heel-over, accelerating and increasing the distance between it and the now distant *Argo*. As he watches his ship retreat toward Lisbon, Captain LeFevre pats Lucien on the shoulder, saying, "Don't worry boy, we'll be fine and home before you know it, with a grand tale to tell." Lucien replies uncertainly, "Thank you sir, but, how do you know it?" "Well," the captain continues, looking down at Lucien and noting the desperate expression on the boy's face, "I've been sailing for the better part of my life, and I've had to deal with pirates since the beginning. In that time, I've learned that at the heart of it, piracy is business and trade, nothing more. The main difference is, rather than buying and selling, as a lawful trader would, pirates take and sell, which makes for a very profitable, but high risk, enterprise. A successful captain, pirate or legitimate, must always be looking for the best return for his ship, otherwise he will not be captain for long. For our new host, the most profitable thing, once he'd seen that the *Argo* was mostly empty, and not fleet enough for his purposes, was to take what supplies he could and set her free, holding you and I to be ransomed, or sold. I'm too old to fetch a good price at the slave market, but, my insurers will pay to have me returned, and this pirate knows it. It's a business transaction, nothing more."

Lucien listens in growing alarm to the captain's explanation, which was meant to allay the boy's fears, but has had the opposite effect, his quick mind jumping immediately to what was not said, "Captain," he implores, "what of Fox and me? We are not so old as you. We do not have underwriters. What will we do? I can't allow my mother to become bankrupt, for my sake, but, Fox and I haven't any money for ransom." The captain looks at him compassionately, "I will have you delivered with me Lucien. Once we are home, your family will settle with the company as best they can. Don't worry."

At that moment the booming voice of their captor demands their attention. "Captain!" They turn to see the pirate captain bearing down on them, "your ship, sir, has borne so little fruit, it was hardly worth my while to board her!" LeFevre replies, "Perhaps if you had given me a bit more warning, I could have spared you the trouble." The other thunders back at him, spiritedly, "Yes! No doubt." "My apologies for the inconvenience!" Captain LeFevre replies, "We were outbound, and had not yet transacted any business. Return me and the boy to our ship and we will be sure to look for you once we leave Barbados, with some silver in our chest." The pirate captain gives a loud laugh, showing off a mouthful of white teeth, "You are a man of high spirits, good! But, to the point, the two of you had better fetch me a good price...Uriah!," he suddenly calls, and a nearby sailor stops what he is doing and comes running. "Show our guests to the compartments near my own." He adds sarcastically, "A stateroom worthy of them." Uriah, laughs, "Yes, captain, a stateroom." The pirate captain then addresses his captives again, "If we are to be shipmates, we'd best be introduced, I am Captain Birdy, no, it's not my given name, and you are on MY ship. Now who might you be?" he says turning to the captain of the *Argo*. "I am Captain Jean LeFevre, lately, master of the *Argo of Bordeaux*," he replies formally. "Your ward?" demands Birdy. But, before LeFevre can answer, Lucien speaks up for himself, "I am Lucien Lehun, and this is my dog, Fox. We were on our way home to Bordeaux, by Lisbon, before you waylaid us. On behalf of myself and the captain, we demand the hospitality that is due us as gentlemen." Captain Birdy looks at this young upstart curiously for a moment, studying him before he replies, "Well young gentleman..." Lucien interjects, "Lucien Lehun." Captain Birdy continues, somewhat impressed with the boy's pluck, "So you said," he goes on, "You say you are a gentleman, eh?" Lucien answers him forthrightly, "My uncle, who is no longer alive, raised me to be a gentleman, and I try to live up to his example. He taught me that civilized people should always give and expect fair treatment from strangers." Birdy is taken somewhat aback by this demand, and snaps, "Well, young Lucien, unfortunately for you, I am no gentleman from Bordeaux," he says, laughing at his own wit, then just as suddenly, barks at the sailor still standing by him, "Uriah, take them below, our introductions are over!" Uriah steps forward and grabs Lucien by the arm to lead him away, when Fox, lashes out at the sailors leg, trying to defend his friend. Uriah, jumps back, exclaiming, "Scurvy cur! I hope your dog knows how to swim!" as he makes a move to grab Fox. Lucien quickly scoops the dog up in his arms protectively. "He was only trying to defend me, leave him be." Uriah, who is accustomed to being at the bottom of the pecking order on the ship, isn't going to waste this chance at authority, and grabs the boy by the arm again, "Or, maybe the two of you would like to have a swim with the sharks together? It would be my pleasure to put you both over the side," he hisses, "and who's to stop me?" Captain LeFevre once more, instinctively, steps toward Uriah, saying, "By God, you will do no such thing," and grabs Lucien's other arm. Captain Birdy who has been watching the exchange, with some amusement, now wades in to end it. "Uriah! Sea-dog!," he bellows, "Not by God, but, by me - which on this ship is the same - you will not do it!" Then calming as quickly as he erupted, he continues with quiet menace. "If you diminish the value of my cargo, you will be the one over the side. Do you understand that, Mr. Uriah, sea dog...shark...bait." He fixes Uriah with that burning gaze that leaves no room for argument. The captain continues, "Take them below. Young gentleman," he adds, turning to Lucien, "it is the tradition of my people to be hospitable to strangers but, control your little friend or I will have Mr. Uriah kill it." With that he turns his back on them and strides off to the helm. Uriah motions them toward a companionway that leads down to the two small, dark and austere cubicles what will become their new home.

Chapter Twenty-four

Veilleux's Report

It's a dreary, sunless day in Bordeaux, a thick ocean fog clings to the valleys and the vineyards, shrouding everything in a damp, foreboding haze.

It's a dreary, sunless day in Bordeaux, a thick ocean fog clings to the valleys and the vineyards, shrouding everything in a damp, foreboding haze. A carriage emerges from the gloom, coming to a stop in front of Madame Marboeuf's secluded country house. The driver jumps to the ground and opens the carriage door for his passenger. A moment later, Monsieur Veilleux, the rotund harbor-master heaves himself out and inelegantly down to the ground. Before he can knock on the front door, it swings open and Phillip greets him. After exchanging a few words, Veilleux is ushered in, with the heavy door swinging shut behind him with a solid thud.

Inside, a warm fire burns in the fireplace in one of the receiving rooms. The harbormaster stands close, letting the heat take the dampness off his clothes as he waits for Madame Marboeuf and Monsieur Raimond to appear. At the sound of his name, he turns to greet them, as Phillip closes the doors behind him as he leaves the room. Madame Marboeuf wastes no time in getting the conversation started, "Monsieur, it is an unexpected pleasure to see you again, dare I hope it is with good news," she says. "Thank you, Madame," he replies. She continues, "This is my husband, Raimond." Monsieur Raimond steps forward to shake the harbor-master's hand warmly, "It is my pleasure to meet you, sir, and to thank you for all your past efforts on our behalf." Veilleux replies, "The pleasure is mine, sir, and as for my past service, that has a great deal to do with my visit today." "I see," replies Monsieur Raimond, "won't you please sit down and give us your news?" Madame Marboeuf, crosses the room to show him to a chair. "Yes, please, sit." she says, motioning him to one of the sumptuously upholstered chairs that flank the large fireplace. "May I offer you something to drink after your long drive? Cognac perhaps to take the chill off?" she offers. "Thank you, but, no thank you Madame," he says. "As you wish," she replies, "In that case, please, proceed. We are anxious to hear your news." The harbor-master leans forward in his chair to add to the gravity of his report:

> "It has been reported to me, that the *Argo of Bordeaux*, the very ship that I pursued into the open ocean and searched for your boy Lucien, has put into Lisbon and is anchored in the harbor there even now. The ship was raided by pirates not far from the Gates of Hercules, which you might know as Gibraltar. The first mate of the *Argo* reported that their captain, as well as a boy and a dog were taken off the ship as hostages, and the ship allowed to go free after being ransacked for treasure. The whereabouts of this pirate vessel is not known, but, since they have taken prisoners to ransom, it is logical to assume that they will pass through the "gates" and put ashore somewhere along the Barbary Coast, in order to facilitate their business."

Madame Marboeuf's face is ashen as she listens to the news. The idea of Lucien possibly being held by Barbary pirates is almost more than she can bear, but, she is a strong and determined woman, and rather than faint away at the news, her protective maternal nature comes out full force as she realizes that this fat, red-faced man has let her son fall into the hands of dark and dangerous men. Addressing the harbor-master curtly she says, "Monsieur, how can this be? Did you yourself, not board the *Argo of*

Bordeaux and search the vessel? Did you yourself, not report to me that there was no sign of Lucien, of my son, and my Fox, on board that ship!" She continues, with rising anger, "If that is true, and you are competent, how can it be so?" Mr. Raimond takes her hand to try to calm her, but, she pulls it away and continues, "You have delivered my son into the hands of ruthless men! How dare you!" Mr. Raimond, knowing his wife's singular determination, intercedes, "Monsieur, we thank you for your report. My wife is understandably upset at this news, as am I, but we are both aware that you acted honorably on our behalf." He clasps his wife's hand tightly in his own as Veilleux replies in a rather officious tone, saying, "I am sorry to be the bearer of what you consider to be bad news, and I am sorry that having risked my own well-being on the open ocean attempting to retrieve your son, I was unable, with all my exertions, to find him aboard that ship. They must have secreted him away in some deep, dark hidden chamber that I would never be able to find, even with all my tireless exertions. It seems to have been a dark plot on the part of the captain of the *Argo* to deceive me when I was onboard. But, remember that your son has been delivered from that hellish vessel now..." He is cut short by Madame Marboeuf, "Into the hands of pirates!" she exclaims. "How is that liberation?" The harbor-master continues, "Madame, pirates, for better or worse, are interested in one thing, gold and treasure. Your boy and Captain LeFevre of the *Argo* are only worth money to them if they are alive and unharmed. Once ashore, it is not so easy to say what might happen. They could be sold to a slaver, or be held for ransom." "Ransom?" It is now Mr. Raimond who interjects, "Yes, that makes sense. The underwriters will pay the captain's ransom, that is all settled before the ship sails, but what of Lucien? They don't know who he is, or his circumstances." Madame Marboeuf interjects proudly, "Surely his upbringing will be self-evident. Any fool can see the kind of boy Lucien is...Oh dear...what if they ask for ransom, and we cannot raise it! What if it is too high! What if he is sold as a..." she can't finish the sentence, the idea of it is too much for her to contemplate. Mr. Raimond tries his best to calm her, "Don't worry my dear, we will raise it." he says with determination, "Whatever it is, we will raise it. I was a poor man at the beginning, and I will gladly be a poor man at the end, if it brings our Lucien back. I've lost one son already, I'll not lose a second for the sake of riches, so help me, I won't."

Chapter Twenty-five

Birdy's Song

Where are
Fox and Lucien?

Turn the page to see.

"...the ship, with me on it, brought back a cargo of furs and tobacco...for your uncle, that people would also pay well for. He did very well on that voyage, and he kept doing well."

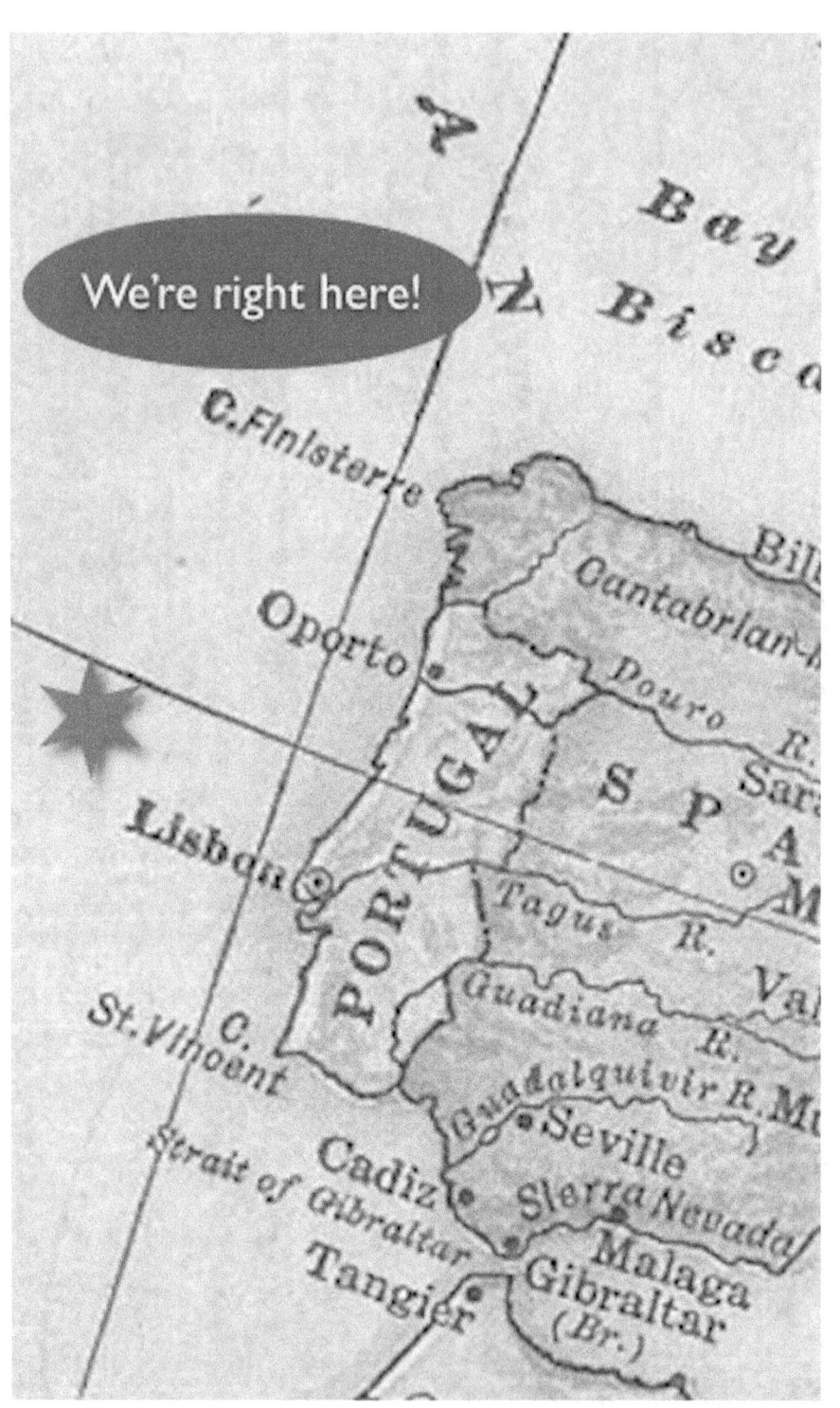

Alone in their "stateroom" as Captain Birdy so lightly put it, Lucien and Fox sit on the hard bed, in the dingy little cabin, taking in their new surroundings. No great efforts have been taken to hide its former role as a storage locker. All sorts of rigging gear is still in evidence, having been hastily pushed to one side of the room to expose the old bed that indicates the room's original purpose, before the ship fell into the hands of its current captain and crew. The small cabin consists of the bed, with a storage drawer beneath it, a plain, but, comfortable wooden chair, and a long disused wash basin, now well-rimed with dust. A small square window, similar to the one in their compartment on the *Argo,* is the only source of light. In fact, Lucien is struck by how similar the two cubicles actually are, right down to the porthole. He observes that other than the clutter around them, they could just as easily be on the *Argo*. As on the other vessel Lucien notices how the little square of light projected by the porthole onto the opposite wall rises and falls with the rocking motion of the ship as it plows on through the undulating swells, putting ever more miles between the two captives and home.

As Lucien gazes out the porthole at the rising and falling horizon, Fox lays with his head on the boy's leg, waiting as always for his slightest communication. After several moments like this, Lucien speaks, more to himself than to the dog, "Don't worry, Fox," he says, idly stroking the dog's head, "We will be home before long, Captain LeFevre has promised it. He is an honorable man." Fox, sensing the boys anxiety, nuzzles in closer to him. "But, I worry that we may be separated from him, or that his insurers will not pay for our release. What would we do then? How would we ever get home?" He pauses, then adds more quietly, "I do so wish to go home, and I know that you do too." Fox just stares up at Lucien, content to listen to his ramblings. "Mother and Father Raimond would surely pay our ransom, they have plenty of money, but how would they know to do so?" He thinks for a moment, "But, we cannot ask them to pay for us. This predicament is of our own making – my own making, it is not your doing Fox." Fox looks at him reproachfully, as if to think, "Don't be silly, we are in this together, like always. If I hadn't shown you the way in, we would not be here now." Lucien goes on, "If my parents were to pay a ransom, I wonder how much it would be? How long would it take me to repay them? I must do better in school Fox. I must be able to pay them back if I have to."

His reverie is cut short when the cabin door bursts open, and Captain Birdy barges into the room. He quickly snatches the chair out of the corner, spins it around backward, and throws a leg up onto the seat, which he then leans on as he gives Lucien a hard look. "I trust you are finding the accommodations to your liking." he booms, amused, "Only the best for our young gentleman." Then, softening slightly, he asks, "Hungry boy?" Lucien timidly nods his head. He is truly overwhelmed by the figure of this pirate, so unlike any person he has ever come in contact with before. The man is large and imposing in stature, but even more so in bearing. Lucien can easily visualize Captain Birdy, sword in hand, wading across the gory deck of some poor merchant ship, fighting through any number of hapless sailors who stand between him and his treasure. Birdy turns to the crewman standing in the passage outside and bellows, "Food for our guests!" He then slams the door closed with the flick of his hand, and turns back to Lucien. "Now, young gentleman, with your supper on its way, we've some business to discuss." Lucien nods, not really knowing why. "You see, young gentleman," Captain Birdy continues, "I'm a businessman, obligated to profit by my actions. My crew are my stakeholders, and they expect me to allow them to profit too. In fact, if I don't allow them to do so, they are within their rights to throw me over the side and take my ship. Of course, there's not a man among them who would dare, but, they'd be within their rights." He pauses a moment, then continues, "I don't want to sell you to some crazy sheik or shopkeeper, but, I'm bound to turn a profit on you. If I can't ransom you, then I'm obliged to take what I can get for you. As an educated boy, you can understand that can't you?" "No sir," Lucien replies forthrightly. "Selling one person to another? No, I do not understand that. My uncle always taught me that God has made us free, and that it is the obligation of every free person to stand up for those who are denied their freedom by scurrilous men." The pirate, impressed by Lucien's recitation, continues, "A grand sentiment, and spoken like a true Frenchman. Fortunately for me, I'm no Frenchman. But, your uncle, does he have any money to back up his grand ideals? Is your family rich boy? If so, perhaps they will have a chance to put their purses to good use, saving

you." "My uncle has nothing, he is dead, sir," Lucien
replies, "but, he took me in when I was in need and raised
me as his own, as a brother to his own son, Gustave." The
pirate listens keenly, suddenly very interested in Lucien's
story.

> "He taught me to be fair and honest with people and
> that generosity is never wasted. When he died, I was
> cast out by Gustave onto the streets of Paris, with no
> one, but Fox to call my friend. It was Fox who reunited
> me with my only family, my aunt, who lived in Paris.
> She moved us from Paris back to Bordeaux..."

Birdy, interrupts, asking hopefully, "This cousin, Gustave,
has he any inheritance? He seems to owe you quite a debt
himself." Lucien replies, "No sir, Gustave owes me
nothing. He has made amends for his actions, and
although he has no money, I would not ask him for it if he
did." "No, of course you wouldn't," Birdy replies
mockingly. "Your aunt then," he goes on, "She must be
wealthy to have moved to Bordeaux with you. What of
her?" he asks hopefully. "I suppose so," says Lucien. "She
and Father Raimond always provide for me whatever I
need and are able to keep their houses and stables well
regulated." The pirates eyes brighten, "Well, there's a
good start boy! We will get you home to your auntie and
your feather bed after all!" "Captain," says Lucien, "as
badly as we want to go home, I could never ask my aunt
and Monsieur Raimond for their money. They have done
so much for me already. That is not the way my uncle
raised me." "Well then boy," roars the captain, "this is
your lucky day, because YOU don't have to! I'll see to
everything!" He then spins the chair around, drops onto it

and commands, "Now, tell me more about this uncle of yours...this man gives me a pain in my head!" Lucien replies, "When I was just an infant, my parents were tragically killed, and I was bound for the orphanage I'm told. But, my uncle Armand, would not allow it, and brought me to his home to live with him and my cousin Gustave..." Lucien is cut short by an outcry from the pirate, "Zounds!" he exclaims, in shocked amazement. "Your uncle, Armand! I know this man! I know him, I say! Armand! My old friend and benefactor! More of a man than me it seems!" the pirate exclaims. Lucien is confused by Captain Birdy's revelation, "You...knew my uncle," he says incredulously, "That is not possible. My uncle was a good and noble man, not a pirate!" At this the captain roars with laughter, "Boy, I wasn't always a pirate, and your uncle wasn't always a gentleman - just more one than I! We all sail many seas to get where we are, your saintly uncle too. I warrant the real man is not as perfectly formed as you remember." Lucien is aghast at this suggestion, and cries out, "No! It's not true! My uncle was a good man, who would never consort with the likes of you! How dare you say so!" With that, without even fully comprehending his actions, he jumps from the bed and charges at the pirate, who grabs him and easily restrains him. "I respect your fire boy," hisses Birdy, "but, have a care, I've put many a real man to a watery rest." With that, he shoves Lucien back against the bed, where Fox is poised at the edge, growling and ready to jump to Lucien's defense. Lucien puts an arm around Fox to calm him down, as Birdy continues his tale, "Now, if we will have no more trouble, I will tell you a story about your uncle, that will give you a clearer picture of him than the one you hold so dear." With that Lucien sits up on the edge of the bed. "Go on," he directs the pirate, adding fearlessly, "nothing you can say will diminish my uncle to me." The pirate regards him thoughtfully for a moment, then begins,

"When I was a younger man, I dreamt of having my own ship and the great fortune she would bring me, no different than most young men. There were fortunes to be made too; cargos that would make a ship and its captain very wealthy indeed. It was at this time, that I first met your uncle. I was a mate aboard a ship that sailed often from Bordeaux. Your uncle, also a man dreaming of riches, decided to make his ashore, as a trader. I'd often deal with him when selling cargos. He was a gifted businessman, and was soon able to outfit a ship to sail to the colonies, loaded with wine and other fine French goods that would pay well. That ship, with me on it, brought back a cargo of furs and tobacco, and other things for your uncle, that the French would also pay handsomely for. Armand did well by that voyage, and he kept doing well, as I said, he was a gifted merchant. Over time, we became friendly and would share a glass of wine when I was in Bordeaux. My own chance finally came, when on another voyage, our ship lost her captain. I as First Mate, took over the vessel, completing the voyage from South America ahead of schedule and very profitably. Your uncle and his partners did very well and my reputation made. I was offered a ship to sail the triangle from Bordeaux. Back then, Bordeaux sent a good many ships to Africa to supply the plantations in the Caribbean, and there was handsome money in it"

Lucien interrupts him, taking an interest in the yarn, "What did they want? What did they need so badly?"

The pirate answers directly, "Young gentleman, they wanted people. They wanted slaves to work the sugar plantations. A ship load of Africans, delivered healthy, could make a captain a tidy sum back in those days...still can. I confided my new opportunity to Armand. He was not happy to hear it, called it a "godless endeavor" that was "beneath my dignity." I reminded him that rich men have far more leeway to worry about their dignity than poorer men do. But, he would not hear of it, and offered right on the spot to commission a new voyage, with me as captain, if I would foreswear the slave trade. It was that very night, making our way home from our favorite establishment at the port, that we stumbled upon a slaver transferring its "cargo", under cover of darkness to a warehouse. It struck me that I wasn't cut out to work in the dark and shadows, so I accepted Armand's terms, and embarked on my first voyage as a merchant captain. It all went well until Charleston, in Carolina. We reached port and had a successful sale of our wares – all the accounting didn't sit well with me, but the money did! We were to use the proceeds to take on a cargo of cotton and pelts for the return voyage, but, I discovered that we had been swindled by an unscrupulous agent, who somehow, after I had recovered my proceeds, ended up in the harbor. We sailed for the islands that night, and it was there that I paid my crew with your uncle's money and decided it would be better to cut out all the greedy middlemen and get my cargos directly from the source, as it were. With all the Spanish gold floating about, it didn't take long to see the profit of it, and once we "exchanged" our old tub for a fine

French frigate, with some nice cannons on deck, we were on our way, and I was the captain of my first pirate ship. I must say the enterprise has gone very well too, and I've got your uncle Armand to thank for it all." "My uncle," Lucien says defiantly, "had nothing to do with it. He helped you and you stole from him. He would never do such a thing, and taught me the same." "Well, young gentleman," remarks Birdy, "be thankful you had your uncle for a mentor, rather than me. The past is past, but, I do think that for your uncle's generosity, I owe you some consideration. What that is, I don't yet know, but I will think about it. In the meantime, I will see to your comfort..." "And Captain LeFevre?" adds Lucien. "Thinking about my old friend Armand has put me in a generous mood...yes, the captain too," says Birdy magnanimously. He gets up to leave, hesitating at the door, "No questions boy?" he says. "Yes," answers Lucien, "What did you do with the ship my uncle outfitted for you?" "Alas," says the pirate, "Scuttled, long ago. You see, the sailors we 'traded' vessels with, were intent on reneging on our arrangement, so, to keep them from endangering themselves somewhere out at sea, I thought it best to burn the ship as we left port." With that, he turns and leaves, closing the door firmly behind him.

Chapter Twenty-six

A Fox Hunt

Where are
Fox and Lucien?

Turn the page to see.

The rat darts behind the open hatchway and disappears from sight with Fox right behind him, totally focused on his prey.

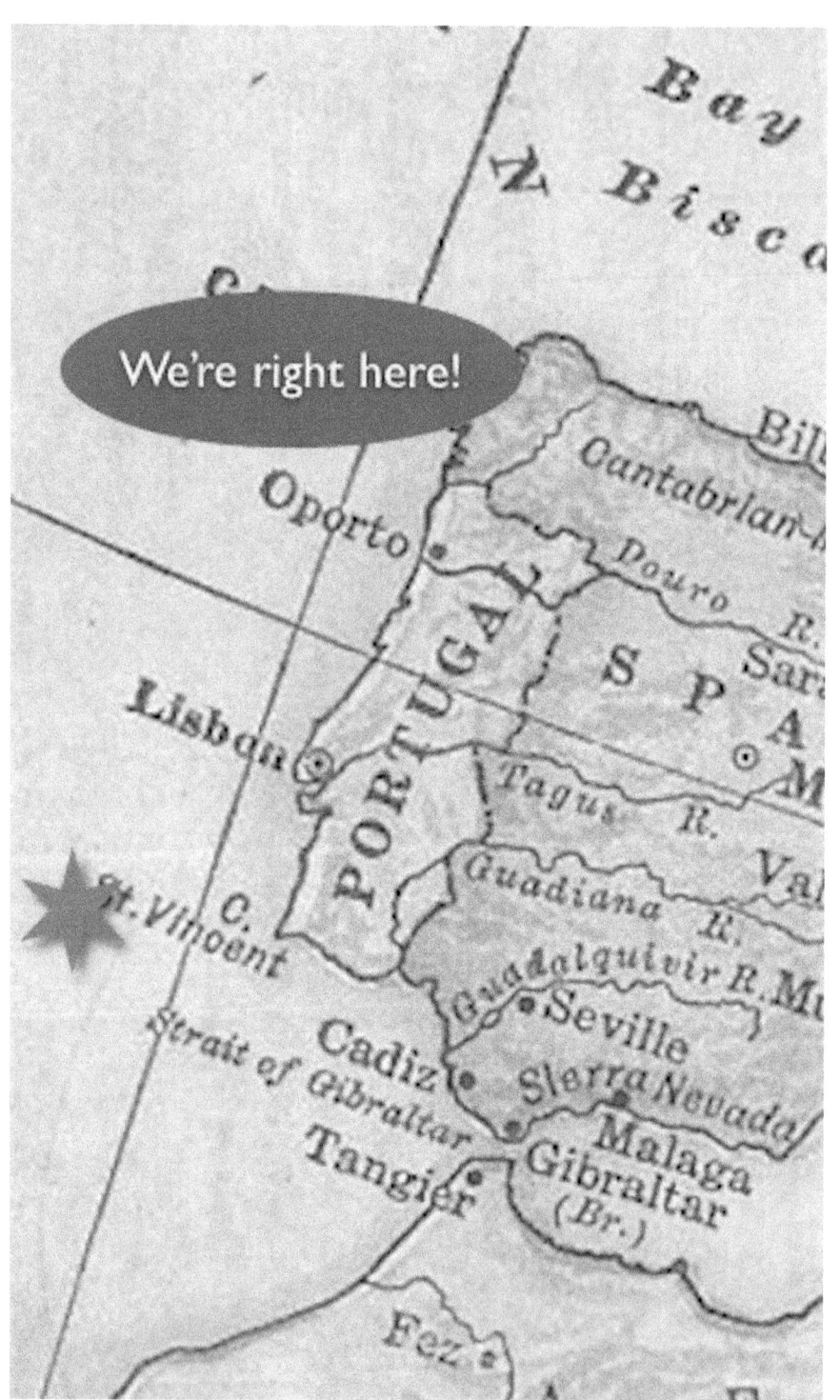

Lucien leans against a mast stay, watching quietly as the ocean swells rise up with the brisk wind, then tumble over onto themselves in a flurry of white, sending salty plumes of mist into the air, which are instantly swept away by the rushing wind. With nothing better to do, as a "guest" of Captain Birdy, he has taken to spending long hours here, enjoying the wind, and watching for a chance glimpse of one of the many amazing sea creatures that seem to escort them. From time to time, he will see a great dark mass rising out of the deepness, off to one side of the ship or the other, checking out the vessel and even accompany it a ways, before disappearing back down into the depths. These creatures are endlessly fascinating to Lucien, and both Captain LeFevre and Captain Birdy have proven to be invaluable stores of information about the ocean's inhabitants. Even one or two of the less surly members of the pirate crew have volunteered a tale when they've seen the boy standing at the rail, gazing intently down into the water at some passing beast. Lucien, is careful however to ask nothing of the crew. Captain Birdy, like Captain LeFevre before him, was very clear in his admonishment to Lucien to keep to the stern of the ship and not interact with his men. Birdy had warned him darkly, "These men are my crew, and I am bound to protect them, as they are bound to follow my orders. But, they are not men to be trusted, not by me, and especially not by you. Keep to the back of the ship and leave the fore-castle to the sailors. If anyone should interfere with you, tell me of it immediately. Do you understand boy?" Birdy's stern gaze would allow no more than a meek nod of acknowledgement, but from then on, Lucien and Fox stayed aft, keeping company with the two captains only. But, even that was proving a bit difficult, as Captain LeFevre had taken mostly to his cabin, coming out occasionally to have a stretch on deck, and then disappearing inside again. Birdy had furnished his peer with several fascinating old books, and LeFevre had taken to them readily, enjoying his temporary "holiday" from responsibilities as a "guest" on Birdy's ship.

And so it was just now, that Lucien was alone at the side of the ship, talking to Fox about what it must be like to live at the bottom of the sea, knowing that his boon companion would listen to every word. The goings-on on deck today were also proving interesting; the captain, always concerned that his vessel remain as fleet as possible, in order to run down potential prizes - or evade potential pursuers, had ordered that the sails should be hauled in close to heel the ship over in the brisk wind. Several of the crew were then sent over the side, suspended above the water on planks, to scrape the exposed hull clean of barnacles. As unenthused as the men were to hang over the side, half in, half out of the water, holding on for dear life with one hand and scraping with the other, they also knew that in their line of work, any additional bit of speed they could muster might be the deciding factor in having a good day, or a very bad one, so, they bent to it without complaint. Peering over the windward side, watching the activity at the waterline Lucien comments to Fox, whom he supposed to be still sitting at his feet, but when the boy looks down for his friend, he is nowhere to be seen. "Fox?"

Lucien calls, "Fox, where are you? Fox, come!" Looking about the deck, he sees the dog aways off forward, keenly eyeing several barrels that are secured to the rail. The dog tenses, ears canted forward, eyes fixed on his unseen target behind the barrels. A moment later he pounces, disappearing behind the stacks. Unfortunately, he misses his mark, and at the same instant, a dark, furry shape darts out from behind the barrels and across the deck toward an open hatch leading down into the ship. The rat darts behind the open hatchway and disappears from sight with Fox right behind him, totally focused on his prey. It is at this moment, that one of the pirate sailors is emerging from the opening, lugging a bundle of line to be used to send another crewman over the side to scrape. He doesn't see Fox, or the rat, nor does he see Lucien bolting toward the dog in a valiant attempt to keep him from causing the sailor to trip and fall with this load. But, as luck would have it, just as Lucien reaches the barrels and as the sailor is stepping through the opening, getting his footing, the rat darts around the corner and leaps down into the safety of the dark interior, with Fox in hot pursuit. The sailor, unaware of either, trips over the dog, losing his balance. Lucien, lunging for Fox, trying to pull him out of the way, instead, gets knocked back across the deck by the falling sailor and his heavy bundle of rigging, causing the boy to fall backward onto the barrels. On his way down, his head strikes the edge of one of the casks, opening a pretty gash, which offers up a robust stream of blood, as head wounds do.

The sailor, still not comprehending what just happened, catches himself quickly, and cursing loudly, sees Fox standing in front of him, barking protectively. The crewman attempts to land a quick boot on the dog, but Fox is too quick for him, evading the blow and running to Lucien, who unaware of his injury, grabs Fox, and jumps to his feet, apologizing to the sailor for the accident. The swearing and commotion gets the attention of everyone on deck, who turn to the melee just in time to see the sailor trying to kick Fox, and Lucien, bleeding from the head.

As Lucien tries to retreat with Fox toward the stern of the ship, he turns and runs right into Captain Birdy, who has also taken note of the commotion. The big man has not seen the whole event, but he does look down and sees the frightened look on Lucien's face, the dark red streak now framing it, and the excited dog barking back at the sailor. He examines the boy's injury, then turns and calls calmly to his second mate, "Take the boy below and get his noggin bound up." As Lucien and Fox are led away the captain turns to his crew and flies into a rage. "Who has done this?" he booms across the deck. "By my soul, I will have their hide!" The captain storms forward, raging for all to hear, "Did I not tell you! The boy is not to be harassed! He has my personal protection! Who says it isn't so? Speak up I say!" He charges up to the sailor, who is standing where he was, with the pile of line and wood at his feet. The poor fellow, still unsure of the event doesn't know what to say, and no one comes to his aid. The best he can manage is to look down apologetically at his feet. The captain bellows, "Seize this scoundrel!"

Chapter Twenty-seven

The Surgery

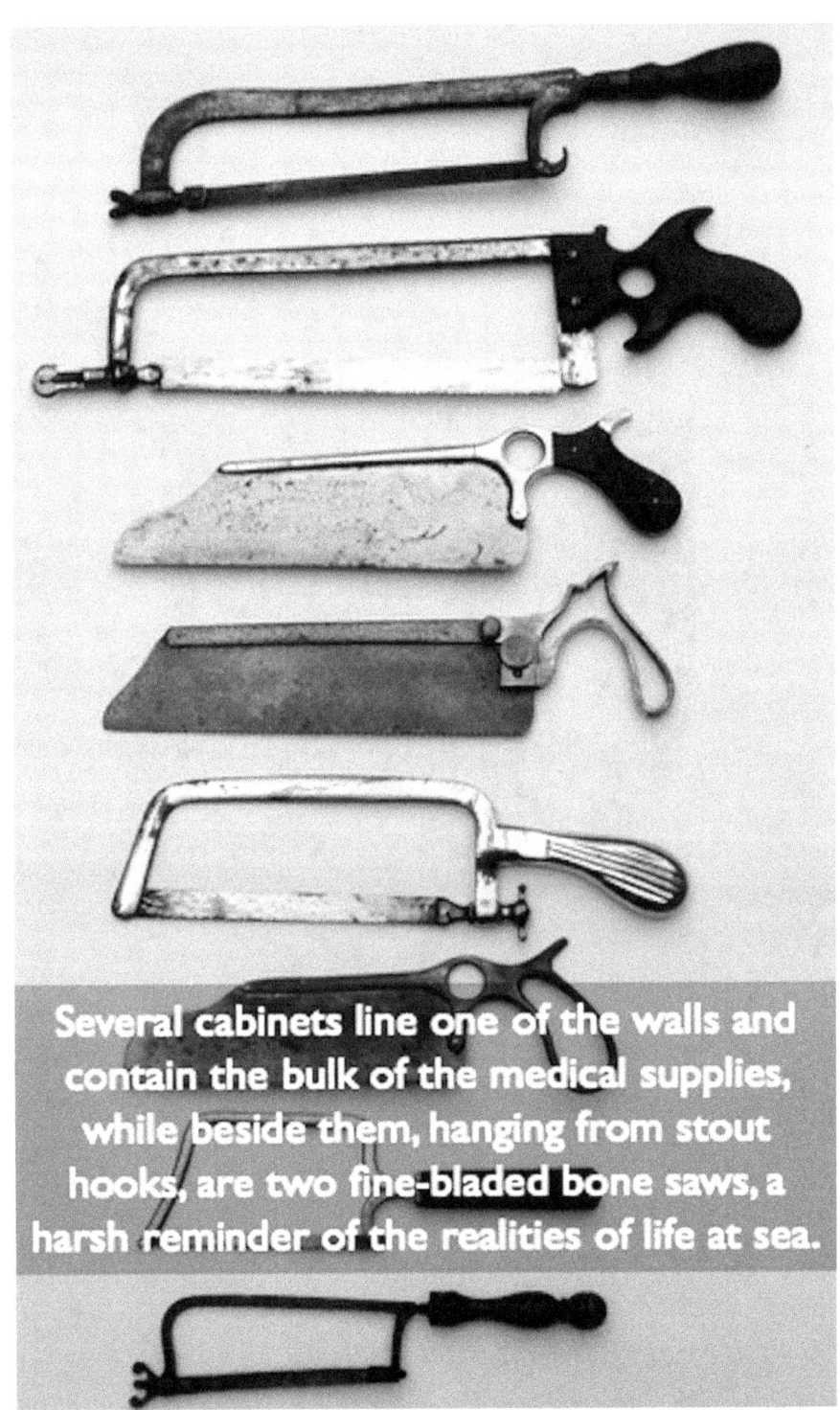

Several cabinets line one of the walls and contain the bulk of the medical supplies, while beside them, hanging from stout hooks, are two fine-bladed bone saws, a harsh reminder of the realities of life at sea.

The ship's infirmary, is well equipped for a pirate vessel and is another hint of her first life as a military vessel. It has been stocked with the supplies necessary to take care of the constant stream of injuries suffered by the crew on a daily basis, whether from a sword or a splinter. Several cabinets line one of the walls and contain the bulk of the medical and surgical supplies, while beside them, hanging from stout hooks, are two fine-bladed bone saws, a harsh reminder of the realities of life at sea for sailors of any stripe. The injuries that occur, must be dealt with then and there, there is no waiting to get to shore. Completing the room's outfitting is a sturdy oak table bolted securely to the middle of the floor, allowing access from all sides. It is fitted with multiple "tie-down" points around its perimeter to secure the arms and legs of uncooperative patients when needed.

The infirmary door swings open and Lucien steps inside, followed by his escort, who motions him to the table. Lucien sets Fox down and jumps up on the exam table, asking the sailor, "Are you also the surgeon?" The sailor replies with a wry smile, "I am...today. So, hold still for the doctor, and I'll get you fixed up good as new." The man's demeanor is reassuring and confident. He is in no way threatening like many of the other pirates, and Lucien relaxes a bit. The "surgeon," turns his back on Lucien to retrieve supplies from one of the cabinets, and when he spins back around he finds Fox on the table beside his friend. "That slab is for the wounded and the dead only, which one are you dog?" he says with a good-natured frown. Fox looks at him uncomprehending, until Lucien interjects, "Fox, go sit on the chair." He points to a rough stool sitting a few feet from the table. "Go on," he repeats, pointing again. With that, Fox turns and leaps onto the chair, landing easily and gently on the seat. Turning himself around to be able keep an eye on Lucien, he makes himself comfortable. The medic remarks, "That's a good dog you've got there, lad. You take care of him." He begins to clean off Lucien's face with a cloth and some fresh water, until he gets to the cut, which is just below Lucien's hairline at the top of his forehead. "Well, that's a good knock. Fortunately, I think you're a hard-headed lad, so, I'm almost certain you will survive." "Will it hurt much?" asks Lucien bravely. "Will what hurt much?" the medic responds. "The stitches? My old friend Father La Tuile once showed me a scar on his leg that he said one of his comrades sewed up for him right on the battle field. It took fifteen stitches, and when I asked him if it hurt much, he said he didn't know, because he had been unconscious at the time, knocked out by the blast that caused it." "Well lad," replies the medic, "You're a lot luckier than your friend, you don't get any sew'n, just some spirits to clean it up. But, I'll guess that the stitches hurt less. Now grab hold and I'll take care of it directly." He pours something from a bottle he had taken from the cabinet, onto a bandage, and brings the wet cloth to Lucien's head, warning, "Hold tight lad!" With that, he dabs away at the cut gently. Lucien, recoils involuntarily at the fiery pain, but, then steels himself and doesn't utter a sound. He clenches his teeth behind his lips, but can't do anything about the tears welling up in his eyes. The medic, seeing this says comfortingly, "All done lad, and that's the worst of it. You're a brave one. Your old soldier friend would be proud of you." He sets the now bloodied cloth down and goes to the cabinet to retrieve a roll of bandages to cover the wound with.

As the medic finishes bandaging Lucien's head, the door to the compartment opens and another sailor enters, asking, "Captain wants to know about the boy," looking from Lucien to the medic and back again. The medic turns to answer, "He's..." Lucien cut's him off, "I'm fine. Tell the captain I'm fine." The sailor speaks to the medic, "Crazy Birdy's lost his sense over this. He's up there right now fixing to haul old Hussein straight away. He's a scary sight and won't listen to any explanation. Who can say what's working him, but not a man has the nerve to speak up, and old "Huss" just gonna have to take it. He doesn't deserve it that's for sure." The medic looks concerned and frowns, "Tell the captain, the boy's good as new, no harm done. Go on, tell him that." The sailor nods and leaves to give his report. Lucien sees the look of concern on the other's face and asks, "What does it mean to 'haul' Hussein?" The medic replies, "He's the one pushed you into that barrel, which doesn't sound like him. He's mostly pretty even-keeled. Anyway, he's gonna pay well for it, and he'll steer clear of you from now on, that's certain." Lucien doesn't understand, "Why?" he asks, "What's going to happen?" The medic explains as he finishes wrapping Lucien's head, "They'll keel-haul him. It's not pretty and I feel for him. He's a good pirate." In growing alarm, Lucien implores, "What does that mean?" The medic pauses in his bandaging and replies in a serious tone, "They will run a line under the bottom of the ship, from one side to the other, and tie Hussein to one end of it. Then, into the drink he goes, and gets pulled out on the other side. Down one side of the hull and up the other. The barnacles do a good job on a man, and the salt water gets in there too. You think it hurt when I worked on that little nick on your head? Poor Hussein gonna wish a shark had taken him by the time he comes out." Lucien, remembering the searing pain he just endured all too well, and visualizing the barnacle encrusted hull that the sailors were busy cleaning off, immediately tries to jump off the table. "No! No! It mustn't happen. It was an accident! He meant no harm!" The pirate grabs him before he can get out the door and stops him. "Hold lad, there's nothing you can do. The captain doesn't change his mind, and he'll want everyone there to see it too, a reminder, who's in charge of this ship." "No!" Lucien struggles, "There's always something a good person can do. Unhand me!" Somehow, he manages to slip the medic's grasp and as he does so, Fox barks and growls, causing the pirate to shift his focus to the dog just long enough for Lucien to slip through the door, with Fox close behind.

Lucien bursts up into the daylight and blinks his eyes in the bright ocean sun. Spinning around to get his bearings, he sees the crew assembled mid-ship. On the port side several of the crew hold the end of a heavy rope, and are making it fast to a cleat. The rope disappears down and under the ship emerging on the other side, where several other men are tying it around Huss's waist.

Captain Birdy and the rest of the crew look on as the man's shirt is removed and his hands are bound behind him. Lucien and Fox plunge into the group of men, calling out, "Captain! Captain! Wait!" The captain hearing Lucien, bellows, "Let the boy through!" The sea of sailors part for Lucien and Fox as they push toward the bound man, standing at the rail. "Captain!" cries Lucien as he approaches, "Please, don't do it. It was an accident, and Hussein meant me no harm. Please Captain! My uncle would be ashamed of me if I were to let another be punished like this!" This gets Birdy's attention, and he turns to Hussein, asking him, "Does the boy speak the truth?" Hussein says nothing, remaining stoic and accepting of whatever fate comes his way. "Captain, Fox was chasing a rat, as he did on the *Argo of Bordeaux*. The rat bolted into the open hatch as Hussein was coming through. I tried to grab Fox and keep Monsieur Hussein from stumbling, but instead, either I, or Fox caused him to trip and he fell into me, which is when I hit my head on the barrel. That is the truth. You must not punish Hussein, or if you do...you must do the same to me," and with that, Lucien steps over in front of accused. The captain considers Lucien's plea for a moment before speaking. "So, you'd like to escort old Huss on his walk, eh? Have you any idea what you volunteer yourself for?" "Yes sir," Lucien replies unsteadily, "I do." "Well then," continues the captain, "Hussein, what say you about this? Would you like the young gentleman's company?" Hussein, who has been silent throughout replies slowly, in a gravely voice, "I need no young gentleman to beg pardon for me. Do what you will, and pity the barnacles, not me." With that, he is silent again, looking straight ahead, emotionless. The captain is left in a predicament. He knows that to reverse his order is to risk his final authority, which cannot be questioned. But, at the same time, he knows Hussein is not guilty of anything but bad timing. The entire company is dead-silent as he ponders the situation, all the while stroking his rough, dark beard as he considers his course of action. Finally, he speaks, addressing Hussein, "The boy has saved you. You are in his debt." At that the old sailor glances down at Lucien quickly, then straight ahead again, saying nothing. "Not very gracious," remarks the captain, who then, in a move to save face, bellows loudly, "One kiss for being an oaf! Five for any man who disagrees! Bring me the 'cat-o-nine!'" Moments later the "cat-o-nine tails" is produced. A dangerous looking device, the thing consists of a long whip, with nine strands branching off at the end. Each of these strands is finished off with a leather knot, meant to give the "cat" its teeth. The captain snatches the whip from the crewman who has fetched it, and the crowd clears back as he practices with it, in preparation for delivering the punishment. Lucien, who is still standing in front of the sailor is pie-eyed at the device and pleads, "Oh captain, no, you mustn't. He is innocent." He is cut short by the hand of Hussein on his shoulder. Lucien looks up at the pirate, who say's quietly, "Innocent? Not Hussein." With that, he pushes Lucien aside, where another crewman grabs him to keep him from being hurt. Once the boy is out of the way, "Huss" stoically turns his broad back to the captain, bracing himself with his now freed hands against the rail, in preparation for his lashing. Lucien can do nothing but watch in shock and horror. The captain gives him a hard look, cracks the whip one more time for good effect, then, raising it high, he makes a dramatic, though ineffective sweep of the whip down on the sailor, delivering an all-together lack-luster blow to the back of the seaman, who barely flinches at the impact. Birdy then throws the device imperiously to the deck and booms, "Now, sea-dogs, let that be a lesson to all of you, that I am the law on this ship, and a good ratter's worth more than the lot of you! Back to work!" With that, he storms off and resumes his station at the stern. Lucien and Fox, rush after him, "Oh thank you Captain! You have done a good thing, the right thing..." Birdy quickly cuts him off, "This is not your concern boy. You have no lot to cast here. I do what I must to regulate my crew. As I told them, you are to be un-harassed, and they must know it. Now, go and have them finish tending to your head, and leave me to my business. Perhaps your friend Captain LeFevre should explain to you the way things are at sea."

Chapter Twenty-eight

Haboob!

With his eyes covered by a raised arm, and squinted almost shut, Lucien heaves himself at the door, and manages to push it closed.

In their compartment later that night, Lucien is pawed awake by Fox, who paces about anxiously as he tries to rouse his friend. As Lucien comes around, he asks tiredly, "What is it Fox? What's wrong?" Becoming more coherent, Lucien begins to hear what Fox is hearing, the sounds of general alarm and excitement above them on deck. Through the heavy planking Lucien can make out the muffled yells and heavy footfalls of the pirates as they rush back and forth overhead. He hears something else too; the wind. It has risen to a furious pitch, and is making a strange hissing noise as it blows through the rigging and infiltrates the ship. It's a menacing sound that Lucien has never heard before, and it prompts him to clutch Fox to him. "Do you suppose we are being attacked Fox? Or attacking another vessel?" Just as the words escape his lips, he is forced to grab hold of the edge of the bed to keep them both from tumbling out onto the floor, as the ship is rocked violently on the rising waves. "We must be in a gale, Fox," he continues with growing excitement. Pausing to listen for a moment more, with Fox tilting his head to do the same, he continues, "Do you hear? The sailors are rushing about to take in the sails and secure ship...Let's go have a look!" With that he slips carefully down from the bed, steadying himself against it as the ship heaves over another wave. Deftly grabbing Fox and placing him on the floor Lucien steps carefully toward the door, but before he can pull it open the ship rocks again, leaning hard, throwing Lucien against it. As the ship begins to right itself, Lucien pushes himself back from the door and tries to open it enough to peek out, but, another sudden lurch of the vessel in the opposite direction sends the boy sprawling back against the bed, letting the door fly wide, and allowing a violent burst of wind through the opening. Lucien winces and shields his eyes as Fox instinctively turns his head away from the open door and the cloud of fine particles that swirl violently through it. With his eyes covered by a raised arm, and squinted almost shut, Lucien heaves himself at the door, and manages to push it closed. Once it's secured, he turns around, blinking his watering eyes and carefully wiping them with his shirt. His vision restored, he wonders aloud, "Fox, what could be happening?" Stepping toward the dog, his feet make a strange scraping sound that gets his attention. Reaching down to the floor boards to investigate, he says curiously, "There is sand on the floor! Fox, the wind has blown sand into our room!" Looking around he sees that the entire space is now covered with a layer of fine white crystals.

His investigation is interrupted when the cabin door bursts open again, accompanied by another burst of wind and sand. Captain LeFevre, on his well-practiced sea-legs, steps in and quickly closes the door behind him. He looks at the boy, holding tight to the edge of the bed, and Fox, struggling mightily to keep his feet, and deftly picks up the dog and puts him back on the bed. Fox immediately crouches as low as he can for balance. "This is a pretty storm," LeFevre says appreciatively, "don't you think?" The old salt seems to actually be enjoying it in some odd way. He continues, "Don't worry my boy, this is a good ship, and her captain and crew, for all their sins are able sea men. Keep to your cabin, secure the door, and you two will be safe, although maybe not too rested, by dawn." He smiles at the boy, trying to disperse Lucien's obvious concern. "Captain," Lucien inquires, "What's this strange storm? There is sand blowing all about. How on earth can the sky be raining sand?" he asks gravely. The captain, realizes that to Lucien, who has no knowledge of the sea, this is indeed a strange event, that needs to be explained. "This storm is called a 'haboob' and sailors in these waters know them well. They are nothing more than great sandstorms from the Sahara." Lucien interjects, "Gustave has told me of sandstorms." The captain continues, "Indeed, I feel for your cousin if he has to endure such things. They can block out the sun for days, and make it difficult to even draw breath. Sometimes, when the storm is big enough and lifts the sand high enough, the winds will carry the desert far out to sea, and rain it down on the water, and any poor ship that happens to be in its way. Vessels have been sunk, just by the weight of the sand on their decks and rigging. The sailors will be busy tonight, that's certain," Captain LeFevre notes. "What shall we do sir," asks Lucien with concern. "You and Fox must keep to your cabin until the storm subsides. If you become afraid, I will be next door, doing the same. Now, climb into your bed and keep each other in good spirits. Come morning we will see how "our" ship has weathered the storm." With that he turns to the door, and steadying himself against it, opens it quickly and slips out, pulling it shut behind him. A few seconds later, the sound of the door on his own cabin closing hard, lets Lucien know Captain LeFevre is just on the other side of the wall. Feeling a bit less ill at ease he lays back on his bed, "Fox, do you think this means we are getting close to...Africa?" He pronounces the word with the gravity and mystery that "the dark continent" deserves. "I wish I had asked the captain, but, I didn't think about it until this very minute." He lies back with Fox beside him, watching a hanging lantern in the middle of the room, leaning magically back and forth. He knows that the lantern is not moving at all, but is staying almost perfectly still as the ship shifts beneath it. "So many strange things at sea," he observes.

Chapter Twenty-nine

The Rogue!

Where are
Fox and Lucien?
Turn the page to see.

It is while Lucien is watching these goings-on, that suddenly, one of the crew up on the rigging calls out a warning. "Wave! Wave!" he shouts "Starboard bow!"

Having spent most of the night wide awake, clutching their bed and one another in terror, as the ship pitched violently and the sand hissed through the rigging, Lucien and Fox are up with the sun, happy to be alive and anxious to see the aftermath of the storm. With the worst of the tempest past, they slip out of their compartment and quietly up the steep steps to the hatch, which had been closed and secured from the inside by the crew as they retreated to their hammocks once the ship was secured. Lucien carefully unbolts the latch that holds the cover, and gives it a tentative shove, but, it doesn't move. He pushes it harder, but is still unsuccessful at breaking it loose. Finally, with one last heave he manages to lift it just a bit, bringing a shower of fresh sand down on his head. Quickly dropping the hatch cover, he brushes the sand from his hair and shirt, then steadies himself for another try. Speaking softly down to Fox, who is waiting patiently at the foot of the steps, he says, "Fox, be ready, I think more sand will fall, stand back." With that he heaves the cover up and moves it over just enough to create an opening that he can see through, letting the little avalanche of sand fall out of the way before peering out at the deck. "Oh my!" he exclaimed at his first glimpse of the aftermath, "Fox, you must see!" With that he muscles the cover aside just far enough to allow him through the opening and pulls himself up and out. Fox, not content to be left at the bottom of the steep treads, bounds up the steps behind Lucien, who grabs his friend and lifts him through. Once outside, they look around in amazement at what the storm has wrought.

The deck is now completely covered with sand. All the rigging sparkles with a rime of white dust. It is piled in small dunes behind every barrel, and hatchway, collecting behind anything that stood in the way of the wind. Other than the areas that have been kept clear by the skeleton crew that is still on duty, and the wet areas around the scuppers that have been washed clean by the ocean water rushing in and then surging back out of them when the larger waves hit, the entire the ship appears covered in a shimmering layer of snow and ice. It is an amazing and alien sight, and the two of them begin to walk carefully about this sparkling wonderland. At the same time, several members of the crew begin to emerge from below to take over for those on the night watch, and start to clean up the ship. Lucien watches as several men climb the rigging and begin to beat the storm sails to knock the sand out of them, sending showers of the white stuff down onto the deck and into the water. Others begin the arduous task of sweeping the decks clean. Using large brooms and pieces of planking as makeshift shovels, they sweep the sand through the scuppers or shovel it over the side. It is while Lucien is watching these goings-on, that suddenly, one of the crew up on the rigging calls out a warning. "Wave! Wave!" he shouts "Starboard bow!" Everyone looks up from their work in time to see a towering rogue wave, rise up out of the ocean and bear down on the ship. The helmsmen makes a hasty course correction to try to get the vessel more head on to it, but, the ship doesn't turn smartly enough and takes the impact on its starboard side, causing it to heave over suddenly to port as water breaks over the rail and blasts in through the forward scuppers, flooding across the deck taking everything not fastened down with it – including Fox! The dog, unable to withstand the force of the oncoming water, and slipping helplessly on the wet sandy planks, is swept up and carried across the deck. He is panic-stricken and barks loudly to get Lucien's attention. Lucien hearing the distress of his friend, spins instantly toward the sound, as the ship begins to right itself. There he sees Fox being swept toward a scupper on the port side of the ship as the water from the wave rushes mercilessly back toward home. The dog claws futilely at the deck, unable to gain any purchase as the water carries him along, until, just as he is about to get taken over the side, his claws grab hold of the the small lip at the bottom of the scupper, where it meets the deck. He strains heroically to hold himself against the water. This is the sight that greets Lucien when he finally locates the dog - his best friend fighting valiantly against the water, but finally, slapped by another wave breaking against the hull, he is pulled free of the vessel and swept helplessly into the cold dark ocean water. Lucien lunges for the dog, without hesitation, but he is too far away to reach him in time, and looks on in horror as his friend disappears from sight.

Jumping to his feet he leans far out over the rail to find the dog. "Fox! Fox! Fox!" he calls frantically, then catches a glimpse of Fox struggling to stay afloat as he is swept quickly toward the stern of the boat. Lucien runs along the rail to keep him in sight, calling out with every step, "Fox! Fox!" as if his words would magically levitate the dog out of the water and back to him. Reaching the stern, a wave rolls the ship again, and the two of them are eye to eye for a moment. It looks almost as if Lucien might be able to reach out and pluck the drowning dog right out of the water. The abject terror in his little friend's eyes plead to him for help, and without a second thought, as the ship begins to roll in the other direction, taking Fox back down out of sight, Lucien jumps up on the rail and leaps blindly into the ocean now far below, determined to rescue his friend or perish trying.

The power of the water is something Lucien, for all his education and natural good-sense could not anticipate. When he hits the water, it knocked the breath out of him, and then, the waves pouring over him, conspire to push him down under the surface. It takes all his strength to fight the waves and reach the terrified dog, who immediately tries to cling to Lucien, scratching the boy with his claws as he works to keep himself above the water and desperately seeks the comfort of the one other being on earth that he trusts with his life. But, Fox's struggles only add to Lucien's problems. The dog, splashing around in front of him, clawing at him, and literally trying to climb onto his shoulders, pushes Lucien down lower in the water, even as he fights to keep his head above it. With the waves constantly hitting him in the face, he tries to grab the dog with one hand to steady him, but that leaves him one less hand to tread water with, making their predicament even more grave. "Fox," he sputters, "calm down, I won't leave you. No matter what." All his words get him is a mouthful of sea water. Fox, for his part, hearing Lucien's voice and sensing their shared fate, tries to calm down, and clings to Lucien's shoulder as best he can. The seriousness of their situation now dawns on Lucien as he realizes that he has no way of supporting the dog, or himself, as another wave breaks upon them, forcing them underwater again, even as he strains to keep Fox above the surface. He gets more and more saltwater in his mouth and throat causing him to cough and allowing yet more water in. He knows too they have no chance of catching the ship, even at its reduced speed under the small storm sails. As all this sinks in, he doesn't allow himself to panic, fighting to keep calm, he thinks to himself, "Don't worry Fox, I won't leave you here. If we aren't able to swim to the ship, we will sink together, while trying." With that he rolls onto his back, so Fox can cling to his chest, and begins methodically kicking with his legs and stroking with his arms, pulling them slowly after the ship. All he can think about now for some reason is his uncle, encouraging him from the edge of a pond near their home to swim across and back on his own, encouraging him to keep going, ever watchful, "Swim Lucien. Don't forget to use your arms! Nice big strokes! You are almost halfway...Excellent!...don't stop until you are there...don't stop until you are there!" The memory, he realizes, gives him another reason to thank his uncle, because he insisted that Lucien be taught to swim, "A proper gentleman," he would say, "must know how to swim, Lucien." Lucien now thought, "Uncle, you were right."

A loud splash, just off to the side of Lucien's head gets his attention. He looks toward the sound and sees, bobbing lightly on the waves a short distance off, a dark, pitch-covered barrel, from the deck of the ship. The barrel is lashed around with rope, which is formed into grab loops at intervals around its entire circumference. A long line is secured to the barrel and then stretches out from it, back toward the ship. There is another splash, and another barrel hits the water further away. Lucien swims furiously for the first barrel, trying to hold Fox and stroke at the same time. He is not making much progress, and as he tires, the barrels, now at the end of their rope, began pulling away from them, towed by the ship. Lucien makes one last desperate lunge for the rope loop, but it is not enough, and the barrel moves farther and farther out of reach. As he looks up desperately toward the slowly receding stern of the vessel, he sees another dark shape come arcing from the deck toward the turbulent surface of the ocean. Just as it is about to hit the surface, it changes its shape somewhat, becoming more streamlined as it enters the water and disappears beneath the surface. A moment later, the head and shoulders of Hussein, the very pirate that had knocked Lucien into the very same barrels that were now so quickly leaving them behind, had come to reclaim Fox and Lucien from the ocean.

After the accident on deck, the sailor had given Lucien a wide berth, not wanting anything to do with what he considered trouble just waiting to happen. But now, here he was, swimming determinedly through the waves toward them, rising up to the top of a crest and then disappearing into the trough before reappearing at the top of the next wave. Lucien was now so tired and numb that he doesn't even feel the iron like grip of the sailor's rough hands on his arm as he is grabbed and pulled roughly through the waves and back toward the nearest barrel. He feels the sailor pulling his free hand out of the water and closing it around one of the grab loops, and giving the gruff command to "Hold!" At that, Lucien summons the strength to tighten his grip on the rope, and on Fox with his other hand, as the sailor pushes off to secure the other barrel, working his way up the line, half swimming and half pulling himself along to get close enough to reach it. Once he has it, holding it with one hand he swims it back to the other barrel and the two castaways, so they all now have something to cling to.

While Lucien, Fox and Hussein have been struggling in the waves, the alarm is raised on board, and the entire crew floods onto the deck with well-practiced efficiency. It takes the first crewman only moments to reach the safety lines attached to the barrels, where he is quickly joined by a host of others. With plenty of raw brawn now arrayed at the lines the men quickly began to haul the barrels, and with them the three castaways, back to the ship. By the time a boat is lowered over the side, the unflinching exertions of the men manning the ropes has brought the barrels within reach of the boat, where several more sailors now stand ready to pull the two victims from the water. A rope ladder had been lowered, and after being pulled into the boat, Lucien and Fox, too tired to make the climb are hauled up to the deck by the pirates, followed by their savior, who makes the climb effortlessly, seemingly unaffected by the ordeal. Lucien and Fox are given blankets and placed in a sunny, dry spot on deck to warm up, and watch as the barrels and boat are brought back up and stowed. Within minutes, everything is back in place and the crew disperses back to their duties. Captain LeFevre, who has witnessed the rescue comes and sits down with the two survivors, saying, "Well, quite a way to start a new day. Are you unharmed?" Lucien, still coughing from the sea water replies, "Yes sir, thanks to old Hussein, who came after us." "All sailors," says the captain, "are very serious about having a man overboard. Most have been out there, all alone, wondering if someone will come for back for them. It's a grave business to sailors, Lucien." As he speaks Lucien watches their savior recoiling the rescue lines and making the barrels fast again, going about his work almost as if nothing had happened. When he is finished, he glances over at Lucien, Fox and the captain. Seeing Lucien looking at him, he comes over to the boy and speaks, "Gentlemen pay their debts, no?" Lucien, understanding what he means replies, "Oui, and you are a gentleman, in your way." With that, the sailor turns to go about his business, saying as he goes, "Stay on the boat." This bit of humor from the sailor brightens Lucien's spirits and he replies, "We will try our best," as Hussein disappears down to the lower deck to retrieve some dry clothes for himself.

Chapter Thirty

Storming The Gates

Where are
Fox and Lucien?

Turn the page to see.

"The English control the 'Gates' and have it
well fortified. Those devils would like
nothing better than to drop a few cannon
balls on my head you can bet."

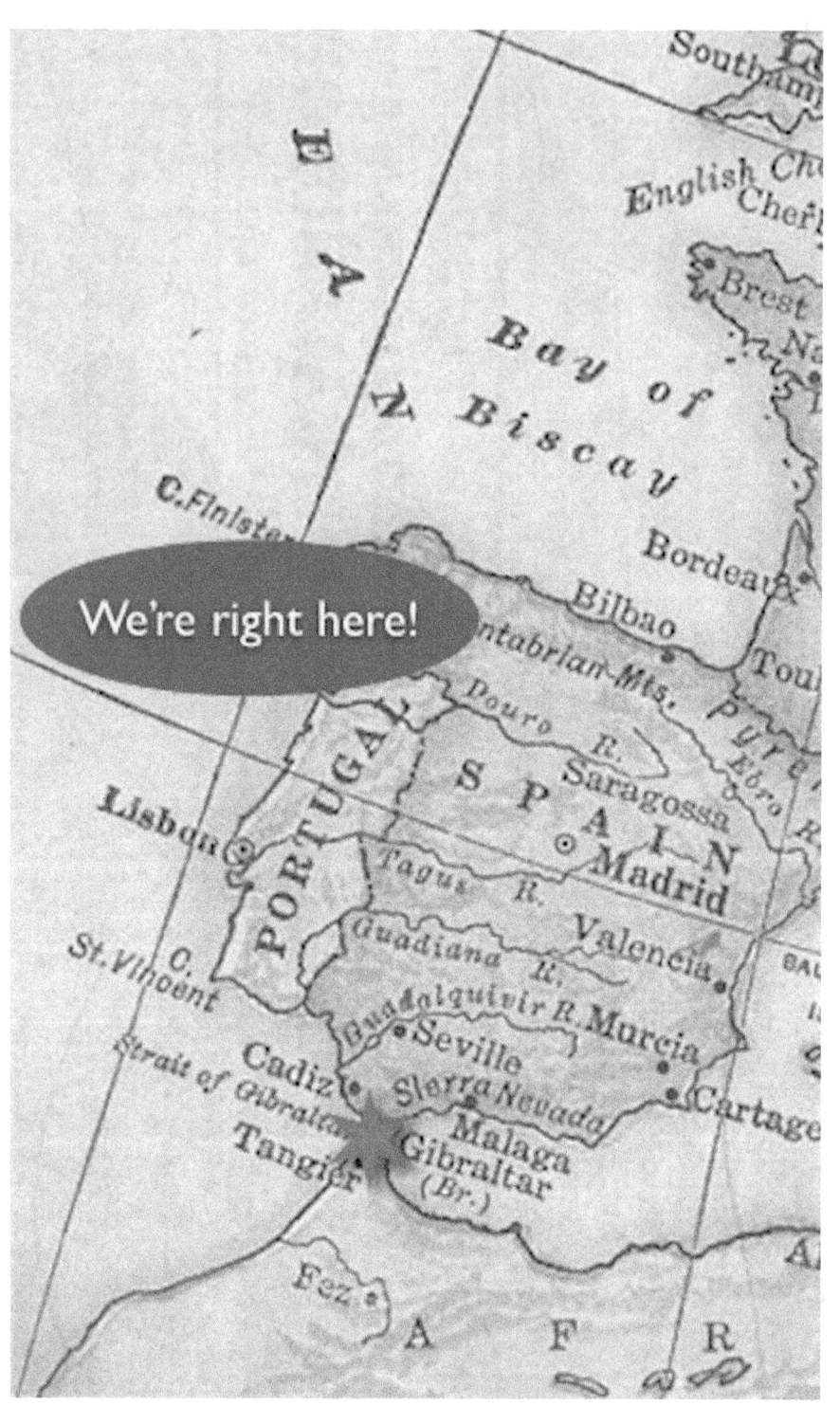

We're right here!

After their sleepless night, spent riding out the haboob, and the morning's terrifying encounter with the rogue wave, Lucien and Fox spent the day gratefully locked away in their compartment, sleeping soundly. Captain Birdy, in an uncharacteristically kind-hearted moment had ordered one of the crew to clean the sand out of their room, and put it back in order so that the boy and his dog could recover from the day's ordeal. Birdy saw that Lucien had a game heart, but the harsh realities of life at sea were something he was clearly not yet strong enough to endure. More to the point, the pirate had not yet decided Lucien's fate, torn between his love of treasure, and the nagging, inconvenient sense of obligation he felt toward the man he had defrauded so many years ago. As far as Captain Birdy was concerned, until he had charted that course, it only made sense to keep the boy in good condition. They were still several days away from Dellys, their current destination, so, any decision regarding the disposal of the duo could wait a bit.

It was not until almost sunset that Lucien and Fox emerged from their compartment and out onto the open deck to see what was what. Lucien was amazed to find that all traces of the haboob had been erased. The sand was gone from every inch of the deck, and the rigging and sails were all free of the heavy load they had carried earlier. He also noticed that, although the wind had died down considerably since that morning, they were still sailing under very light sails, just poking along eastward. This seemed peculiar to him, since up to now the captain had insisted on piling on the sails, to get the best speed they could out of the ship. Seeing Captain Birdy standing with his helmsmen, beside the wheel, looking out into the distance in front of the ship with a spyglass, Lucien decided to ask about their sluggish pace. He knew better than to interrupt Birdy, having learned that the captain could explode into a rage at the slightest provocation, so he simply stood beside him and waited to be noticed. When the captain had finished his scan of the sea ahead he lowered the glass and addressed Lucien, "Well boy, I see you've got the water out of your gills." Lucien replies, "We are both feeling much better now, sir." "The cook has set aside some food for you below, when you're of a mind to eat," the captain replies. "Thank you, sir," says Lucien, "we are quite hungry now." Then, sensing an opening, he continues, "Captain sir, if you don't mind my asking, why, now that the storm is past are we traveling so slowly? Has the ship been damaged?" The captain looks pained at the questions, responding with, "It's the captain's business how he sets his sails, not his cargo's. But, no harm in it, here," he says, thrusting the spyglass to Lucien, who puts the eyepiece up to his eye while the captain points the other end for him in the direction he was looking. "There now, do you see that? Do you know what that is?" Through the eyepiece Lucien sees nothing at first but the unbroken ocean, shortly though, after adjusting the aim a bit, he makes out what looks to him like distant islands jutting up from the ocean. "I see an island. Is that where we are going?" the boy inquires. The captain retrieves the spyglass and returns it to its case as he answers. "Not islands, and, yes, that's where we are going." Lucien says nothing, waiting for further explanation. The captain continues, "That is Gibraltar, the Gates of Hercules. Call it what you will, it's all the same. To port, on the north is Europe, to starboard, south, is Africa. We've got to sail between them to get to our destination." Lucien asks, "Then why do we travel so slowly if we are so close?" "Fast is not always best," continues Captain Birdy. "The English control the 'Gates' and have it well fortified. Those devils would like nothing better than to drop a few cannon balls on my head you can bet." "Because you are a pirate ship?" Lucien interjects. Captain Birdy corrects him, " 'independent merchant vessels'...are not well liked by the tariff collectors who fund the kings and queens of Europe, and so we are not generally given a cordial welcome. I've found it best to run the 'Gates' in darkness, to lessen the opportunities for the artillery on shore. We sail with light canvas so that we don't get too close too soon. We will remain beyond the reach of their guns until after dark, then pile on all sail. With luck we will slip right through the 'Gates' unscathed." Lucien looks concerned, "They will be trying to sink the ship?" The captain sees the boy's distress at the thought of having the ship sunk and being back in the water again, so he tries to allay his fears, "Little gentleman, I know my business, and I have transited the 'Gates' countless times; even if they do decide to try to drop a ball or two on us, they can't hit what they can't see. Don't concern yourself. Go below and get some stuffing for yourself and your little squire. Come back on deck after dark and watch as we make our passage. The Gates of Hercules are a fine sight, night or day."

Heeding the captain's advice, Lucien and Fox head below to find some food. The cook fills them both up well, and the food, plain as it is, makes Lucien feel much better. Later that night, long after the sun has set, Fox, Lucien and Captain LeFevre are standing at the rail taking in the show. The ship is eerily dark and quiet, Captain Birdy having ordered that all lights be extinguished and no more than a whisper from anyone until they are past the English artillery. All sails are flying now, and the ship is moving along at a furious clip. The moon, though not nearly full is still shedding enough light to illuminate the high rocky cliffs that they are gliding silently beneath. The captain had reminded Lucien that, "if you can see them, then they can see you." and it made him uneasy, realizing that at any moment a bright flash of light and a distant boom might signal their end. But, at the same time, he is transfixed by the steep, sheer walls of stone rising in front of them. Flickering torch lights can be seen at various spots, moving about on the great monolith, and once in a while, he is sure that he hears voices drifting down from above. It is thrilling and terrifying all at once.

They sail on this way, in dark silence for what seems to be hours. The constant low hiss of water off the bow, as the ship surges forward, seems deafening in the complete lack of sound coming from its inhabitants. Everyone is on edge and aware that any misstep might give them away to the gunners they know are stationed atop the rock, and it is with a palpable sense of relief that the rocky sentinels on both sides of the ship began abruptly to fall back. They soon find themselves once again in open water, no longer in the Atlantic, but now sailing on a brisk wind into the Mediterranean Sea. Lucien knows from his studies that France would soon be just to the north of the ship, but even so, he feels as though he is in another world from the one he and Fox left behind so many days ago.

Chapter Thirty-one

Dellys

Where are
Fox and Lucien?

Turn the page to see.

Several hours later the captain, looking a bit tense, returns and disappears into his state room, summoning both Lucien and Captain LeFevre. They find Birdy in a rather agitated state, pacing anxiously about the room.

We're right here!

Lucien wakes the next morning to find the ship riding quietly at anchor in a secluded cove, ringed by a sand beach that rises quickly upward into steep green foothills. The foothills, in turn, rise abruptly into the rugged, desolate Atlas mountains of Algeria. Trees and plants of all sorts grow in a continuous carpet from the edge of the beach up into the hills, but stop well short of the distant sun-parched peaks, creating a verdant border for the mountain range. Not far from the ship, a noisy little waterfall tumbles into the back of the bay where they are moored, the end of a rocky river that can be traced far back up into the hills, where it disappears into the tumultuous, dry, terrain.

Although still early, the sun is already bitingly hot, but the pirates are in good spirits, being back in friendly, familiar territory. A boat has been launched, loaded with water casks to be refilled from the cascade, and as they work, the sailors all take advantage of the cool, fresh water to clean away the accumulation of months of sea salt and sun burn. Captain Birdy's boat is also launched, and Lucien and Fox watch from the ship as he and two dark sailors push off and row toward the water's edge. They don't join the others at the waterfall, instead pulling straight for the beach. Lucien squints to watch as the sailors land the boat and steady it for the captain, who climbs out and wades the last few yards through the mild surf. He crosses the beach purposefully, disappearing into the trees, leaving his oarsmen to make themselves comfortable on the sand in the shadow of their boat, to wait for his eventual return.

Several hours later the captain returns and disappears into his state room, summoning both Lucien and Captain LeFevre. They find Birdy in a rather agitated state, pacing anxiously about the room. The two captives take a position on one side of the the chart table, which also serves as the captain's desk, while Birdy positions himself on the other. He throws Lucien a distressed look and then plunges right in, "My friends, we have made Dellys, and are doing some provisioning ashore. Once that is done, we will set out again. Captain," he says, addressing LeFevre, " you will remain aboard for a bit. I have arranged to have your agent contacted as to your condition and ransom, and I hope to have my leave of you at our next port." Captain LeFevre replies rather calmly, "I understand, Captain. But, what of Lucien and Fox? What do you plan to do with them?" Lucien jumps in abruptly, "Are we not going with the Captain?" The pirate glares at him, "No. I am not confident that LeFevre's insurers will pay for you. Further, I have no way of knowing if your family has the means to, so, in deference to your uncle, my old friend Armand, I have decided to give you your freedom. You, and your little squire will be taken ashore immediately. I will give you money enough to get you to Algiers where you can buy passage to France." "But..." Lucien begins before being cut off by LeFevre, "You cannot simply cast the boy up on shore and leave him in this foreign and hostile land. He doesn't know the language, or the customs and is defenseless! It is barbaric!" Birdy appears unconcerned, "Perhaps, Captain, you would like to escort him?" The other replies immediately, "Yes!

Of course. I insist on it." Birdy feigns consideration then responds, "But, what of your ransom? You ask me to tell my crew that they will forfeit their shares? That won't sit well with them, which won't do well for me..." LeFevre shoots back, "I am a man of some means, I will give you my word that once I am home, you will have your ransom." "Yes, I'm sure you will," is the unimpressed reply from Birdy who continues, "But, honestly, not only do I not believe in 'honor among thieves,' I don't subscribe to honor among sea captains either. What I do believe in is not depending on honor to make my fortune for me. You will stay aboard until your ransom is paid...and counted. Then you will be released, and you may go searching for the boy to your heart's content." "You are a barbarian," sneers LeFevre. "I am a barbary pirate," is Birdy's quick reply, "Would you prefer the boy be sold as a slave?" Lucien takes the hand of his friend to calm him, "Captain, Fox and I have made our way before. We will make our way now. In spite of what this man says, my uncle always taught me that people are good at heart, and I have found it to be true. Fox and I are not afraid." The captain looks down at his young friend, "You are a brave boy Lucien, but this is not France." Birdy interrupts, "Enough, my boat will take you ashore. You are free of me, and I am free of further obligation to my old friend, Armand."

Minutes later, Lucien and Fox stand with Captain LeFevre, waiting to disembark the ship. The cook, in a kind gesture has given them a canvas sack full of food to get them by. As they are about to depart, LeFevre pulls a gold coin out of his coat and presses it into Lucien's hand,

"Take this Lucien, it is all I was able to hide away from these men. It is all I have for you." "Thank you, sir, but, Captain Birdy has given me a small purse of coins, I can't take the only gold you have left, it would not be right." "Lucien," replies his friend, "I do not need it, you may. Having gold enough to buy the good fortune you need will never hurt you. Get to Algiers as quickly as you can. If we are near Dellys, Algiers is to the west." A loud shout from below cuts off their goodbyes, "Aye! Come on little gentleman! Time to pull for shore!" LeFevre continues in a rush, "The french forces are garrisoned there, reach them, and they'll help you. When we meet again, you may repay me if you wish." Lucien looks over the side, then turns back to LeFevre, and gives him a warm hug. "Thank you, sir. I hope to be able to do that." With that, he climbs over the side onto the boarding ladder. The captain picks up Fox and hands the dog to Lucien, who props him over one shoulder. Fox now teeters there precariously, but doesn't move as Lucien, who has become accustomed to the steep stairs and ladders of ship board life, throws one last uncertain smile to the captain, then begins a careful descent to the launch bobbing below, ready to face whatever this new adventure has to offer.

Chapter Thirty-two

Castaway

...then turning back toward the shoreline, he watches as the pirate sailors waste no time in pushing their boat back into the surf, making ready to abandon them there without another word.

The short journey to shore seems to take hours, and be farther than Lucien ever imagined. With each pull of the oars, the little launch lurches forward, bringing Fox and him a few feet closer to that unknown country, while sending Birdy's ship, their home for the last – he can't even remember now – farther into the distance behind them. Their friend, Captain LeFevre, stands at the rail watching their long slow departure and waving his sad goodbyes to them the whole way to the beach.

A few minutes into the trip, Lucien becomes aware of the low whispers of one of the pirates as he complains to his shipmate. "Birdy's a fool...could sell the boy and make a good profit...why should we give up our share, we worked for it." His companion is silent, content to just let the other rant on. "What if we take the little skipjack ashore and do him in, and we split his purse? Who would know? We're hauling anchor soon as we get back." Frightened by what he overhears, Lucien turns to face the sailors, and is surprised to find that one of them is Hussein, the pirate who saved him from the ocean. Obscured beneath his broad-brimmed hat, Lucien had not even taken notice of him as they left the ship, distracted as he was by his departure. "Good sailors," Lucien begins, "you must deliver us safely to shore. That is what you have been charged with. I would be happy to pay you if that is what it will take. We will share what he have with you." The disgruntled sailor continues "Share? What's to share? I say we do him in and take his money. We've earned it. What do you say Huss?" The other sailor regards him darkly from under his hat, finally replying, " I say, perhaps

I do you in, take your purse and give it to the boy." The other pirate looks surprised at this response and stumbles, "Will you now?" Hussein replies tersely, "Oui. No honor in robbing young boys." With that the exchange is over and they go back to their rowing in silence.

When he feels the swells begin to stand up beneath the little boat, Lucien knows they are finally nearing shore. As he turns to see how far from the water's edge they are, the boat is picked up by one of the waves and sent careening into the back of the next one, spraying everyone in the boat. As soon as the wave roars past and breaks, one of the sailors jumps out with the bow line and sloshes up onto dry ground, pulling the boat in behind him. Lucien feels the little craft grind to a stop in the sand, signaling Hussein to jump out as well and grab the side of the boat. As the now lightened boat floats higher again the two pirates give it a solid, well-timed heave, to nestle it firmly on the beach. "Well, little prince, what you waiting for?" yells Hussein. Lucien stands up, steadying himself on the gunwale, then, swinging his legs over the side he slips down into the knee deep water. He turns to retrieve Fox, who looks more than a little hesitant to leave the safety of the boat, but Lucien coaxes the dog to him, "Come on Fox, come on. I'll catch you, don't worry. I won't let anything happen to you." Fox steps up on the gunwale timidly, then, before Lucien can grab him, he jumps into the surf and bounds for shore, leaving Lucien to wade the rest of the way on his own. Fox greets him with a joyous reception when they are both on dry land again.

Walking up the beach a ways, with Fox at his heels, Lucien looks around at his new surroundings, then turning back toward the shoreline, he watches as the pirate sailors waste no time in pushing their boat back into the surf, making ready to abandon the pair there without another word. Looking past them, out to the ship resting at anchor so far off shore, he thinks he can make out his friend Captain LeFevre, still standing in the same spot, watching his progress. Looking off down the beach in one direction and then another, not knowing what to do or where he should go, he is suddenly overwhelmed by his predicament, and sinks down into the sand putting his head in his hands, tears welling up in his eyes and running down his face. Fox, sensing his friends distress, does what he has always done, he walks to Lucien's side and leans into him, as if to say, "Don't worry, no matter what happens, you won't be alone. We will be together, and together we will be all right." Lucien reaches out and drapes an arm over the dog, rubbing his damp fur absently as he tries to make sense of their predicament.

He is startled as the sack of food, given him by the cook, lands with a dull thud beside him on the sand. Looking up, he sees Hussein towering over him, peering down at them from beneath his broad, dark hat. "Even little French gentlemen need to eat, no?" the sailor says. Lucien had completely forgotten about the food in the boat, and knew it would have been a terrible thing to have been left there on the beach without it. He was immediately grateful to the man for bringing it back to him. "Thank you sir," he offers weakly. The pirate, seeing the distress on the boy's face offers, "Eat first boy, then worry. It will make things easier." Lucien just stares blankly at Hussein, totally lost, squinting into the bright sun to see him. Hussein squats down in front of them, and speaks quietly, "After you and your little friend have had your food, walk this way," he points toward the east, "to Dellys. There is a man there that I know. He is an Ottoman, and he can help you get to your people. His name is Karasu. Tell him that the pirate" he corrects himself, "the sailor Hussein has sent you. He will help you, but, don't trust him...he's Turkish." Lucien, listening intently asks, "How will we find this man?" The sailor again points down the beach, "He lives beneath the walls of the casbah. The people know him."

Lucien looks down the beach in the direction Hussein points and sees the dark outline of an old fortress far in the distance, clinging to a hillside, overlooking the water. He also notices that it is surrounded by other buildings that comprise the town of Dellys. The sight of the distant town, and realizing that he is not stranded in the midst of some dark African wilderness, but rather, close to the company of other people, lifts his spirits a bit. The pirate stands up saying, "It's a long walk, don't waste the day...the sun is hot here, take this too." With that, he pulls the hat he wears off his head and places it on Lucien's. "It will keep the sun off." Without another word the sailor turns and starts toward the boat where the other sailor waits impatiently. Lucien calls after him, "Thank you sir! You are a kind man...a gentleman!" The sailor doesn't respond, and Lucien and Fox watch helplessly as the two pirates turn their boat around and shove off through the waves, pulling hard back toward their ship, shrinking slowly into the distance.

Chapter Thirty-three

A Walk on the Beach

Fox barks again, turning his gaze down the beach and then back at Lucien. He does it once more, as if to say, "Come on! Get up! Being afraid won't take us home. Get up!"

Finishing their sparse meal of hard biscuits, dried meat and water, Lucien reminds himself of how fortunate they are that the ship's cook, out of fatherly concern for them, provisioned them so well, giving them plenty of biscuits and salted meat, and even some fruit to help them along the way. Though their lunch had been tough to chew, and at present, he had to force himself to eat anything at all, it had helped buoy his spirits. As he now carefully repacks their food bag and ties it securely shut, Lucien cautions Fox, "We must be careful with this, it may have to last us several days." The dog doesn't seem to hear, as he is already off sniffing at every rock and bit of driftwood he happens on, getting acquainted with their undiscovered new world. After a bit of exploration, he notices Lucien sitting silently, looking out at the ship, the launch now stowed back aboard, and the crew raising the sails to get underway. Lucien speaks quietly, as much to himself as to Fox, "What sort of person would just leave us here on this beach, so far from home? Gustave did as much, but at least we were still in France, and knew the ways of the country, and he has tried so hard to make amends..." He stops speaking, his thoughts now turning black, as the enormity of their predicament creeps back in and freezes the boy in place. Fox, somehow sensing what is needed, breaks off his sniffing safari and trots back to Lucien. He nudges him with his nose, but gets no response. He does it again, but still his friend is lost in his own thoughts. Finally, he's had enough and lets out a loud, impatient bark. Lucien starts and turns to the dog, "What is it, Fox?" Fox barks again, turning his gaze down the

beach and then back at Lucien. He does it once more, as if
to say, "Come on! Get up! Being afraid won't take us home.
Get up!" Lucien replies to Fox's unspoken coaxing,
"You're right Fox. We should be on our way, no matter
what." He gives his friend a hug, continuing, "I think that
so long as I have you with me, I'll be fine, and you know I
won't let anything happen to you, don't you?" Fox replies
with a look that says, "Don't be silly of course I know."
With that, Lucien gets to his feet, brushes the sand off,
slings the bag of food over his shoulder, and together they
begin their long walk along the beach to the distant,
ancient fortress.

Chapter Thirty-four

The Shopkeep

Where are
Fox and Lucien?

Turn the page to see.

Lucien just stares...stupidly as she picks up
her basket and starts back toward the...
buildings that now frame the beach. Just as
she disappears into their midst, she turns
and looks back, ever so slightly, to see if the
clumsy boy is still watching her.

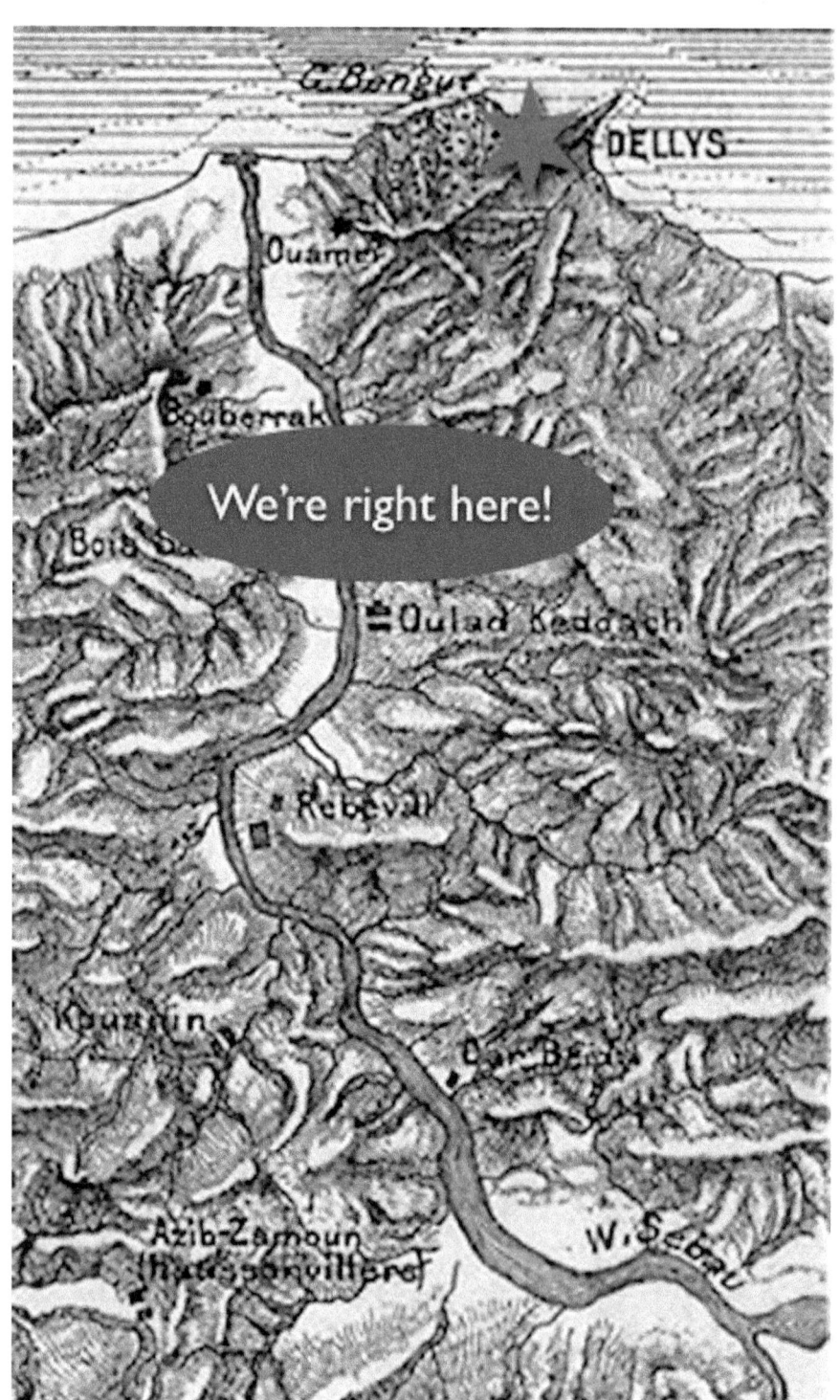

Hours later Fox and Lucien find themselves on the outskirts of Dellys, but, even as hot as it is, their time on the beach had passed easily. Birdy's ship being anchored far outside the town, the two had had the beach to themselves. The sound of the surf and the screech of the birds, along with a full stomach and the sheer joy of being back on solid ground, conspired together to help them forget their troubles for awhile and enjoy their long stroll along the water's edge. Fox had even taken time out from chasing the sea birds to coax Lucien into a game of tug-of-war with a prized piece of driftwood he had decided would be perfectly suited to it. Their trek was a calming balm to them both, and Lucien especially was feeling much more hearty, and ready for whatever lay ahead for them in the strange town they were now approaching.

Rounding the point of land that had blocked their view of anything but the old fortress nestled up on the hillside, they could now clearly see not only the ancient casbah, but the rest of the town spreading out below it too. The fortress's old weathered stone walls seemed to grow right out of the bedrock on which it perched so ominously. Although the casbah had at one time contained most of the town's people, commerce and government within its walls, the population had long since outgrown it. Buildings now spilled down the hillside all around it, almost to the water's edge, stretching out along the shoreline in both directions. The fringes of the settlement are marked by the small fishing boats pulled up on the beach, their nets spread to dry in the sun. In the artificial harbor in front of the town, larger boats and some trading ships ride quietly at anchor, behind the protective breakwater that defines the harbor's borders.

Lucien and Fox now pass more and more people on the beach as they move further into the town. Lucien doesn't notice the curious looks he and Fox are getting, he was too busy marveling at the gleaming white buildings and houses with their courtyards and archways and iron gates to notice. Then, something special catches his eye. Seeing it, he knows what it is, but, never imagined that he would be face to face with one. But, there it is...a camel! He had learned about them in school, how they could store enough food and water right on their own backs to be able to trek across the great deserts of Africa without a care. Gazing at the picture in his school book he remembers thinking, "What a strange thing that is." Now, here was a camel, right in front of him, being led along patiently by its owner. Fox notices the animal too, and creeps cautiously forward, sniffing the air to get a sense of it. The camel's head, swinging on its long neck, pivots around to check out Fox as well. Not knowing what to make of the beast he gives an uncertain, blustery little bark, which the camel ignores. Lucien admonishes the dog as he watches the strange animal being led off, and remarking, "Fox, we are SO far from home!"

Continuing along in silence, Lucien, awed by their strange new surroundings is not really comprehending where he is going. Fox, equally distracted by all the new sights and smells, is eagerly zig-zagging ahead, smelling everything he can as they continue toward the casbah. It is in pursuit of one of these strange new odors that Fox darts in front of Lucien, who, eyes fixed on the towering casbah, which now seems to rise right up over them, fails to see the dog and trips over him, losing his balance and sprawling onto the sand. Fox is just as startled, and yelping, bolting several feet to get out of the way. Picking himself up from the ground, and brushing himself off, Lucien hears laughter. He looks around and finds a strange girl staring in their direction and laughing. She looks to be about his age, wearing a long brightly patterned skirt that reaches the ground, a billowy, long sleeved blouse, and a sort of vest over that. Her head and hair are wrapped in what looks to Lucien like a scarf that drapes down below her shoulders. The head wrap partially covers a necklace made of gold coins carefully strung together and draped around her neck. But, it is her intense green eyes, outlined by heavy black makeup, and the gleaming white teeth that flash so brightly as she laughs at Lucien's stumble, that grabs his attention most. Not knowing what else to do, he stares at her. She playfully mimics Lucien falling, but does so with an artistic grace that makes Lucien think of a dancer, rather than a mocking recreation of his own clumsiness. She laughs again, her wide happy smile sparkling beneath her pale green eyes. Lucien just stares stupidly as she picks up the basket she had been carrying and starts back toward the buildings that now frame the beach. Just as the girl disappears amidst the crowds, she turns her head, ever so slightly to see if the clumsy boy is still watching her, then she is gone.

Fox's impatient bark snaps Lucien out of his stupor, reminding him, "She's gone. We need to get on with it."

Lucien replies, mostly to himself, "Perhaps that strange girl can help us to find this man Karasu? Let's run after her!" With that Lucien takes off after the girl, with Fox right at his heels. But, when they reach the spot where he lost sight of her, they can see no trace of her on any of the streets that swirl away into the old town like a maze. He looks in every direction, but sees nothing, "Fox, she has disappeared. No matter," Lucien continues, "someone will surely know this Karasu. Hussein said to look for his house beneath the walls. So...," he continues, tying a leash onto the dog, "let's go this way, toward the fortress." With that, Lucien starts along a narrow twisting street lined with gleaming white houses and shops, toward the towering citadel walls.

The serpentine streets they are wandering have become a crowded carnival of vendors of all sorts and throngs of people partaking of the many exotic offerings they have. The smell of cooking lamb is heavy in the air, and Fox is quick to notice. Lucien must keep a tight hold of his leash to keep the dog from visiting every stall they pass. Lucien is not immune to the temptations either, and after wading through this sea of spices and food and delectable tidbits that he knows any French patisserie would be proud of, he succumbs and stops at a stall to buy a little treat for them both. Standing at the entrance to the little shop, Lucien looks in, amazed at all the offerings, not knowing what to try. Fox knows what he wants, and pulling at his leash, rears up on his hind legs to reach for the oily lamb sausage hanging on a string from overhead. Lucien remarks laughing, "So, you've already made up your mind have you! Well, they do look as good as anything. Do you think that is what we should buy?" An enthusiastic yip from Fox is the unmistakable answer. The proprietor watches suspiciously from the back of the shop as they make their way over to him. Without thinking, Lucien addresses the man, "Hello sir, we would like to buy two of your sausages, if you please." A blank stare and a slight shrug of his shoulders to indicate that he doesn't understand is the shopkeeper's only reply. This catches Lucien off guard; he had not considered that the people here would not understand him. "Parle vous Francais?" he asks. Again the man shakes his head and shrugs. "Oh my, you don't speak French? No, why would you. How rude of me to assume it." Lucien takes a few steps toward the sausages hanging near the door and points at them, then holds up two fingers, saying "Deux, s'il vous plait." The shopkeeper smiles in comprehension, and gets up from his chair to join them at the front of the stall where he picks up a knife and deftly cuts two of the dark red sausages down from their perch. He wraps the meat in coarse brown paper, and ties it with a string, holding the finished package out to Lucien, while at the same time asking him for payment. Now it's Lucien's turn to be at a loss. Realizing that the shopkeeper must be asking for payment, he pulls out the purse given him by Captain Birdy and extracts a coin, which he holds up for the shop owner. The man eyes the gold coin for a moment without taking it. It is obvious to him that Lucien has no idea that the coin is a gross overpayment for the food, but, greed gets the better of him. He takes the coin and shoves it into his pocket, thrusting the neatly wrapped package into Lucien's hand in return. "Merci," says Lucien politely as the shopkeeper nods agreeably and rushes back to his chair, anxious to have the transaction concluded.

Once back out on the street with their package, Lucien abruptly stops and turns around. The shop keeper, watching the pair come back his way, assumes they have figured out his cheat and will be demanding money from him. When Lucien reaches the store owner he says, somewhat unsure of himself, "Sir, I know you cannot understand me, but, hopefully I can find a way, for we do need your help." The shopkeeper, assuming he is being asked for a refund immediately jumps to a defensive posture, responding, "How dare you say I have cheated you. Out of my store! Out!" He gestures them toward the door angrily, but Lucien and Fox have no idea what he is saying to them, or why. They only know that he sounds irate, and Lucien doesn't know what he has said to cause this outburst. He tries again, continuing, "Sir, I don't know what I have said, but, I am sorry if I have offended." The shopkeeper stays with his ploy, demanding again, "Out, out of my shop." Lucien, having nothing to lose, goes on, "We must find a man named Karasu. Do you know KARASU?" The shopkeeper suddenly pauses and steps back, thinking, "Karasu. Why does this infidel ask for Karasu?" Lucien is encouraged by this and continues, "We have been sent to find Karasu, he is to help us go home. We were sent to him by Hussein the pirate. He had given me his hat." says Lucien, pointing to the black, wide brimmed chapeau on his head. At this the shopkeepers demeanor completely changes. He recognized just three words out of the boy's mouth, "Karasu," "pirate" and "Hussein", and that hat looks familiar as well, and that is enough for him. He knows both those men, everyone knows them. What's more, he knows what might happen if either of them thought that he had somehow interfered in their business. "Allah," he thinks to himself, "why have you sent this boy to me. I have done nothing. I have..." he quickly pulls the gold coin from his pocket and offers it up to Lucien, who is now confused, "No sir, I do not want my money back, I am sure that your sausages will be fine. I need to go to find the man named KARASU." He turns and gestures toward the street, waving his arms to try to indicate the entire town. "Where does Monsieur KARASU live? Hussein the pirate has sent us to him."

Finally, it clicks with the shopkeeper; they are asking directions to Karasu. He hurriedly grabs Lucien by the arm and walks him out of his stall, and points up the street further and says "Karasu." "Where?" asks Lucien. The man points again and tries to speak the directions, but it is no good. Seeing that Lucien is completely lost and confused, the shopkeeper gestures for them to stay where they are, as he disappears back into his shop. He reemerges a moment later with a pencil and paper, which he shows to Lucien and begins to draw on, making a mark to indicate his store, then traces a path for Lucien and Fox to follow to reach Karasu's home. When he is done, he folds the paper in half and puts it in Lucien's hand, along with the gold coin. He closes the boys fingers around it, thinking to himself, "Better to give away two sausages to the boy, than to risk angering those he keeps company with." Lucien assumes the man's assistance is simply a reflection of his good and generous spirit, rather than a function of his fear, and responds, "Thank you sir," to the shopkeeper, "you have been very kind, and we are in your debt." The shopkeeper nods and smiles as he nudges them along into the street, anxious to have them gone and play no further part in whatever it is they are up to. He has done what he can, and if anyone comes around to ask questions, he can tell them so.

As the pair trudge off up the street, Lucien turns and waves to the shopkeeper, who plasters an insincere smile on his face and waves back tepidly.

Chapter Thirty-five

The Old Turk

The grey-haired man smiles, and looks amused. "I am Karasu," the man says to Lucien, in well-practiced French, "and I have been told that you are looking for me."

Using the shopkeeper's crudely drawn map as their guide, Fox leads the way through the ancient streets of the old town, slowly closing in on their destination. The growing rumblings in Lucien's stomach remind him that their breakfast on the beach had been hours ago and they still had not eaten the sausages given to them by that rather strange shopkeeper. Feeling more confident that they will soon find their destination, Lucien decides this is as good a time as any to try their new delicacy. "Fox," he says, "lets find a place to sit and have our sausage?" The dog wags his tail excitedly. "I thought you might like that idea," continues Lucien. "Let's see what we can find." Continuing along the narrow, curving street, as it winds ever higher up the hill, they don't have to search for long. To their relief, they soon come upon a spot where the old fortification the street has been following has collapsed leaving a gaping hole. Whether the breach is the result of simple neglect, or a cannon ball launched against the ancient casbah in some long ago war is unclear, but, no matter the real reason, Lucien has already decided that the gap is definitely the work of a cannon ball. "Only a terrible pirate like Captain Birdy would do this. What else could it be," he thinks to himself as he surveys the rubble, conjuring up images of that ancient battle.

The hole provides the perfect spot to stop and eat, presenting them with an unobstructed view of the harbor and the wide Mediterranean Sea spreading beyond it. "Fox, this is a grand spot for our lunch!" Lucien remarks. "Look at all the boats in the harbor and sailing past. This is where we will eat." Having made his decision, he steps into the breach and sits down on one of the large stones strewn there, pulling out the paper wrapped sausage as he does so. Fox immediately noses hungrily up to Lucien, demanding his lunch. "Now just wait a moment Fox. You know I won't forget you," Lucien says, as he carefully unwraps their lunch and breaks up one of the sausages into the paper which he then sets on the ground for Fox, who pounces on it immediately. "There. Now, don't bother me about mine." Fox can't hear him, he is already too busy gobbling up the tasty bits of well-seasoned lamb meat. Before Lucien gets even half-way through his, Fox is there, nudging him for another piece. "You are going to make yourself sick Fox," admonishes Lucien, "We're not accustomed to this spicy food." Fox barks at him impatiently. "Alright you glutton, here..." Lucien says, breaking off another bite of the sausage and holding it out for Fox, who gladly gobbles it down.

Watching as the dog finishes off the sausage, Lucien says, "Well Fox, here we are again, eating our lunch out on a busy street in a strange city that we don't know anything about. How do you like that?" he says, handing the dog his last bit of the meat. "At least it is warmer here than Paris. Do you remember how we had to huddle by the fire sometimes to stay warm? But, our little "island" there was not so bad, and it was ours to do with as we pleased, with no one to ask us why. Maybe that is what we should do...just stay here. Think of all the wonderful things we could grow in a garden here! What do you think?" The dog gives him a quizzical look, which Lucien interprets to mean, "Thank you, but I prefer my nice soft bed at home, if it's all the same to you." "Yes," Lucien replies, "for all our longing for a new adventure, now that we are stuck in one, I just wish we were back home again." He continues more thoughtfully, "I do so miss our mother and everyone at the house. Martine was always so good to us...I wish we could go home." He falls silent, turning his back to the sea, and staring forlornly out at the street with all its mysterious dark people rushing past, not even giving the two of them a second look. It makes him feel even more lonely to realize that no one there cares at all that they are alive or dead. His head sinks into his hands as he contemplates home and how very far away they are. Fox, sensing his friend's sadness comes and sits down beside him, looking up at Lucien, patient as always, content to be by his side.

After a few moments of blankly staring into the crowded street, Lucien suddenly jumps to his feet. "Fox!" he exclaims, "I didn't even realize where we are. In all my hunger and sadness," he says as he excitedly checks their little map, "I didn't see that we have been sitting right across from the street where Karasu lives!" He quickly repacks their food sack, and ties it shut, continuing, "I hope this man can arrange passage for us back to France. Oh how exciting it will be to see home and tell the story of our adventure! Come on!" He scoops the dog up and dashes through the people and the carts to get across the street, then disappears up the little side street running beside the walls of the citadel.

As they make their way up the congested little street, Lucien refers to the map given him by the shopkeeper and locates their destination; a small, dingy and unimpressive little store-front. A bearded man sits in a chair by the front door, watching Lucien and Fox as they cross the street and approach him. "Excuse me sir," says Lucien as he stops in front of the man in the chair, "are you Monsieur Karasu?" The bearded man shakes his head and says something that Lucien can't understand, gesturing for them to be on their way. Frustrated once again by his inability to communicate with the local people, Lucien tries again, speaking more slowly and clearly - although he knows it will make no difference. "I am looking for Monsieur Karasu. The pirate Hussein has sent me to him." The man, like the shopkeeper recognizes the names and puts the rest together for himself. He looks Lucien and Fox over, then motions for them to stay where they are as he gets up and disappears through the dark doorway. "Fox, I think this man will be able to help us get home. I am sure of it," says Lucien to his friend.

The fierce looking fellow is back at the door quickly, opening it and motioning them in. The room they enter is dimly lit, the light from the street fading quickly toward the back of the room. Lucien notices several other men sitting in large, comfortable looking chairs, talking amongst themselves and glancing suspiciously over at Lucien and Fox. A large, ornate water pipe sits on a low table between them, smoldering and giving off a stream of fumes as they take turns drawing from the tubes that extend from the central body of the pipe, causing it to emit a muffled bubbling sound whenever one of the men puffs from one of the mouthpieces at the end of each tube.

The two are shepherded to the back of the room by the guard who had brought them inside, and now points them through an open doorway hung with a beaded curtain that separates the adjoining rooms from the storefront. Beyond the beads, they find themselves in a comfortable sitting room, with rugs on the floors and heavy furniture, covered in colorful fabrics and pillows arranged throughout the space. A grey-haired man reclines in one of the large chairs, and motions for Lucien to approach. Stepping toward him, Lucien tries to introduce himself, now quite aware of the fact that no one can understand him, nor he them. He tries to compensate by over-articulating, and using his hands as much as possible, in a desperate attempt to be understood "My name," he says, indicating himself, "is Lucien Lehun. This is my dog," he says, purposefully patting Fox on the head, "Fox." The grey-haired man smiles, and looks amused. "I am Karasu," the man says to Lucien, in well-practiced French, "and I have been told that you are looking for me." Lucien is surprised and thrilled that he is hearing someone speaking his own language. "You are French!" Lucien exclaims. "No, of course not," counters Karasu "I am from Constantinople. There are many fine schools there, teaching many languages. Now," he says, getting right to business, "why has that scoundrel Hussein sent you to me?" He motions Lucien to a sofa near him. Lucien sits, and recounts their adventures since leaving Bordeaux. Karasu listens intently. When Lucien has finished telling his tale Karasu remarks, "I think I understand now why you are here. Hussein is a rough man, but, he is not without common sense." "Yes, sir," Lucien chimes in, "I forgot to tell you that he has given me his own hat to protect me from the harsh sun on the beach. I do not believe him to be a bad man." Karasu replies, "What is "bad" after all? No matter, you are here now, and I can help you get to your people. God willing, we can have you reunited with them in a short time, but, tonight, Monsieur Lehun, you will stay with me and my family, as my guest." Lucien is overjoyed at this news and can hardly contain himself. "Oh thank you sir, thank you!" Karasu smiles kindly at Lucien, then turns toward another door and calls out in Turkish, "Melek, are you there? Bring some tea and sweets to your father and our guests, and a bowl of water too," he adds remembering Fox. A girl's voice answers, then, several minutes later Melek emerges, carrying a tray that holds a pot of tea, with several cups and a platter covered in little, sticky pastries. She hesitates ever so slightly when she sees the young stranger sitting there with her father. As she gracefully places the tray on the table in front of them, Lucien immediately recognizes her as the girl who made fun of him on the beach that very morning. Melek gives no indication of recognizing Lucien at all, instead continuing to pour tea into the small cups. She hands one to Lucien, and then to her father, who is obviously pleased by his beautiful daughter's attentiveness. "Merci." Lucien says stiffly as he takes his cup. She seems to not understand him. Karasu interjects, "This is my daughter, Melek, who looks to be about your age Lucien. I dote on her too much, but, she is a good girl. Please greet our guest in French, Melek." The girl looks at her father, then at

Lucien and says, "I am very pleased to meet you." She then places a piece of the pastry on a small plate and hands it to Lucien, who is already holding the tea cup in one hand. He takes the plate in the other, looking rather awkward now, sitting there with his arms outstretched to support the tea cup and the plate. Seeing this Karasu furrows his brow, "Melek!" he says firmly, in Turkish, "What do you think you are doing. Put his plate on the table so he can drink his tea. Do not embarrass your father." Melek looks at her father innocently, "I am sorry Father," she replies, as she sets another plate of pastry in front of him. She then turns to Lucien and retrieves the little dish from him, placing it on the table, adding coyly, while leaning close to Lucien's ear, "There, now you won't drop it." She giggles softly then stands up and rushes out of the room. Karasu has witnessed the interaction, and is appalled. "I beg your pardon Lucien. My daughter has not been well-instructed by her mother. She will be punished." Lucien immediately jumps to her defense, "Oh please sir, don't punish your daughter for our sake," he says. "She was simply having fun. You see sir, I met your daughter, after a fashion, this very morning, just as Fox and I arrived at the village. She was down near the water, and she saw me trip over Fox and fall down on the beach. I am sure I looked very silly, and she teased me for it. Just now when she came in, I thought she did not recognize me, but, I see now that she does. She meant no harm." After hearing Lucien's explanation Karasu says, "Just the same, she will apologize for being disrespectful. Melek!" he calls sternly. The girl appears, rather sheepishly, at the doorway.

"Come in here. You will apologize to our guest for being unkind and impolite." She enters the room reluctantly and begins, "I am sorry..." her father cuts her off, "In French, Melek," he warns. She pauses to think for a moment, then goes on, " I am sorry that I spoke disrespectfully. I meant no harm, and I apologize. May I go now, Father." "Yes, Melek. Help your mother make preparations for our guest." She turns to go and smiles a wry smile at Lucien, who seems quite taken by her. He watches her as she leaves and just as she disappears through the door, she feigns a stumble, pretending to catch herself on the door frame, laughing innocently as she disappears into the next room. Lucien smiles and turns back to Karasu who has not seen his daughter's parting stunt.

Chapter Thirty-six

Melek

A heavy necklace of gold coins hangs from her neck, swaying back and forth as she moves, accentuating the graceful motions of her shoulders and arms.

The young dancer swirls and glides around the room, her bare feet making no sound, as the rest of her body illustrates the melody of the song being performed by a group of four musicians perched off to one side of the space. The girl's mother, sitting nearby, claps in time and coaches her daughter along, as the girl flows and gyrates around the room. Melek is dressed in light, billowy skirts that soften all the movements of her hips and legs. Her blouse shimmers iridescent in the dim light, while the heavy bracelets and anklets she wears add their own voice to the music and the rhythm of the dance. The heavy necklace of gold coins, hanging from her neck, sways back and forth as she moves, accentuating the graceful motions of her shoulders and arms. Several men sit nearby at a low table, taking in the performance and enjoying the music. Karasu looks on with pride at his daughter Melek as she glides fluidly about, looking to her mother from time to time for encouragement and guidance on executing the subtle dance.

Lucien sits on a cushion beside his host, pie-eyed. He is transfixed by the pretty young girl, but his upbringing and limited life experience have not prepared him for this performance. He is embarrassed by it, but at the same time unwilling to look away. He also knows that even though he doesn't understand what he is looking at, it seems to be meant as an honor for him, and he knows better than to risk insulting his hosts. But, he was fairly certain that he would not have averted his eyes in any event, after all, this girl, with her brilliant green eyes, surrounded by heavy black eye makeup and colorfully painted face, framed by her long dark hair, was the most unsettling girl he had ever come across. He could not ignore her whether she was dancing unashamed in front of him, or making fun of him for falling on his face at the beach.

After several more minutes of mute observation from Lucien, the musicians bring their song to an end, and Melek being familiar with their playing, finishes her dance in unison with them. All the men applaud and shout encouragement to Melek, who then walks to each of them in order to accept a coin. The men are aware of Karasu's eyes on them, so they are quick to pull out their purses and produce payment for his daughter. Lucien, seeing this, fumbles for his own purse and pulls out a gold coin, which he holds out for her. When Melek arrives at Lucien, she pauses, but after considering for a moment moves on without taking his coin. He looks confused and turns to his host for explanation. "Should I not pay your daughter as well?" he asks Karasu. The old Turk smiles at him, "You are an honored guest tonight Lucien, it would be rude of her to take money from you." "I did not mean to make her feel bad, I only wanted to do the correct thing," explains the boy. Karasu laughs, "You have done no such thing, and, I think my daughter may like having you here." Lucien looks over at Melek, who is now seated next to her mother, who is dressed in similar fashion to Melek, and immediately gets embarrassed and looks away. The other men notice this and laugh, one of them says something which Lucien doesn't understand, and they all laugh again. Karasu interprets for him, "He says that 'if our girls overwhelm you, wait until you have to deal with our women!" Lucien, not knowing the right thing to say, replies simply, "I am not accustomed to such things as this. In Bordeaux the girls do not dance in such a fashion. I appreciate Melek's skill, but I admit that it has embarrassed me. If my mother knew I was watching such a dance, she would scold me thoroughly." Karasu tries to interpret for his other guests, who laugh heartily at Lucien's discomfort. Everyone seems amiable and happy to be with him, so Lucien takes no offense at their laughter. "You are a well-mannered boy Lucien," Karasu offers reassuringly, "your father will be proud of you. I think the French will be eager to have you back." "I am just as eager," Lucien replies, adding, "Melek has danced so wonderfully. I would like to entertain you and your guests as well. If you have a violin, I could play that for you." Karasu looks at him approvingly, "So, you are a musician. Music is a fine thing." The white haired man then turns to the musicians and says something to them, they all shake their heads in answer, and Karasu addresses Lucien again, "I'm sorry my friend, but none of these men has a violin, but do not feel compelled to do anything tonight but enjoy the hospitality of my house. Tomorrow we begin a long trek, in hopes of reuniting you with your own people." As he says this, the musicians begin to play again, and Karasu gestures for his wife to come forward. She immediately rises, and walking to the middle of the room strikes her starting pose. In time with the music, she begins her own dance, more understated and elegant than her daughter's, her long years of training show as she begins to glide around the room, bringing the music, and Karasu's older guests, to life with her movements.

Chapter Thirty-seven

Under the Desert Sun

**Where are
Fox and Lucien?**
Turn the page to see.

Hours later, as the sun threatens to disappear again behind the towering peaks above them they come to a damp river bed...It is decided that they will set up their camp for the night here.

345

We're right here!

As the first hints of the sun begin to streak the eastern horizon, Fox and Lucien are gently nudged awake by Karasu's wife. She hurries them out of bed as best she can and leads them outside into the cool morning air, where a string of camels and donkeys wait patiently beside the house, loaded with the provisions they will need for the trip. Melek and her father are already there making ready for the trip, as are several of the men who had been at Karasu's the day before. They busy themselves with the animals, having apparently been recruited by Karasu to join their party. Not yet fully awake, Lucien and Fox are loaded onto one of the camels, which is led by one of these men. Melek sits atop another of the beasts, whose reins are held by her father. Once everyone is assembled and in order, Karasu gives the signal, and the lead man starts off down the street with everyone else falling in behind. Now fully awake, Lucien looks out over the train from his perch high on the camel's back, and thinks excitedly, "It's a real caravan!" Melek's camel, being just in front of his, as they start off down the narrow street, the girl looks back at him asking playfully in her broken French, "Do you think you can not fall from your seat?" Lucien just smiles as she turns back around to watch the road ahead. He can't help but notice how her body shifts fluidly from side to side with the gait of her mount, keeping her upper body relatively steady. He watches for a moment, then makes a conscious effort to copy her, in order to smooth out the swaying ride.

Minutes later, they pass through one of the ancient gates in the wall surrounding the old city, and out onto a larger boulevard, lined by countless dark shops and houses.

As the minutes pass and they move further and further away from the city's old walls and toward the distant mountains, the buildings quickly thin out. Before long, as the sun is just beginning to break above the horizon, they are out in the open, and commence the long climb up into foothills that will take them high into the Atlas Mountains.

As the long hours pass, it feels to Lucien like they are climbing forever. His back hurts from sitting in the strange saddle used on the camels, and the higher they go, the hotter the sun seems to get. His European eyes are not accustomed to this brilliance and glare, and the shade the wide-brimmed pirate hat provides is a blessing for which he is very thankful. He notices too, that as the sun climbs higher in the sky it gets more intense, but the air temperature stays about the same. Karasu had been smart to time the journey so that they would be high in the cool mountain passes before the hottest part of the day.

Both Fox and Lucien are relieved when the little caravan finally stops for lunch. It gives Lucien a chance to stretch his aching back, and for them both to drink a bit of much needed water. Melek anxiously watches his none-to-graceful dismount from his camel, a bit disappointed that he managed it so well and that she would have nothing new to tease him with. Instead, she has to satisfy herself with helping her mother prepare their meal, which once more is composed of foods totally unknown to Lucien, except for one, dates. His uncle had once brought him some as a special treat. Lucien remembered how he had not wanted to try the strange little brown lumps, which he complained reminded him of beetles. His uncle had insisted, sitting with him until the boy relented, all the while enjoying the exotic delicacy himself. When Lucien finally took his first tentative taste, he had been amazed at how sweet the little "beetles" were, and before either of them knew it, the entire packet had disappeared. From that day on, according to his uncle's wishes, he had always been willing to try new foods, and since their often hungry adventure in Paris he had made a point of trying everything. But today it would take no coaxing. Melek and her mother had prepared their sumptuous meal perfectly, and Lucien ate everything with relish. Of course, he also knew that he was doing it to impress Melek. He didn't know why, but he wanted her to approve of him. He wanted the strange, uninhibited desert girl to like him, and no longer tease him for stumbling and falling at their first meeting. It bothered him, but, her approval was important.

After their meal, while preparing to resume their trek, Lucien asks Karasu if he can walk for a bit. The Turk is concerned that the boy will not be able to keep up for long, but Lucien insists that he will have no problem, and wonders if Karasu's wife might like to ride his camel for a time. Karasu finally relents, and his wife gladly accepts, expertly mounting the animal and taking its lead from the man who had been controlling it for Lucien. Seeing her, sitting tall on the camel's back, wrapped in her Bedouin robes and headscarf, Lucien imagined she could hold her own against just about anything. She reminded him, more than a little, of his own mother, Madame Marboeuf, in her quiet, strong manner. The thought brings on a sudden rush of homesickness for her, for Mr. Raimond, for Martine, for his school mates, for everything. As they begin their journey again, Lucien walks along in silence, thinking about all the things left behind in France, barely noticing the magnificent, jagged landscape they are traversing. They continue on this way for hours, with Lucien catching an occasional glimpse of Melek swaying to and fro on her camel; she too lost in her own thoughts and apparently not noticing Lucien at all.

Hours later, as the sun threatens to disappear behind the towering peaks above them, they come to a damp river bed with a few palms growing along its banks. It is decided that they will set up their camp for the night here. Karasu's men quickly pitch a spacious tent for him and his wife and daughter, the rest of them will sleep outside, beneath the stars. With the camp set up, Melek and her mother quickly set to work on their evening meal, which they all enjoy together, sitting outside in the waning light, under the magnificent vault of the desert sky. Once the sun and their evening meal is but a pleasant memory, the travelers relax around the small fire that burns at the center of their little encampment. The men are engaged in quiet conversation, while Melek and her mother busy themselves sewing the coins the girl earned with her dancing, into her heavy necklace. Karasu, noticing Lucien's keen interest in what they are doing remarks, "I see you are curious about my daughter's necklace." "Yes," Lucien says "why do they do this?" Karasu, looking at his wife and daughter for a moment, responds, "I can't say I approve, but among my wife's people it is a custom, which she wants her daughter to know about, and I have learned the hard way that a man does not cross an Ouled Nail woman." Lucien asks, "What is an Ouled Nail?" "That is my wife's tribe Lucien. I am a Turk, from Constantinople. I was first sent here in the service of our Sultan, but, my wife's people, the Ouled Nail have lived here...always. The daughters among them are taught to dance in their traditional way, and then go out to the towns and dance to earn money, usually under the guidance of their mothers, or aunts. They sew the coins into their clothes and jewelry so they can better safeguard it. When a girl has earned enough, she comes home and uses the money to buy a house and start a family. I met my wife just when she was ready to return home. I saw her dance one night, and of course, paid her well. I followed her home to her village and convinced her to marry me. I must have been very convincing, because she had quite a few fine choices." "So, will Melek go out to dance for a living?" Lucien asks. Karasu bristles at the suggestion, "I would prefer she not, I can well afford to give her what she needs, but, the tradition is important to my wife, so I indulge her, to a point. But lately, I have heard stories of the..." he pauses to choose his words carefully, " 'infidels' killing Ouled Nail women to steal their necklaces and other money they have saved. This will not happen to my daughter," he says with conviction. Lucien looks at him quizzically, "Who are these infidels? Where do they come from?" he asks. Karasu considers for a moment before answering, then says gently, "Where are you from?" Before Lucien can answer Karasu continues, "I apologize Lucien. I have said something that I should not. Please, forgive me." Changing the subject he goes on, "I have a gift for you." Lucien looks surprised, "A gift, no sir, you have done so much for us already, I could not accept a gift from you." "My boy," says Karasu, "if you accept this gift, I expect you to return a gift from it to me." Without waiting for Lucien to reply, Karasu turns and calls out to Melek, who immediately jumps up and disappears into their tent. She returns a few moment later carrying something dark in her arms which she brings to her father who takes it and presents it to Lucien. Lucien looks down in happy surprise at the old, worn violin case Karasu holds out to him. "Oh sir, what is this?" he asks. He opens the case and lifts out the instrument inside. The violin has seen its share of performances, and it shows, but Lucien carefully plucks the strings and listens carefully. The sound sits well on his ears. "This is a beautiful violin. Do you hear how it resonates?" He takes the bow from the case and draws it across the strings. They make a terrible noise and he quickly stops. "Let me tune this, and then, may I play for everyone?" "That is the bargain I was hoping for Lucien," Karasu replies.

In short order Lucien has the violin back in good tune and the bow well rosined. With everyone looking on in anticipation he decides on the song, and draws the bow across the strings creating a beautiful clear note. His long, stubborn practice back home pays off handsomely as he flows seamlessly from song to melodious song with ease. Everyone listens in contented silence to the lovely melodies coming from the old violin, that then waft off into the silent, crisp night air. Even Fox, hearing Lucien play the familiar songs again, just like back home has relaxed and is laying contentedly on Melek's lap. The girl seems more than happy to have the little dog there, and she strokes him fondly while Lucien plays on.

Chapter Thirty-eight

The Homecoming

It's no different, Lucien realizes, than this little lion carving, to the person who had once carried it. He understood that now, and is ashamed of himself for his arrogance.

The little encampment is quiet. Karasu and his family have retired to their tent, while the other men lay about on the ground either talking or sleeping. Lucien, still wide awake, the music having stirred up longings for home in his heart, has walked to the edge of the little rocky river, where he sits, looking solemnly up at the amazing display of stars that play out over head. They are even clearer and brighter than he remembers them being when they were far out at sea, before being captured by Captain Birdy. Taking notice of their positions and using the lessons he learned from Captain LeFevre, he is able to estimate that this spot must be far east of Bordeaux, and it gives him some satisfaction to know it. "Uncle," he says quietly, "I think you must be here helping us along. How else is it possible that we have found Karasu and so many others, who are helping to get us back to Bordeaux? I think you must be watching out for Fox and me." Without warning he is almost knocked from the rock he is sitting on by a dark furry shape, that rushes him out of the darkness. Managing to catch himself before he falls over, he finds himself eye to eye with Fox, who immediately gives his friend's face a lick. Lucien smiles, "There you are Fox. I thought perhaps you had decided to live with Melek and her family now and leave me on my own!" As if in answer, Fox dips his head under the boy's hand, coaxing it onto his head. Lucien pets the dog fondly, saying, "Oh Fox, you know I wasn't serious. Don't be cross." Then, just as suddenly as he appeared, Fox turns and trots back into the darkness, leaving Lucien to wonder why. It only takes a moment to get an answer, as Fox is back in an instant with

Melek close behind. Lucien jumps to his feet, suddenly feeling as awkward and clumsy as he did back on the beach. As Melek approaches, she says, "Don't worry, Fox is a good dog. As soon as he realized you were gone, he wanted only to come and find you. I followed because this land harbors many dangerous things that you would not see in the dark. You must be careful." Lucien just stands there awkwardly, at a loss for words, feeling that same helpless feeling he did back on the beach in Dellys. Melek, aware of the strained silence continues, "You played the violin beautifully, you are a talented musician." Lucien replies, "I have to practice very hard. I don't think I could ever be a real musician. I think you dance better than I play." It is now Melek's turn to feel awkward, not knowing how to respond to Lucien's compliment. The moment hangs in the air for too long, until the girl finally blurts out, "I am sorry, for teasing you on the beach and at my father's house." Lucien responds, "You have already apologized Melek..." she continues, cutting him short, "yes, but, I did not mean it, not then. I said it only because my father bade me to. Now, I apologize because I want to. You are a stranger here, all alone, with just Fox for a friend, and I was unkind." She looks at her feet, not knowing what else to say. Lucien continues, "Thank you Melek. You are kind. I owe you and your father a great debt of thanks for your help. If not for you I don't know what Fox and I would have done." At this, a distressed look crosses the girl's face, as if she wants to say something more, but dares not do it. Lucien goes on, "I wish there was something more I could do for you, or give you, but, I have nothing but the clothes on my back." She smiles, "I would take Fox." Lucien looks stunned, not understanding that she is joking with him again. "Oh no! I could not do that! I could not give Fox away, because I do not own him. Fox is my friend. I care for him as best I can, and he does the same for me. We are determined to go home together." Melek, sensing his distress responds apologetically, "Silly boy. I was teasing you again. It is easy to see, Fox has only one home, and that is with you. He would never leave you, and I would not take him from you." Suddenly Lucien brightens, "Melek! I do have a gift I can give you," and with that he reaches inside his shirt and lifts something from around his neck that he presents to the girl. "Fox and I found this little statue, buried in the ground at the old slaver's warehouse. One of the sailors on the ship helped me to make the necklace for it, and I have had it with me ever since. I was told not to give you money, so, I would like you to have this." Melek takes the little figure and marvels at it, trying to see every detail in the pale starlight.

Gazing intently at the little lion dangling from the end of the elegant braided cord that now supports it, she is startled by the sound of her name being called. "Melek. Melek!" "We are here Mother," the girl calls out in her native tongue. A moment later, Karasu's wife appears out of the darkness, and speaks sternly to her daughter. Lucien doesn't understand the words, but, it's apparent from the woman's tone that she is not happy to find Melek alone with Lucien and Fox. Melek, defiantly explains things to her mother, holding up the lion necklace for her to see. The woman takes the necklace and studies it closely for several moments, before shaking her head. "No," she says, handing the totem back to her daughter as she launches into an explanation, all of which is lost on Lucien. When the woman finishes speaking to her daughter, she casts a suspicious look at Lucien, then turns back to Melek and gestures for her to explain to the boy. She then turns and disappears back into the night.

Once her mother has left, Melek holds the necklace out to Lucien saying, "My mother says I cannot accept this from you." Lucien, looking crestfallen replies, "But why Melek? It is a gift." Melek continues, "She has told me that this does not belong to you to give. It is a spirit totem, carved by the hand of the one who used to wear it It can belong to no one else. She said it comes from beyond the Sahara, far, far to the south, from the tribes who have been taken. My mother says this totem has brought you here. It wanted to come home to its native land and used you to deliver it, so it may guide the spirit of its owner home again." Lucien is confounded, "This little lion did not bring us here! A pirate ship brought us here. We found this buried in the ground in France! Our journey is an accident." "Maybe," Melek continues, "the totem wanted to be found, and maybe the totem caused you to be brought here, in order that it might be brought home." Lucien doesn't know what to say, this all sounds so strange to him. Melek goes on, "I told you, there are strange things in the desert, things you won't understand. My mother says that we can not return the totem to its actual home, it is too far away, but, we should bury it here, in Africa where it came from. To do otherwise will bring bad luck to us all." Lucien takes the necklace back from Melek, "I don't believe in such things. Luck is created by effort, nothing more." Melek looks at him a bit frustrated, and tries to explain, "In France things are not the same as things are here. This spirit totem was the guardian of the person who made it. They might have believed it was one of their relatives, who would help and protect them. You may not believe this, but, that doesn't mean it isn't true. If this totem was yours, and it was important to you, would you not wish that it would be treated with respect?" Lucien thinks for a moment about what she has said. "It's just a little statue," he tells himself. But then a thought pops into his mind, and he see's his old copy of "Robinson Crusoe," and remembers how much that has meant to him over the years, and he remembers that only minutes earlier he had been thanking his own uncle for all this help and protection on their journey. It's no different, he realizes, than the little lion carving was to the person who had once carried it. He understood that now, and was ashamed of himself for his arrogance. "You are right Melek," he says. "How can I not understand when I myself have felt the very same way? We must bury this little lion right here by the river. It is not perfect, but it is the best we can do." Melek smiles appreciatively and says, "Where shall we dig?" Lucien looks around for a moment and then points to a rock, "Over here, that big rock will protect the lion." Walking to the spot they have chosen, Lucien hands the necklace back to Melek. Kneeling down on the ground he uses his hands to begin scooping out a hole. Seeing how poorly his friend is doing at the task, Fox jumps in to help, going at the dirt with his stout front claws, and sending it flying out behind him. "Good dog Fox!" Melek adds, as Lucien sits back, more than happy to have the dog help him. "You're a great helper Fox," he says. "Keep digging." Fox happily obliges, digging until he has created a nice hole several inches deep. He stops and looks to Lucien, who says, "That's perfect Fox. Good doggie." Melek then bends over the hole and slowly lowers it in. Once the little lion is resting on the bottom of the hole, she lets go, letting the rest of the necklace drop in on top of it. "You are home now Lion. Lucien has brought you home. You must now help him get home too. Then you are free." With that she gently begins pushing the sandy soil back into the hole. Lucien joins in and they have it restored in short order. Melek, wasting no time says, "I must go now. My mother is waiting for me." She hesitates, uncertain of what she should do next, then reaches over and kisses Lucien on the cheek, saying, "I'm sorry." Without another word, she stands and rushes off to her tent, leaving Lucien and Fox to ponder what she could mean.

Chapter Thirty-nine

The Smala of al-Qadir

Where are
Fox and Lucien?
Turn the page to see.

...off in the distance Lucien spies a tent city of sorts, resolving itself out of the heat waves rising from the quickly warming earth.

The final day of their journey dawns just like the all the others since their arrival in Algeria; cool morning air beneath a brilliantly transparent blue sky, and then, heat. Today, descending from the protection of the cool mountain passes, the sun has become an even more hurtful companion. Throughout the day, as it climbs through its arc, it increases so in intensity that Lucien is convinced it could cook the skin right off him, were he not now covered from head to toe by a set of traditional robes given to him by Melek several days before. The fierce heat makes Lucien all the more homesick for the warm, misty mornings among the grapevines in Bordeaux. The desert sun has even banished his treasured "pirate" hat from his head, stowed away now in exchange for a traditional head wrap that keeps him more comfortable in the intense daytime heat of the desert. Fox too, is now wrapped up for protection, bundled happily in Melek's lap. But, as content as he looks, he always has one eye on Lucien, never letting his friend completely out of his sight, on edge because of the tension he senses in the girl's body as she idly strokes him. Her hidden stress makes him uneasy.

The nature of the landscape has changed as well. They have come down onto a plateau and the ground has become a hard, windswept, rocky pavement. In places sand has been piled high by the wind into dunes that resemble frozen ocean swells, but there is almost nothing to offer shelter from the sun's heat. Their little caravan still follows the shallow river-bed as it snakes its way downhill, and Lucien thinks he can actually see it evaporating as the sun climbs overhead. After traveling for several hours along its banks, stopping only once for water, off in the distance, resolving itself out of the heat waves rising from the quickly warming earth, Lucien spies a tent city of sorts. As they get closer, he counts a great number of shelters, arranged at the inside of a bend in the river, surrounded on three sides by the shallow water. As their caravan enters the encampment, Karasu and his family are greeted with the familiarity of family. It's clear they are not strangers here. No one seems to pay any mind to Lucien, but are drawn to Fox, who is now standing up on Melek's lap atop the camel, taking in the new surroundings and barking at the people who venture up to say hello.

Near the center of this smala, they arrive at a large tent that has a banner flying over it, decorated with strange Arabic letters that Lucien can't decipher. A man standing in front of the tent greets Karasu warmly. They confer quietly for a moment, then disappear inside. Melek and the others dismount, as several boys come to take their animals for water at the river. She walks over to Lucien and hands Fox to him, "Here, your friend has missed you. I think I am a poor substitute." Lucien takes the dog, and sets him on the ground, where he commences a nose-survey of the area. "Oh no, Melek, Fox likes you very much," replies Lucien. "I could tell that he was very happy to be riding with you, rather than walking with me." The girl smiles, adding, "You have walked a long way...good for a boy who falls so easily," she teases. Lucien smiles at her jibe saying, "Fox and I would go for wonderful long walks together back home. I like to walk, of course its not nearly so hot back home," he says. Melek looks kindly at him now, "I am sorry," she offers weakly. Lucien replies lightly, "Melek, I don't think you can control the sun!" "No," she replies, "I am sorry you have to stay here." He doesn't understand, "Why? This looks like a fine camp, and if it brings us closer to going home, then, I thank you for bringing us." Melek is obviously troubled by something and replies, "No, do not thank me for it, please!" She looks at the ground and manages only to reply with, "Clumsy boy," as she abruptly turns and walks over to her mother who has been watching their exchange from a vantage point beside the tent. Melek says something to her mother and indicates Lucien, but he can't hear what is said, seeing only that his new friend Melek is unhappy about something. At that moment Karasu and the other man emerge from inside and walk over to him. Karasu speaks,

> "Lucien, I have brought you to the camp of my friend al-Qadir. He is the man, if there is one, who can return you to the French. This man," he says, indicating the person with him, "has told me that al-Qadir, is not in the camp now, but, will return shortly. You and Fox will stay here until his return. He will know how to best deal with you. Do as these men tell you and you soon may be safely back with your own people. I and my family must continue on to my wife's village, which is still two days journey. I am sorry that you can not come and see it, it is a beautiful oasis, but this is where you will be most useful. It has been my privilege to look after you."

"But sir, how will I get to my countrymen?" Lucien asks. Karasu replies, "al-Qadir and his men will see to that. Do not trouble yourself about it. God willing, you will soon be home."

Later on, their farewells having been said, Lucien and Fox stand by, looking on as the little caravan that has been their refuge for the past several days departs the camp. Melek looks back at them unhappily and waves. Fox barks his good-bye, as Lucien waves back, saying to him, "Well Fox, here we are again, cast off and on our own. I am glad I have you with me." A tap on Lucien's shoulder gets his attention, and he turns find the man Karasu had introduced him to standing behind him. He indicates with a gesture that Lucien and Fox should follow him, then turns and starts back through the rows of tents and people. As they walk, Lucien notices that many of the men are sharpening swords and tending to muskets and other weapons, but thinks nothing of it. Their guide stops at a tent, not too far from edge of camp, and pulls back the flap indicating that they should enter, then follows them in. He indicates that they are to stay here, then excuses himself and disappears back through the flap, leaving Lucien and Fox alone to survey their new quarters.

The tent is a spacious, round affair, and though spartan, looks quite comfortable. The floor consists of a beautiful mosaic of hand-woven carpets laid over the ground. Several small oil lamps hang from the support poles that hold the tent up, promising a comforting light after the sun sets. The sleeping area is comprised of a low bed, covered over with colorful tapestries and cushions that promise warmth and comfort during the cold desert night. A table has been set with food and drink for both of them, and Lucien and Fox, famished from the morning's activities waste no time in finding it and digging in. Lucien looks at his new surroundings and the artistic presentation of the delicious food, not knowing that it was Melek who prepared it so carefully for him, and thinks to himself, "I guess we French are not the only people who know how to live well." He speaks to Fox between mouthfuls, "What do you think Fox? Will you be comfortable here?" To which the dog answered by picking out a particularly plump pillow to plop himself down on as if he were back home in Bordeaux.

It is some while after they have eaten and drunk their fill, as they are resting on their comfortable new bed, warm and satisfied, that Lucien suddenly sits up with a start, jarred from his peaceful afternoon rest by a frightening realization: "Al-Qadir!" he says with alarm, "That is the name of the cruel outlaw that Gustave spoke of in one of his letters to me! How could Karasu not know who this man is?" he asks the dog emphatically. "We must leave this place," he exclaims, "But what shall we do? Where can we go?" he asks the dog desperately. Fox, for his part sits up waiting for Lucien's decision, ready, as always, to go with the boy, no matter where that might take them. "We must try to catch up with Melek and her family," he continues. "They will help us and we can go with them to their village and make our plans from there. They can't be so far away, and I know the direction they were traveling. If we are quick, we will catch them, and let them know they have been deceived." Jumping up from the bed, he grabs all the left over food from its platter, wrapping it up in the cloth that covers the table, and tying the corners together to create a sack to carry it in. Water proves more difficult. There is still a good amount left in the pitcher, but nothing to transfer it into for traveling. Lucien looks through their belongings and finding nothing to use, spies one of the hanging lamps and is struck with an idea. Going to the tent pole where it hangs, he quickly shimmies up the pole high enough to unhook the lamp and bring it back down. Working quickly, he unties and unwinds the lamp from the lashing cord that it is wrapped in, then taking a small square rug from the ground, he places it over the top of the pitcher and ties in place with the lamp cord, wrapping it around the rim as many times as he can before knotting the two ends tightly together with one of the strong knots he learned from the crew on the *"Argo of Bordeaux,"* creating a sling for the water pitcher that he slips over his shoulder. It's not perfect, but it will keep most of the water from spilling out as they run. He loads up with the supplies, pulls on his wide-brimmed "pirate" hat, and quietly creeps to the door of the tent to peek out. There is no guard outside, evidently his captors think it unnecessary to guard their two guests, who have no idea that they are not among friends. Lucien thinks, "Yes, why would I try to run away?" So, the two of them creep carefully out of the tent, trying not to look suspicious, and it seems to work. There are few people out in the hot mid-day sun, and those who are outside don't seem to pay the two any attention, after all, there is nowhere for them to escape to. So, weaving their way through the tents, they quickly arrive at the edge of the camp, where Lucien pauses to look out over the vast rocky emptiness between him and the only people he knows in this entire country,

Melek and her father. "Fox, we must be quick about this and very quiet." He puts the dog on the ground, and makes ready by checking his gear and looking to see that no one is watching. Satisfied that they are unnoticed be begins to walk quickly out into the open desert with Fox beside him. Once they are clear of the tents he breaks into a run, aiming for the shelter of a large boulder that he sees a ways off. "Come Fox, if we can get to that rock unseen we will be free. Run!" The two take off in a full sprint out into the open, in the direction that Karasu's caravan took, aiming for the protection of the big rock.

In their mad dash for the boulder, Lucien struggles to keep the water pitcher stable, trying valiantly to preserve as much of its contents as he can. He puts the food satchel on top of it, and tries to hold it all together with one hand, leaving the other free to run with. So intent is he on this problem, and keeping track of their target, all while not tripping and falling, that he doesn't even hear the sound of the beating hooves racing up behind him, drowned out as they are by the sound of his own racing heart. It is not until a huge white shape sweeps past them that he sees the horse, which pulls up several yards in front of them. The rider draws his long scimitar and points it at the two fugitives. They turn to run the other way, just as two more riders swoop up behind them, blades drawn to cut off any chance of escape. Fox barks furiously and growls as Lucien reflexively scoops him up. They are surrounded, and have no chance of escape.

Chapter Forty

The Battle

The Moorish fighters begin shooting wildly out into the darkness, as return fire rains into the camp.

After their failed escape attempt, Lucien and Fox had been berated terribly by their captor. Though neither of them could understand a word of the fiery-eyed man's rantings, his threatening posture and frightening habit of constantly grabbing the hilt of his scimitar as he reprimanded them, left no doubt about his anger at their attempt to flee. But, no matter how irate the man seemed to be, he did not actually harm them in any way, instead, placing them firmly back in their tent, with a guard now posted outside at all times. Imprisoned now in their tent, it became clear to Lucien that he and Fox had some sort of value to these men, that their leader al-Qadir, would be able to use once he returned. He also realized, to his relief, that it was important they be turned over to the mysterious mystic-warrior in good health. So, there in their "cell" they had remained, under guard, awaiting their fate, but treated well enough all things considered.

It was on another cool morning, before dawn, several days after their failed escape attempt, that Fox woke Lucien early, nudging the boy awake just before sunrise, then lifting his nose to the air, trying to discern a new scent. Lucien watched half asleep as the dog circled the tent looking for a spot where he could better smell whatever it was that was out there somewhere. Fox would sniff a bit, then come over to nudge Lucien again, before moving to the other side of the tent, nose raised, trying to let Lucien know that something was in the air. For his part, Lucien hears nothing, but trusting the dog's judgement, gets up and creeps silently to the door, which he draws back just far enough to peek through. Even in the dim waxing light the broad back of their surly jailer is easy to see, parked as always just outside the door. Lucien drops the flap and creeps carefully back over to the bed where Fox is still pacing about, whispering, "Fox, what's the matter with you? What do you smell?" In response the dog leans against him anxiously. Lucien, still clueless as to what Fox is trying to tell him, sits uneasily back down on the bed, holding his friend. The answer to the mystery comes in the form of a high pitched whistling sound and then a loud explosion that shatters the silence of the camp. As alarmed voices fill the air all around them, another loud concussion – closer this time – shakes the tent and the ground beneath it. Men shout and run for their weapons and horses as several more concussions wrack the air. Lucien, who has jumped to his feet, with a firm grasp on Fox, is knocked to the ground by the next blast. Not knowing what else to do, he stays right there. The tent flap is thrown open and the guard lunges in to quickly check that Lucien and Fox are still alive and accounted for, then he turns and rushes out, shouting something into the growing din.

Then, as suddenly as the explosions started, they stop, but as the last blast fades, it is replaced by another sound, like rumbling thunder. Lucien and Fox can both feel it coming up through the ground beneath them. As the low vibration grows stronger, Lucien realizes it's coming closer, and in a flash of understanding cries "Horses!" As he says it, the sound of gun fire is added to the confusion. The Moorish fighters shoot wildly out into the darkness, as return fire rains into the camp, striking with impunity. One of these dangerous little missiles rips through their tent above their heads, smashing into one of the lamps and sending it crashing down in pieces. Lucien lays flat on the ground, holding Fox next to him as the panicked cries from outside the tent are intermixed with the sound of horses galloping through the camp, the clashing of steel on steel, and more musket shots. Adding to the terror, a horse gallops right behind their tent, and a long straight sword pierces the side, opening a huge gash as the horse and rider streak by. In all the chaos of yelling, hoof-beats and gun fire, Lucien whispers urgently to Fox, "Fox, we must run and hide in the rocks! If we stay here we will be murdered by these thieves. We must get out of here. Come on." He crawls to the back of the tent, pulling Fox along with him, and listens carefully. After looking back toward the door for any sign of the guard coming in again, he pulls the carpets back from the edge of the tent and begins to dig the rocky earth out from beneath the well staked edge of the shelter. It doesn't take long to excavate, as Fox, understanding the peril, joins in and begins to dig right beside Lucien, his claws tearing into the packed ground. "Good boy, Fox. Dig!" In short order the dog wiggles through the shallow opening he has made. Lucien follows, but isn't so lucky, getting caught under the edge of the tent. In an attempt to create more space for himself, he pushes himself up for all he's worth, hoping to gain a bit of slack and get untangled. With Fox pulling him from the other side, he squeezes through the gap, and the two of them disappear together, into the maze of tents. Remembering their path from their last escape attempt,

Lucien guides them quickly and cautiously toward the edge of the camp. Fortunately, at the moment, the bulk of the fighting is focused behind them and they make it to the perimeter unseen, quickly darting off into the open desert undetected. Staying low, Lucien runs for the big boulder they had tried for during their first escape, but the path is blocked by the swirling horses and fighting men, who are raising a sea of dust. The cloud obscures the details of the battle, but also helps to hide the two refugees. "Fox, this way," Lucien calls to the dog as he plunges off in a new direction. Fox, as always stays right at his side. Lucien quickly grabs Fox and dives down behind another boulder that is closer to the camp, but still provides good protection from the fighting. They huddle there together, pressed to the boulder, trying to make sense of what is going on around them.

Chapter Forty-one

The Horseman

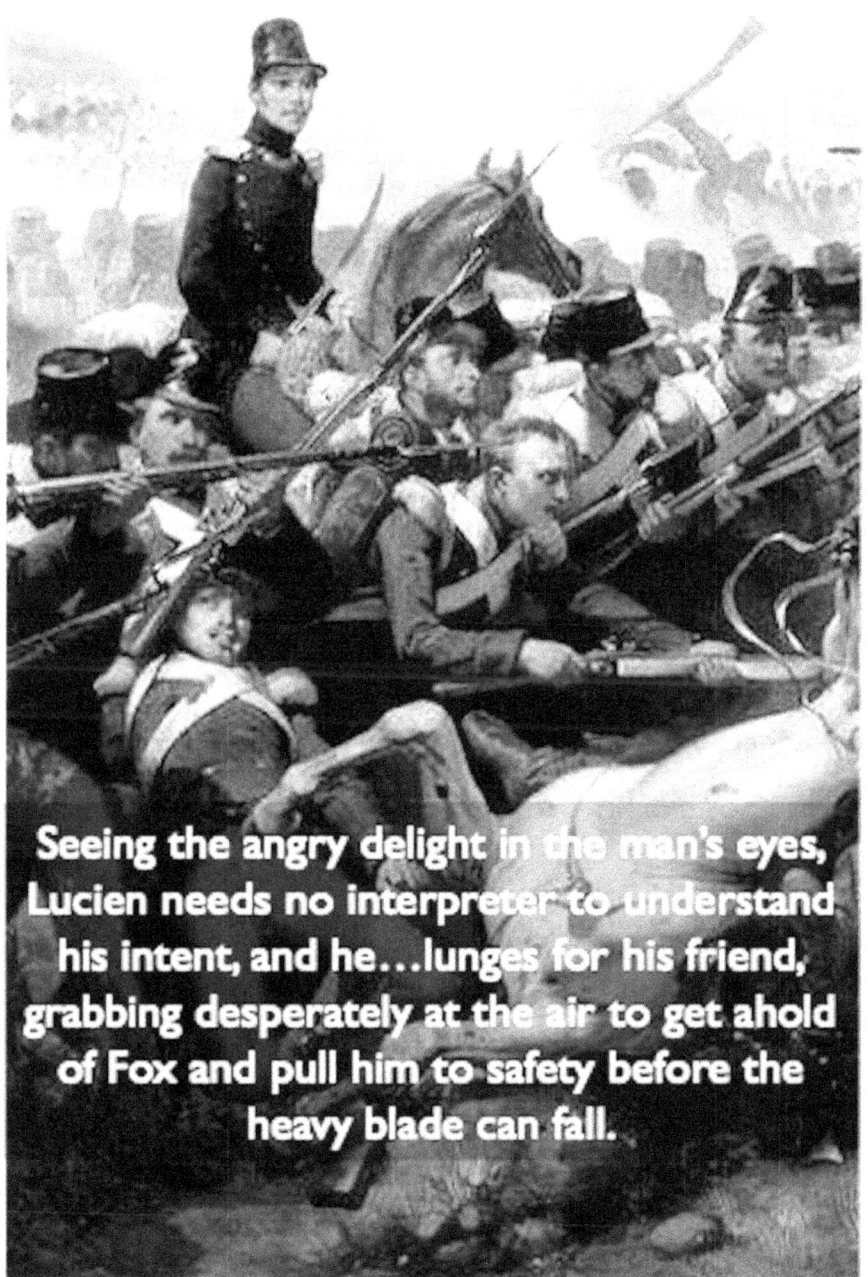

Seeing the angry delight in the man's eyes, Lucien needs no interpreter to understand his intent, and he…lunges for his friend, grabbing desperately at the air to get ahold of Fox and pull him to safety before the heavy blade can fall.

As the battle spreads, creeping ever closer, Fox and Lucien stay low behind their boulder, trying their best to remain invisible to the growing chaos of suffering and fighting that fills the air on the other side of their haven. On several occasions musket balls glance off the edge of the rock, startling Lucien, who grabs Fox and tries to sink down even lower, afraid to move. It is while they are huddled there on the ground, in terror, that Lucien first hears it. A familiar cadence catches his ear and he turns his head to listen again, but the noise of the fight makes it almost impossible to discern anything at first, and he is unsure. With his brain now working hard to sift through the mad welter of noises filtering in, he hears it again, and it makes him sit up in spite of his fear. "Fox," he exclaims, "do you hear it?" Listening more intently, it is now unmistakable, entwined in the beating of horses hooves, the blasts of muskets, and the general mayhem, he hears French! He hears it clearly now; commands being called out and answered in his own language! In their panic to escape the attack, he had not even noticed that the attackers were his own countrymen! "Fox, they are French!" he shouts excitedly. "We must get their attention! You stay down, and I will look." With that he slowly rises to his feet, leaning close to the boulder to peek around the edge at the battle beyond. He attempts to shout out for help, waving his arms at the same time, "Help us! We are French! Help us!" But, his voice is thoroughly trampled out by the noise of the fight. Then, another errant musket ball, having missed its intended mark, sends him diving back down behind the rock for protection. "I could not see anything Fox," he says to the dog. "I need to climb up on top of the boulder so they can see me, and I will call for help. Stay right here. Don't be afraid...we're saved!"

As he begins to carefully pull himself up the face of the rock, which stands about six feet tall, and is well-weathered and broken with age, making it easy to climb. He takes his first tentative step, then finds another hand hold and begins to pull himself up a few feet further. He shifts his weight and reaches out for another one, but before he can find it, he is suddenly yanked off the stone, spun around and pinned against it. The bloodied face of the Moor who had been guarding them in their tent glares into his. Lucien gasps involuntarily as the Moor speaks, "Little infidel," he seethes, "do you think you would so easily escape me? You will be very useful to us after today. Al-Qadir is expecting you, and I will deliver you." Lucien tries furiously to break free from the guards iron grip, "Leave me alone! Unhand me!" he shouts in a futile attempt to be understood by the man, who just holds him tighter. Fox, seeing the struggle, immediately rushes the Moor, sinking his teeth into the guard's calf. The pain is enough of a distraction for Lucien to pull himself free, but the boulder is behind him and he has nowhere to go. Fox, letting go of the Moor's leg, tries to jump in front of Lucien, snarling and snapping at the now enraged Moor, who reflexively steps back, and instantly draws his vicious looking scimitar, saying, "You are coming with me, little Frenchman...alive, your little protector...perhaps not." Seeing the raised blade and the angry delight in the man's eyes, Lucien needs no interpreter to understand his intent, and he instantly lunges for his friend, grabbing desperately at the air to get ahold of Fox and pull him to safety before the heavy blade can fall. The Moor steps into his swing, just as Lucien finds Fox's collar, and yanks the dog toward him. Fox yelps as the blade falls, and Lucien crouches reflexively, raising his free arm, trying to protect them both from what's to come. He closes his eyes, even as Fox continues to struggle and snarl, determined to the last to protect his friend.

A moment later, Lucien hears nothing but the odd sound of the Moor's sudden heavy exhalation accompanied by the loud thundering of horse's hooves right on top of them, rushing past and quickly receding. Realizing that the blade never came, he opens his eyes just in time to see the enraged Moor being dragged away by the neck behind a powerful war-horse, and disappearing into the swirling dust. It is all over so fast that Lucien can scarcely believe what he has just seen. Was it his imagination, he wonders? One second he is cowering on the ground, protecting Fox, waiting to die, and a moment later, he looks up and his attacker is disappearing into the distance, dragged away behind a horse. He stares, for what seems an eternity at the spot where the Moor disappeared, as the sounds of the fight come flooding back in. It is a terrible scene, but he is too stunned to look away. Then, out of the smoke and dust of the battle, a shape begins to form. A stout, muscular horse, with a cavalry soldier on its back charges back toward him, unburdened of its former cargo. Lucien is in shock and almost insensible as the sweaty, bloodied horse charges up to him and the rider jumps off and approaches. The cavalry soldier pauses for a moment as Fox, breaking free of Lucien's grasp, begins barking and snarling his challenge to this new threat. The horseman says something, and Lucien begins to hear French again. "Don't be afraid," Lucien thinks he hears the voice say. "You've done well and protected your friend." Lucien senses the dog calm down as the voice begins again, and he hears it more clearly now, "Get up now," the rider says urgently. "Get up," he repeats, "We must go! Grab your dog! Quickly!" Lucien is frozen in place and not comprehending, so the soldier quickly grabs Fox and shoves him hurriedly into Lucien's arms, commanding him to, "Hold onto your dog!" Then swinging himself smoothly into his saddle, he roughly hoists the two onto his horse with him. The rugged animal, without complaint at the added burden, immediately bolts ahead, carrying them all swiftly back into swirling dust of the battlefield.

Chapter Forty-two

The French Camp

The French camp in contrast is austere and geometric, populated only by soldiers moving purposefully about the tents, attending to their horses, or their weapons, or themselves in one way or another.

Where are Fox and Lucien? Turn the page to see.

We're right here!

The long straight rows of angular tents make an easy contrast to the haphazard arrangement of the camp of Al-Qadir. The Moors' smala seemed much more village-like, with women, children and even a few pets living there with the men. The French camp in contrast is austere and geometric, populated solely by soldiers moving purposefully about the tents, attending to their horses, or their weapons, or themselves in one way or another. It is orderly, military, "well-oiled". Toward the end of one of its long straight "avenues" is a large hospital tent where the battle-wounded are brought for treatment. To the surgeon's continual despair, the aid and comfort he can offer is often times not much better than the wounds he is attempting to repair (the tools of the surgeon's trade in such places, as they were aboard ship, are mostly scalpels and saws). So, it is a happy relief for the doctor when Lucien is brought in, along with his protective little comrade. Here are patients he can minister to without resorting to any of his more unwelcome tools and techniques. After giving the boy, and the dog a thorough examination and treating a few scrapes and bruises – many of them acquired during their harrowing race through the battle on horseback – the surgeon pronounces them "in need of rest and a real meal, but otherwise fine" and has them escorted to a tent of their own to sleep and recuperate. It is into this now empty surgery that Gustave rushes, in search of his cousin, whom he had turned over to a field medic, while he returned to his unit to finish their business. The surgeon, noting happily how nice it was to have a fine young Frenchman brought to him in such a good state of heath, directs him to their tent. Gustave impatiently salutes his talkative senior officer, and once dismissed, bolts down the long avenue to find his two long-lost family members.

When Gustave pulls aside the tent flap and walks in, it takes Lucien a moment to recognize him, covered in the dirt and grime of the fight as he was. But, more than that, actually seeing him there in his uniform, and how different he looked since they had bid him "Bon Voyage" in Bordeaux, was startling to Lucien. This Gustave was nothing like the spoiled cousin he had once lived with, nor was there any sign of the poor beggar he had become. Standing before him was a man who seemed to have escaped from the inside of that other person, and now stood there, tall, mature, and worn with experience. Although he looked almost as he always had, the transformation was profound in a thousand little ways. Gustave also noted how different his cousin now looked. Gone was the blindly trusting little boy. Here sat a young man, who rather than being bowed by his adventure was bigger and better for it He was more ready for the world than he had ever been, and that gave Gustave great satisfaction.

Lucien, shaking off his initial disbelief was quick to spring from the bed, "Gustave! It really is you!" he exclaims, throwing his arms around his cousin. "All this has happened so fast, it was like a mad dream! I began to doubt that I had seen you at all!" "Yes, Cousin!" Gustave replies, "it is me and I thank God for him letting me find you. I must confide to you that when I heard from home that you were lost at sea, I thought I would never see you again. This weighed so heavily on me, all I could think about was the wretchedness of my actions towards you; taking your home from you and casting you to fate in Paris. I will be marked by that forever." Lucien takes his cousin's hand and says earnestly, "Perhaps Cousin, but, I have forgiven you long ago, and you are not the person now that you were then. I think maybe God, by sending you to save Fox and me from a terrible fate, is telling you that it is time for you to forgive yourself. May we not speak of this ever again?" he asks. Gustave considers this for a moment, appreciating his cousins words, and the burden they are helping to lift from his heart. "No Lucien," he counters, "it is you and Fox who have saved me." "Well then," replies Lucien cheerfully, "I think it is time that we consider all our debts settled. All I want now is to go home." At this Gustave perks up and smiles, "I have already requested leave to accompany you safely home to Bordeaux. I am going home with you! If I wish, I have been told that I may petition for an early discharge as well." Lucien is overjoyed at the news, "Cousin! What a homecoming it will be! I can hardly wait!"

Chapter Forty-three

Marseilles

Where are
Fox and Lucien?
Turn the page to see.

There is no one there to greet them as
they descend the gangway, just a handshake
from the captain as they disembark...so, they
are just three anonymous travelers amid a
sea of anonymous people surging through
the streets of...the city.

Marseilles is aglow in the radiant Mediterranean sun that fuels the warm, gentle breeze that wafts so easily amongst the ships, shops and warehouses that crowd the port. Standing on the upper deck of the French frigate that has brought them here, Fox, Lucien, and Gustave are drinking in the sight of their long absent homeland, as they anxiously wait for the gangway to be lowered and secured. Gustave looks magnificent in his dress military uniform, which he has taken pains to keep spotlessly clean for this special occasion. Lucien too, has gotten himself scrubbed clean, and, with help from the surgeon, his clothes mended. He also wears a fresh white shirt that Gustave acquired for him from the Quartermaster, which Lucien insisted on saving for their arrival today. Even Fox looks renewed, the result of a good scrubbing by Lucien, and some much needed attention from the camp's barber, who had taken a liking to the brave little dog, and had insisted on giving him a fine haircut so they would all make a good impression upon their arrival home. The three now stand, beaming with anticipation, as they impatiently wait their turn to set foot back in their own country.

There is no one there to greet them as they disembark the ship, just a handshake from the captain. They had arrived in Algiers in the nick of time to catch the frigate, which was sailing for Marseilles, and were unable to send word ahead of their imminent arrival, so, they are just three anonymous travelers in a sea of anonymous people surging through the streets of the beautiful port city.

Once off the ship, they hurry down the wharf to stand once again on the solid ground of home. "Come

Lucien," Gustave calls, "let's find a coach line to Bordeaux, I am as anxious as you are to see home again." Lucien, in his happy excitement, adds, "And you will purchase tickets for both of us this time?" Gustave shrinks at the unexpected comment, suddenly overcome with guilt. Lucien instantly understanding the terrible thing he's said is immediately ashamed of his words, and implores, "Cousin, I apologize for my thoughtless remark, especially after insisting that we never speak of it again. I spoke carelessly, out of excitement at being home. I am ashamed. I hope you will forgive me." "Of course Lucien," says Gustave, regaining his composure with his cousin's heart-felt apology, "We are all excited to be almost home, and rest assured that I will not leave you. I will carry you on my back if that is the only way." Lucien laughs, lightening the mood, "I am a bit heavier now than I was Gustave, are you sure you are up to it?" Gustave smiles, "Yes, perhaps it would be best to hire a coach after all. Come on."

As they walk along the docks, searching for a coach office, Lucien suddenly sees something and stops. "Look there," he exclaims pointing down the line of merchant ships. There, amidst the forest of masts and tangle of rigging, Lucien spies the word *Argo* visible on the transom of a ship not far from where they are. "Could it be?" he wonders aloud. "Gustave, we must go look at that ship before we go anywhere," and with that he sets Fox on the ground and starts off for the ship.

Reaching the vessel, he looks up at the transom, and there, spelled out proudly across the stern is the name, *Argo of Bordeaux.* "This is our ship." exclaims Lucien as he runs for the gangway to try to go aboard. He is stopped by a gruff sailor that Lucien doesn't recognize. "Hold on there lad. What business have you here?" the sailor asks. "I must see Captain LeFevre, if he is here. Has he come home? Is he aboard?" Lucien asks. The sailor replies gruffly, "The captain might be aboard, but he is a busy man, with no time for wayward boys." Gustave hearing what the sailor said, interrupts and speaks up for Lucien, "Sir, this is no wayward boy. He was aboard this ship when it was taken by pirates. He and the captain were taken prisoner together." The sailor replies, "Well, that may be true, or it may not, I wasn't there. My job is to keep control of who goes on and comes off, so you'll..." He is cut off by Lucien's shouts up toward the ship, "Captain! Captain LeFevre! Are you there? It is Lucien Lehun and Fox! Are you there? Captain! It is Lucien Lehun and Fox!" Just then the tall proud shape of the captain comes to the side of the ship, and waves to Lucien in surprise. "Lucien! Good heavens! Can it be! Come aboard! You there sailor, bring those people aboard." With that the sailor steps aside and Lucien, Fox and Gustave re-board the ship that began this whole adventure.

On deck the captain makes no secret of his relief at seeing Lucien and Fox alive and well. "My lad, I can't tell you how overjoyed I am to see you both. The angels must truly surround you," he says giving Lucien a warm hug. "And who is this fine soldier you are with? Could it be your cousin?" "Yes Captain," replies Lucien, "This is my cousin Gustave, and my savior. Believe it or not, it was he who actually rescued us from our captors. If not for him, I fear to think what might have become of us." The captain turns to Gustave, "Well then, I am very honored to make your acquaintance corsair." Gustave replies, "The pleasure is mine, sir. Lucien has told me of your kindness toward him, and for that I am truly grateful." "But, Captain," interrupts Lucien, "how is it you come to be here?" The captain replies enthusiastically, "Lucien, I was not in that pirate's custody more than two days after they left you on the beach. Birdy and his ship were seized by the navy, and as luck would have it, I rejoined the *"Argo"* before any ransom was paid. But, you will all dine with me tonight and tell me your whole story. I insist." Lucien looks at Gustave and down at Fox who is looking up at him anxiously. "Sir, we thank you most kindly for your invitation, but we have been so long from home that we are anxious to finish our journey to Bordeaux. I hope you will understand, it's only out of longing for home that we decline your invitation." The captain replies graciously, "Of course son. I am dissappointed, but I well understand the call of home." Gustave steps forward, "Captain, when you are next in Bordeaux, which I hope is soon, you will be our guest and I'm sure we will gladly recount the entire adventure for you." "I accept," comes the hearty reply from LeFevre. "In that case," says Gustave, "we will take our leave and be on our way. If has been my pleasure to meet you." "And mine as well," replies LeFevre. Lucien holds out his hand formally to the captain, saying, "Now that I see you are home safe and back on your ship, I can travel home without a care. Good-bye sir." The captain clasps the boys hand warmly, and when he releases it he finds that Lucien has slipped his old gold coin into the palm of his hand. The captain holds it up, "What's this?" Lucien replies, "Sir, I could not keep it. It brought us good fortune, but now I return it to you, in case you need it yourself someday." The captain doesn't protest. He slips the coin into his vest pocket. "Good luck to you both. I look forward to our reunion in Bordeaux."

Shortly thereafter, they have found the Bordeaux coach office, and rather than spend another night in Marseille, buy tickets on the last coach of the day, preferring to sleep on the bouncing carriage than to spend one more minute away from home than necessary. As the coach rolls out of Marseille, Lucien and Fox hang out the windows taking in the sights of the beautiful city, so happy to be back in France and almost home. As the evening light fades, and the coach leaves the Marseilles behind, Lucien suddenly calls his cousin, pointing to something out the window. "Gustave, look here. Do you see?" Joining them at the window, Gustave looks out just as the stage rolls past a brand new, glittering train track, the first ever laid into Marseille. The work crew is just finishing for the day, and the big steam engine that is hauling the steel rails sits idly by. The steam in the boiler is being bled out for the night creating a huge white cloud around the impressive machine, making it look as if it is emerging from a storm cloud. Gustave remarks, "Who would have thought such a thing possible." Lucien, still transfixed by the massive machine says to Fox, "Fox, would you like to have a ride on such a thing? I think I would." With that,

Gustave settles back into his seat, as Lucien and Fox strain to get a last look at the gleaming new locomotive. The waning light and billowing steam conspire to make the huge engine slowly dissolve before their eyes, and fade away into the receding cityscape.

Chapter Forty-four

Home

Where are
Fox and Lucien?
Turn the page to see.

It takes her a moment to process the unexpected sight that confronts her, and after staring a moment longer, it is Fox's exuberant rampaging that focuses her perception. "Oh my. Oh my!" she exclaims with growing excitement.

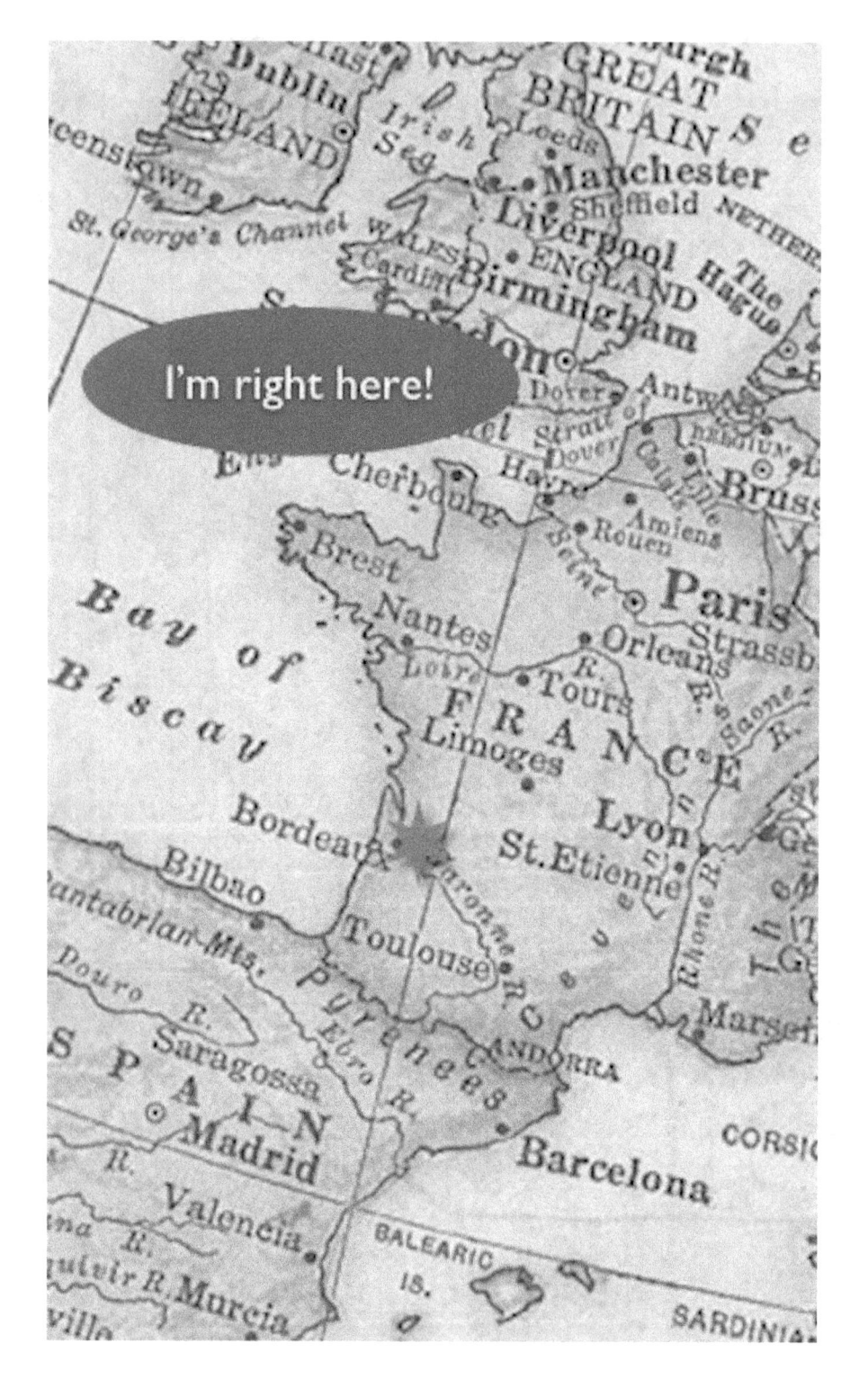

I'm right here!

As the cab comes through the gate and rolls onto the long drive leading up to the big old country house, the driver brings his team to a stop. One of the cab's doors swings open and, in a shot, out pops Fox, beside himself with excitement at the familiar sights and smells of home. He tears off ahead of the carriage toward the house, barking wildly, and is already stationed at the front door, continuing his vociferous announcements as the carriage rolls to a stop behind him, and the two passengers climb out. At the same moment, the heavy front door of the old house creeks open and out charges Martine determined to find out what the racket is all about. It takes her a moment to process the unexpected sight that confronts her, and after staring a moment longer, it is Fox's exuberant rampaging that brings her to her senses. "Oh my. Oh my!" she exclaims with growing excitement. "Madame! Monsieur!" She quickly darts back into the house to raise the alarm. "Madame! Monsieur! Come quickly! Come to the front door quickly! Quickly!" From inside the open door the now somewhat frail voice of Madame Marboeuf can be heard, "Martine, what on earth is the matter with you? Have you finally gone mad?" "Yes Madame, of course!" Martine replies exuberantly. "Now please, come outside. Monsieur come outside." "We are doing our best Martine," comes the calm voice of Monsieur Raimond. A moment later Martine steps back through the door, moving aside to make room for her employers, as Madame Marboeuf and Monsieur Raimond emerge into the brilliant sunshine of late morning. They look toward the carriage and, like Martine before them, stop dumbfounded, momentarily unable to process the tableau that greets them, as there, at the edge of the drive, looking haggard from their journey, but smiling slyly, stand their two lost boys, come home again, with Fox bounding joyfully between them all.

Madame Marboeuf, seeing them there actually faints into her husband's arms. Monsieur Raimond, for his part is so stunned by the vision of Lucien and Gustave standing so casually beside the cab, as if they have just returned from running errands, that he almost lets his wife fall to the ground before grabbing her, and pulling her to him. At the sight of her faint, Lucien instantly rushes to her, crying "Mother!" Gustave is right behind him, with Fox bypassing them both, to be the first to arrive at her side. "Mother," cries Lucien again. "My dear," says Mr. Raimond, getting hold of himself, "we must get you inside to lie down." At the sound of Lucien's voice she opens her eyes and begins to come around. "Lucien?" she says weakly, reaching out to grab him, even as she is being supported by her husband. "Dearest," Monsieur Raimond says, "we will take you inside to lay down, and then you may greet our arrivals." "Yes Mother, please.." interjects Lucien with concern, only to be immediately cut short by Madame Marboeuf. "Nonsense," she says, suddenly regaining her composure. She pushes herself back to her feet, continuing, "Our sons will not be welcomed home by an old woman on a fainting couch!" It is clear to everyone that she has regained herself, and a moment later, she exclaims, "Lucien! My beautiful boy! You are home!" and she throws her arms around him, pulling him to her.

"Gustave too! How is it you are here? And safe! Oh what a wonderful day!" she exclaims pulling Gustave to her and hugging them both. Monsieur Raimond interjects, "My dear, will you not let me greet our two adventurers?" He embracing Lucien warmly, adding, "Lucien, we had never given up hope of getting you back." Then, clasping Gustave's hand warmly, he continues, "Gustave, to have you home as well is a blessing beyond words!" Fox, not to be ignored, now barks loudly, as if to say, "I have been along for the entire adventure, what about me?" Madame Marboeuf looks down at him, exclaiming, "...and Fox, my poor Fox! You are back with us! I can't believe it! Come..." she lets go of Lucien and opens her arms and Fox doesn't waste a moment, jumping up into her waiting embrace. Lucien now takes notice of Martine, who has been standing quietly beside them, waiting her turn. Seeing the tears running down her face, he gives her a hug as well, adding, "Martine, you are the face of home to me, and I have never been happier to see it." It is Mr. Raimond who takes charge of the moment and decides it is time to continue their welcome inside. "Come, we should go inside and let our travelers refresh themselves before hearing their tale." As they are about to go inside it is Lucien who remembers the cab man, who is still waiting at his cab. "Oh my! Father Raimond, I am embarrassed to say it, but, Gustave and I have no money left to pay our fare. We promised the driver his fee upon our arrival." Mr. Raimond replies, "Of course Lucien, gladly," as he pulls out a coin purse and hands a coin to Martine saying, "Martine, will you please give this to the driver." "Yes of course sir," she replied cheerfully. Before she can take a step Monsieur Raimond stops her, "Wait Martine," he says, taking another coin from the purse, he continues, with a smile, "and this one too."

Once they are all inside, Madame Marboeuf flies into a joyous panic seeing to it that Lucien's room is prepared and another for Gustave. Having her son home again has re-animated her, with a joyful energy she has not felt since he was lost. Once she has made sure the rooms are being properly prepared, she turns her attention to having a suitable dinner planned for them, the whole time waging a happy battle with Martine, who is equally excited at the homecoming, over the best way to do this or the proper way to do that. Between the two of them, the entire staff is driven to distraction. Madame Marboeuf, aware of her demands on them, and being in such high spirits tells the house staff that once things are in order, they can have the rest of the day off to go home to their own families, or do as they please. For her part, Martine elects to stay on duty noting that, without her, "Madame may burn the kitchen down and leave everyone hungry." Madame Marboeuf, graciously accepts, knowing that Martine is just as anxious to spend time with her newly reunited family as she is, and to hear the tale of their long adventure.

Epilogue

The Party

After their initial reunion Madame Marboeuf had determined that there would be a suitable welcome home party for Lucien and Gustave, and immediately set about making it happen in her usual, determined fashion. Mr. Raimond too, with Gustave's permission, set about having his early discharge from the Legion approved. He had a great many contacts in Paris, and elsewhere, and worked to make it happen, determined that his newly reunited family not be separated again. Thanks to his efforts, Gustave's request was granted, and he even received a citation for his part in the battle and the rescue of his cousin.

On the night of the party, the big old house was positively bursting with life, full as it was with party guests and house staff. Madame Marboeuf had made sure all of their friends and acquaintances from Bordeaux were there, and had even surprised Lucien and Gustave by secretly arranging for several of their old friends from Paris to be brought to Bordeaux for the big event. She had been able to keep it a secret right up to the moment the three guests of honor had made their entrance. Lucien and Gustave were completely surprised to see all the old familiar faces, even Fox seemed overjoyed at the reunion with his old acquaintances. Gustave and Father La Tuile, both well turned-out in their military uniforms – Father La Tuile's being a bit tight after so many years as a civilian – spent the rest of the evening regaling all the pretty young women with tales of their many daring battles. Meanwhile, Lucien had been surprised to see Marie and her father there, and having already grown tired of endlessly recounting his own recent adventures, listened attentively to stories of their new life in Paris.

Sometime later, after the excitement of the reunions had subsided, Lucien wandered over to listen to the musicians who had been filling the house with such lively music throughout the evening, and hesitantly asked to join them for a song. The ensemble welcomed him enthusiastically, and Lucien rushed off to his room to retrieve his violin, returning minutes later, to take up a spot beside the other musicians.

Looking around the room, he sees Gustave lost in conversation with old Father La Tuile, and their adoring audience. Marie and her father are seated by the fire with Mr. Raimond at their side. Madame Marboeuf bustles about happily, hovering over her staff, and making time to converse with everyone she can. He looks at Fox, plunked down on his favorite pillow not far from Mr. Raimond, and close by the fire, not at all concerned with the crowd that fills the house, but as always, following Lucien's every move. Lucien catches his faithful little friend's eye and thinks to himself, "Yes Fox, we really are home."

Outside, a warm glow pours from every window of the house and the sound of conversation and laughter fill the air, drifting out across the garden and down through the grapevines. That loud murmur is now joined by the voice of Lucien's violin, leading the other musicians, sending a happy song out into the night sky, and eventually floating out over the dark, ever-present Atlantic ocean, that shimmers, patiently, in the distance.

The End

Acknowledgements

As is always the case, I could not have pulled this book together on my own. There is a stalwart band of friends and relatives who stand ready to keep me on the right track and apply their talents to the job of not letting me mess things up.

First and foremost, I'd like to thank my Tiersa, who is on call 24/7 to supply needed editorial advice and support at a moments notice. She's the one who has to tell me when my "divine inspiration" isn't actually as divine as I like to think it is. That can't be fun.

My friend John for his indefatigable technical, artistic and spiritual assistance. He's always there to "pull me out of the ditch" when I need it. His film work at "www.eternalways.com" is splendid and inspired (check it out), as is his much-appreciated help on this book.

Sherry Wright, painter and artist, who supplied not only the cover art for this book, but also for the original, "A Fox in Paris." She doggedly worked through my many little "tweaks" to her paintings to get us where we needed to be, and then some, and has created a stunning visual identity for these stories.

Finally, to my great, great grandmother, Mary Nelson Carter, who got the ball rolling and seemed to be there to help every step of the way.